THE BRAMBLE PATCH CRAFT SHOP

SARAH HOPE

Boldwood

First published in 2020. This edition first published in Great Britain in 2023 by Boldwood Books Ltd.

Copyright © Sarah Hope, 2023

Cover Design by Head Design Ltd

Cover Illustration: Shutterstock

A CIP catalogue record for this book is available from the British Library.

Paperback ISBN 978-1-80549-119-4

Large Print ISBN 978-1-80549-121-7

Hardback ISBN 978-1-80549-120-0

Ebook ISBN 978-1-80549-122-4

Kindle ISBN 978-1-80549-123-1

Audio CD ISBN 978-1-80549-114-9

MP3 CD ISBN 978-1-80549-115-6

Digital audio download ISBN 978-1-80549-116-3

Boldwood Books Ltd
23 Bowerdean Street
London SW6 3TN
www.boldwoodbooks.com

For my children,
Let's change our stars
xXx

1

'Mum! Ellis is being annoying! Can you tell him to stop copying everything I say?'

'Mum! Ellis is being ann...'

'Ellis! Stop! Just stop teasing your sister.' Glancing in the rearview mirror, Molly Wilson raised her voice.

'I'm only being annoying to her because she's being annoying to me. Did you hear what she keeps calling me?' Folding his arms, Ellis pouted.

'I did, and I've already told her off for that. Lauren, like I said, please don't be horrible to him.'

'But he *does* smell. He's stinking the back seat out. You don't have to sit next to him, if you did...'

'Stop. If neither of you has anything nice to say to the other, then don't. Just try to be nice. In fact, just be quiet. Have a bit of quiet time. Look out of the window or read or something. We'll be there soon.' They'd be there already if it hadn't been for the roadworks on the motorway and the ridiculously slow average speed limit.

'I bet we won't. You said that ages ago.'

'That was before I knew about the roadworks, Ellis.' Molly looked at the satnav. 'All being well we should be there in twenty minutes.'

'Yeah right.'

Breathing slowly out through her nose, Molly reminded herself that this was a massive change for them too. They were not only moving from the house they had lived in their entire lives, but they were also leaving their schools, their friends, and the bustle of town life they were used to. To top all of the changes off, they would have to get used to Molly working around them. However much Molly was looking forward to opening the craft shop, she knew it would be harder work than the 8.30-4.00 work-life she was used to. This would be 9-5 every day apart from a Sunday, plus fitting all of the admin and ordering in.

* * *

'Here we are, Payton-On-The-Water.' Winding the window down, Molly took a deep breath. 'Just smell that country air.'

Twisting in his seat, Ellis copied his mum and wound his window down too. 'Yuck, Pee-On-The-Water stinks!'

'Ellis, please?' What was the point in telling him off yet again? He'd only ignore her anyway?

'You're such a baby. It's Payton-On-The-Water.'

'No, I'm not! I'm nine now, so I'm definitely not a baby! Mum, Lauren called me a baby!'

Stop acting like one then. Gritting her teeth, she ignored their argument. 'I can see the craft shop up ahead. Look!'

'I thought we had to pick the keys up from the estate agents first?' Chewing her nail, Lauren looked out of her window.

'No, we were going to but because we're so late now, they're meeting us here.'

'Oh, okay.'

Pulling the car into one of the parking bays outside the small shop, Molly yanked the handbrake up and turned to look at her children. 'Right, you two, let's go and begin our new life!'

Huffing, Lauren unclipped her seatbelt and grabbed her rucksack from the footwell. 'Yep, let's get this over and done with.'

Shutting the car door behind her, Molly walked up to Tania, the estate agent who had shown them around before they'd put an offer in. 'Tania, hi. Sorry again that we're so late. The roadworks on the motorway were a nightmare.'

'Molly, evening. Hello, kids, I bet you're both excited, aren't you?'

'Ecstatic.' Rolling her eyes, Lauren looked at the floor.

'Sorry, they're just tired.' Molly looked back at Tania.

'Of course. I bet it's been a long day.'

'Yes, it has.'

'Well, here are your keys and I wish you all the best in your new venture.'

'Thank you. And thank you again for waiting for us.'

'You're very welcome. Bye, kids.'

Standing still, Molly watched as Tania sauntered back to her sports car and disappeared down the road.

'Well, here we are.' Putting her arms around Lauren and Ellis' shoulders, Molly gently twisted them so they were looking at the front of the shop. 'Welcome to our new life at Bramble Patch Craft Shop.'

'It says "Diane's Dresses" on the sign. Are you sure this is the right one?' Glancing up, Lauren looked back down and began picking at a loose thread on the sleeve of her jumper.

'We're having a new sign coming tomorrow morning. Are you excited?' Glancing from Ellis to Lauren and back again, Molly chewed her bottom lip.

'Umm.'

'Okay, let's go inside and start cleaning before the removal van gets here. I think they're only about half an hour behind us.'

* * *

Pulling Ellis' bedroom door to, Molly stepped over the boxes stacked in the small hallway before making her way towards Lauren's bedroom. After insisting on unpacking every last Lego set he owned, Ellis had eventually given in to sleep. Molly was just relieved that the idea of wrapping the sets in towels before placing them into the removal boxes had preserved them. She had been half-expecting Ellis to insist on rebuilding any broken ones before going to sleep, but apart from a missing wheel on one of the trucks, they'd done surprisingly well.

Carefully inching Lauren's door open, Molly stood in the door-way. 'Try to get some sleep, sweetheart.'

'Mum, can't you see I'm on the phone?' Lauren narrowed her eyes and glanced across at her mum before turning her back and speaking quietly into her mobile.

'Sorry. Night, love you.' Pulling the door shut behind her, Molly went into the small galley kitchen and switched the kettle on. When had her sweet, caring baby girl transformed into a hormonal four-teen-year-old who thought, no, knew, that the entire world conspired against her?

Molly had lost count of the number of times Lauren had argued with her over the past few days. She knew that Lauren was upset over the move. And she didn't blame her, she really didn't. She couldn't imagine having to up sticks and move away from school, friends and clubs at that age, especially when hormones would be running rife. It was an age when feeling awkward and self-conscious was at an all-time high.

Pouring the boiling water into her mug, Molly mixed the hot chocolate powder a little too vigorously and watched the hot brown liquid dribble into a puddle on the work surface. Shaking herself from her thoughts, she wiped up the mess and held her mug in her hands, breathing in the hot steam. Switching off the kitchen light, she made her way downstairs.

* * *

Standing in the doorway from the flat to the shop, Molly surveyed the shop floor. The large counter lined the back wall and the shelving units she'd sourced from various charity shops and closing down sales were stacked in front of the large window opposite. The stock would be arriving tomorrow afternoon and she still had so much to do.

The shop looked as though it had been empty for at least a year, if not a few, so everywhere needed a good clean and she needed to arrange the shelves and units before the delivery.

On top of that, the flat above looked as though a tornado had torn through it and she wanted to get that looking and feeling more like home before the kids started their new schools after the half term holiday.

Bringing her mug to her lips, Molly took a sip of hot chocolate, hoping the sweetness would give her the comfort she craved.

'Mum?'

Jerking her head around, Molly braced herself for a torrent of abuse as Lauren walked through the doorway.

'I'm sorry.' Stepping towards her, Molly could see she was carrying two mugs. Lauren held one out to her. 'I've made you a hot chocolate although I can see you've already got one.'

'Oh thank you, sweetheart. I've finished this one anyway, so that's great.' Gulping the last of the hot chocolate she'd made, Molly placed the empty cup on the counter and took the fresh one. She couldn't remember the last time Lauren had made her a drink or done anything remotely nice for her, in fact. Definitely not since Molly had announced their move. 'Thank you.'

'I'm sorry I had a go.' Joining Molly behind the counter, Lauren stared into the mug in her hands.

'That's okay. I know this is difficult for you.' Placing her hand on Lauren's forearm, Molly smiled.

'That was Olivia on the phone. All she could talk about was how she's going to the Roller Disco with everyone else tomorrow and that, apparently, Hayley might invite them all for a sleepover on Sunday night for her birthday.'

'You can still go. I can drop you off at the Roller Disco tomorrow, if you like? And you can definitely go to Hayley's birthday sleepover.'

'It seems silly driving all that way for a Roller Disco. You won't be able to do that every week or every time they meet up to go to the café after school, will you?'

'Maybe not after school, because by the time we get there, it'll be time to come back but, yes, I can drive you back at the weekends. You can still meet up with your friends.'

'I guess. But it won't be the same. They'll all be talking about things that had happened at school and I won't be able to join in, I won't know what they're talking about. Anyway, we're going to Dad's tomorrow so I won't be able to go to Hayley's sleepover.'

'You will. If you want to go, we can always swap weekends. Daddy will understand. He wants you to be able to do things with your friends too, remember.'

'I know, but we're going to Jessica's parents' house for their anniversary party so I can't really say I don't want to go and that I want to go to Hayley's instead.'

'Yes, you can.'

Biting her bottom lip, Lauren looked at her mum and then back into her mug. 'No, it's fine. I'll go to Dad's.'

'Okay, but just say if you want to change your mind. Daddy can always drop you off early.'

'Umm. There's not really any point, though, is there? I'm not really going to stay friends with them, anyway.'

'Why not?'

Lauren rolled her eyes and looked around her. 'Because of this. We've moved. We're going to be living two-and-a-half hours away from them, I will be going to a different stupid school and my old friends will just forget about me.'

'No, they won't. Loads of people stay friends with people when they move schools. You can still meet up with them.'

'Yeah right.' Putting her mug down on the counter, Lauren pulled the sleeves of her pyjama top down over her hands and used the spotty pink and white fabric to wipe her eyes.

'Oh, sweetheart, it will be okay. Everything will be fine, you'll see.' Placing her mug next to Lauren's, Molly wrapped her arms around her daughter. Resting her head against Lauren's, she waited as the sobs wracking through her body turned to hiccups.

'It won't be. I didn't even want to come to this stupid village. I wanted to stay in our home. I was happy, I had my friends, my acting club, my school. I've lost it all. It's all gone and now you expect me to rebuild my life here. I'm never going to have friends like I did back then. I'd known Olivia since we were toddlers. It's never going to be the same.'

'It will. It will take time, but you'll make friends here. You'll make good friends and your new school will be just fine. You said you liked it when we went and looked around. You said it had good after-school activities too. And we'll find another acting club here. We can have a look on the internet tonight, if you like? Try to find one you can start next week?'

'No, there's no point. I don't want to go to another acting club, it won't be the same. I had my friends who went to the one back home.'

'I know. But you *will* make friends here.'

'I shouldn't have to. You shouldn't have made me move. I'm almost an adult now, I have rights. I have a right to be happy, and you took it away from me. I don't want to go to another stupid school. I want to go back to Meadow View High. I want to go back to my friends. I want to go back home.'

'I know you do, but it's just not possible, sweetheart. I'm sorry.' Rubbing Lauren's back, Molly blinked back the tears stinging her eyes.

'We didn't have to move. We could have stayed where we were. Things didn't have to change.'

Taking a deep breath, Molly momentarily closed her eyes. 'We did, you know we did.'

'Yes, because you and Dad got a stupid divorce. But he moved out seven years ago, and we've been perfectly happy living there since then.'

'It's a bit more complicated than that.'

'Why? Why is it more complicated? It doesn't make sense. He moved out, we stayed there, and now we have to move. It's ridiculous.' Pushing her mum away, Lauren stepped back and stared at Molly.

'Well, I...' Looking at Lauren stood in front of her, her eyes red-rimmed through crying, her pale face highlighting dull shadows under her eyes, Molly could see exactly what this move was doing to her daughter. She couldn't very well tell her that, yes, Molly and her dad had been split up for just over seven years now, but because he hadn't wanted his own children to be able to stay in the house they had grown up in until they were eighteen, they'd had to go back and forth through solicitors who had finally ruled that Trevor was entitled to thirty-five per cent of everything so the house had had to be sold.

'Yes, I know, you had to sell up to give Dad his share. He told us that, but you could have bought a house there. There were loads for sale before you decided we had to come to this stupid place.'

'Oh, I didn't know he'd told you that.' If he had admitted to Lauren it was his fault they'd had to sell up, why was she still bearing the brunt of Lauren's anger? How come he'd seemingly got away scot-free?

'Yes, he did. I was moaning at him about you when you told us we were moving and he told me.'

'Right.'

'I mean, I get it. Why shouldn't he have some of the money from the house? He's still got to live, but why did you have to make us move out of Tipston?'

Molly scoffed, trying to hide the mixture of anger and amusement behind a cough. That sounded like his excuse, his reasoning word for word why he had wanted the house sold. So she knew he'd wanted them, his own children, out of their home and yet Lauren was still blaming her? Molly shook her head. 'You know the house prices in Tipston and all around there are super high. The only place we'd have been able to afford was a two-bedroom flat. You wouldn't have wanted to share a bedroom with Ellis, would you?'

'If it meant I could stay with my friends, I wouldn't have cared.' Crossing her arms, Lauren pursed her lips.

'Yes you would. You can't even spend a car journey together without teasing each other, there's no way you'd have tolerated sharing a bedroom with him!'

'I would. It would have been better than having to leave everyone back home and start again here.'

'Lauren, I... I'm sorry.' What else could she have done? The house prices in and around Tipston meant that in order to afford somewhere they'd have had to have moved about thirty minutes away anyway and then more than likely Ellis wouldn't have got into the same secondary school as Lauren. That, plus the fact that Lauren would have had to have taken the bus to school and back every day and Ellis would have spent longer in childcare each day to give time for Molly to travel to and from work had meant that they'd have been struggling for money.

'It's a bit late now.'

'Lauren. Honestly, I had no choice. This way we get to live in a nice little village and I get to run this place meaning that I'm here for you both instead of going out to work.' Molly held her hands up. 'I know it means getting used to a new school and making new friends, but I really think this will work out to be the best thing for all of us. We just all need time to get used to it.'

'Huh. It's not like you had any friends back home anyway, and you don't have to go to a new school. I'm going to be surrounded by people I don't know, teachers I don't know. What if I'm put down in a set? They won't know what I can do or not, what I've learnt already or not. What if they're learning about something we hadn't covered yet at Meadow Hill? I'm going to look really stupid, and on my first day too.'

'Your old tutor will have passed all your grades onto your new school. They'll use those to put you in the right sets and, besides, they'll be doing tests again at the beginning of term. And, once you know what topics you're learning about in the different subjects, if you haven't covered them yet then we can do work at home. We'll get you up to speed and it will just mean that they're teaching things in a different order, so you'll be way ahead of the other students when they get round to teaching the topics you've already covered.'

'I suppose so.' Picking up her mug, Lauren wrapped her hands around it and took a sip.

'We'll sort it. And you *will* make loads of new friends. The new person at school always has people who want to be their friend. It will be fine.' Picking up her own mug, Molly looked around. 'We've got the half term to get settled before you start school so maybe we could have a wander around the village tomorrow before Dad comes? There might be a youth club or somewhere teenagers hang around that you could go to?'

'I'm not really just going to go up to a group of people and ask if I can be their friend, am I? I'm not that sad.'

'Okay, I just thought you might feel better about going into school if you get to know someone beforehand.'

'Yeah right. That's not going to happen. And I don't want to "wander around the village"...' Placing her mug momentarily down, Lauren used her fingers to make quotation marks. '... I don't want the first impression people get of me to be that I "wander around" with my mum and kid brother, do I?'

'It was just a thought.' Shrugging, Molly opened a notebook she'd placed on the counter earlier. 'Maybe we can just try to get this place straightened out a bit then. We've got a big stock delivery coming tomorrow afternoon so I want to get this place ready so I can just fill up the shelves. The sooner we open up and can get some money coming in, the better. I've been thinking I might start a Knit and Natter group. You know somewhere people can come and learn how to knit or just knit and talk?'

'I know what a Knit and Natter is, Mum. The name kind of gives it away.' Rolling her eyes, Lauren glared at her mum.

'Of course, you do. Well, what do you think? I thought it'd be a nice way of me getting to know the locals and then hopefully once they see what we have in stock, they'll start using this place to get their wool and things from?'

'Yes, it's a good idea, I guess. I see *you've* got what you've dreamed of. You've got your perfect life opening this place up, but you've ruined mine and Ellis' in the process.' With anger flashing across her face, Lauren slammed her mug back down on the counter before wiping her eyes again with the sleeve of her top.

'Lauren, I... This wasn't my dream life.' How could she tell Lauren that her dad had smashed through her perfect life seven years earlier? Yes, she had always wanted to open a craft shop, but not like this, not under these circumstances. And she certainly hadn't meant to ruin her children's lives. 'This isn't how I had envisaged my life turning out either. But you know that after having to sell our home I just couldn't afford to buy again, not near our old place and this,' Molly waved her arms around, encompassing the shop floor. 'Buying a shop was one way I could get a big enough mortgage to get a place with three bedrooms. If I could have bought close enough to our old place so you two could have carried on at your old schools, you know I would have, don't you?'

'Umm, I guess. I just...'

'You're just nervous about starting a new school, aren't you? And you're missing your old friends.' Holding her arms out towards Lauren, Molly signalled her to come closer.

Nodding, Lauren stepped forward, resting her head on Molly's shoulder.

'And it's natural to feel that way. It's totally normal, and it's okay, I understand if sometimes you feel so completely angry with me, as long as you know deep down that I'm just trying to build a good life for you both. Try to see this as a way of starting over. You can be who you want to be, act how you want. No one knows you here, so it's a completely new start.'

'I guess so.'

'And there's no more Davina. You won't have to see her again.' Davina was Lauren's age and had been their next-door neighbour for the past six years and for some reason had taken an instant dislike to Lauren, picking on her at school and trying to turn her friends against her.

'That's true. She'll no doubt move in and replace me in our group though.'

'Let her. Who cares? You can meet up with your friends and you won't have to meet up with her. You won't have to put up with her snide remarks every day.'

'I suppose so.'

'If we try to treat this move as a positive, as a way to make our lives better then I think we could be really happy here. I know you're worried about starting a new school, but when we looked around, it looked as though they had fantastic resources. The science lab was new last year, wasn't it? And the computer suite and art studios looked amazing. They're really high on the league tables and get great results too. I think you'll do really well there. If you go in with the right attitude, then I'm certain you will be super happy there.'

'They also said they put on a pantomime at the village hall each year too.'

'Yes, they did, didn't they? And didn't they say they take the drama club to join in with a theatre production in the next town?'

'Yes.' Stepping out of her mum's hug, Lauren wiped her eyes and smiled. It was a small brief smile, but it was a smile.

'There you go then. And actually joining the drama club will be a really good way of making friends with people who have the same interests as you.'

'Umm.' Nodding, Lauren looked down at the counter, picking up a stray staple. 'I will still miss my friends though.'

'I know, but you'll make new friends and still have your old friends so you'll have double the amount.'

'I guess.'

'I wouldn't have moved you here if I didn't think it could work, if I didn't think you'd like the school.'

Nodding, Lauren squeezed the staple between her thumb and forefinger.

'Right, do you want to see what my plans for this place are?'

'Suppose so.'

Leafing through the notebook in front of her, Molly turned to a page full of scribbles and drawings and slid it across the counter towards Lauren. 'Here is a very rough plan I've drawn. So, we'll put the shelves against the walls and then have those big baskets I got from the car boot weeks ago up here by the counter, they'll be full of wool. And then here in the middle we'll have a bit of space where we can have some comfy chairs grouped together so people can come in and sit and craft for a bit. I can offer free tea and coffee too to get them in and then we can make the chairs into a circle when we have events like the Knit and Natter. What do you think?'

'It looks good. Do you think people will really come in and sit though? It's a shop, not a café.'

'I hope they will. If I can make it as inviting as possible then I'm hoping people will want to spend some time here. If they don't, then we can have a rethink.' Smiling, Molly could imagine the sort of place she wanted to turn the shop into. In her mind people would travel from the next town and surrounding villages to shop here. It would be somewhere friends could come to have a catch-up and still do their crafting. 'I'm just trying to think of ways to be different from the other craft shops and to attempt to compete with the big online stores.'

'I think it's a good idea then.' Lauren circled the chairs drawn on the paper. 'Where are you getting the chairs from?'

'Not sure. I'm hoping we can get out to a couple of car boots on Sunday and then I'll try to find some on the social media sites too.

I'm thinking it might add to the charm if they're all different, anyway.'

'Okay.'

'So, what do you think? Would you like to come and check out some car boots on Sunday instead of staying in bed all day?'

'We're going to Dad's tomorrow, remember?'

'Drat. Yes, of course, you are. I had completely forgotten.' Taking the notebook back, Molly smoothed the page before closing it. She'd been looking forward to having Lauren and Ellis' help and input in designing the layout of the shop, but she guessed, in reality, they probably wouldn't have wanted to help, anyway. 'Hopefully, I can get the shop all set up, and the flat unpacked before you get back then.'

'If you can find enough space to put everything up in the flat.'

'I know we're used to a house, but it's actually only a little smaller than our old place. It's only missing a dining room.'

'And a downstairs loo, a utility room, a conservatory and a garden.'

'We've got a sweet little courtyard here remember, and the green is opposite.'

'Yes, a courtyard, we used to have space for a trampoline and a swing set.'

'Which you never used to play on.' Smiling, Molly raised her eyebrows at Lauren.

'I guess. Ellis used to, though.'

Molly nodded. 'Yes, I know, but he's getting older now and as long as he has a bit of space to kick a football around I think he'll be happy. And the swing park is only down the road, anyway.'

'But you'll be busy working in here all the time so you won't be able to take him.'

'We'll make it work.' Patting the palms of her hands against the cover of her notebook, Molly copied Lauren as she yawned. 'Right, it's been a long day, I think you should hop into bed now and try to get some sleep.'

'Are you coming up?'

'In a minute.' Wrapping her arms around Lauren, Molly kissed the top of her head. 'Night, night. Love you.'

'Love you too.'

Watching as Lauren disappeared through the door adjoining the shop to the stairs leading up to the flat, Molly yawned again. It could work, their new life. It *would* work. She'd make sure it did. She just needed to try to immerse them all into village life and they could be really happy here, away from the traffic and rush of Tipston. Away from the memories of happier times and arguments which lurked in every crooked shelf and mark on the wall in their old place. This was their chance to start afresh. This was their chance to build a new life.

Taking a last look around the shop floor, she tried to block out the thought of all the work that had to be done and made her way up to bed.

2

Pausing, Molly checked the time. It was only just gone nine. It felt a lot later. Putting her hands on her hips, she glanced around the shop floor. The shelves were all in place, she just needed to drag the big wicker baskets through from where the removal men had dumped them in the back kitchen behind the counter and the shop floor would be almost ready. There were still the pictures to be hung and the chairs to be bought and put in place, but she was almost there.

'Mum!'

Twisting her neck, Molly watched as Ellis raced through the door. 'Mind the mop bucket!'

'Oops! Sorry!' Kicking the edge of the bucket, Ellis jumped to the side as dirty water dribbled to the floor as the bucket tipped and thankfully steadied itself.

'Don't worry, I'll mop it up again.' There was no point in making Ellis tidy up the mess he'd made, he'd only make it worse. 'Why are you in such a hurry, anyway?'

'What time is Dad coming to get us?'

'About half ten, I think. Have you packed?' Picking her way

across the tiled floor, Molly was careful not to tread in any of the split water. Picking up the mop, she squeezed it out and dried up the floor.

'Yes, no. He's just messaged Lauren, we need to take our swimming stuff and I need new trunks.'

'You've got trunks. You've got the ones with the sharks on.'

'No, they're too small. Remember, I told you after swimming at school?'

'Oh yes. Okay, we'll have a look when we go into town next. Or else I'll order you some.'

'I need them now.'

'I'm sure they can wait.'

'No, I need to take them today. I told you, Dad's said to bring our swimming things.'

'All right, I'll speak to him and I'm sure he can pick you some up. Don't worry.' Shrugging, she smiled at him.

'No, he can't. We're going straight to Jessica's parents' house and they've got a hot tub. Dad told us to bring our swim things so we can go in. Max and Freya are going too, and they'll be going in. I want to have a go too.'

'Don't worry. I'm sure your dad won't mind stopping off and picking you some up.' Frowning, Molly watched as Ellis' bottom lip quivered.

'He won't. He's said if we don't bring them then we can't go in.'

'Really?' Actually, it probably *was* something Trevor would say. He wouldn't want any inconvenience. 'Could you borrow some from Max? He's only a year younger than you?'

'His will be too small too. Please, Mum, can we go and get some new ones?'

Checking her watch, Molly looked at Ellis. It wasn't fair if he had to miss out because she'd forgotten to replace his trunks when he'd outgrown them and his father wouldn't buy any new ones.

After all, that's what maintenance was for, wasn't it? An endless pot of money that magically grew and grew when the children outgrew their clothes or a school trip needed paying for. Molly rolled her eyes. She was sure that's what Trevor believed. 'Are sure you can't just squeeze into them? Just for one day? Your dad will be here in just over an hour.'

'We gave them to Harry, remember?'

'Drat.' Of course, trying to declutter before the move, Molly had given a huge bag of clothes Ellis had outgrown to his friend Harry. 'Okay, okay. Go and get your sister but we'll have to hurry.'

'Thanks, Mum.' Turning on his heels, Ellis rushed back upstairs shouting Lauren's name.

Pulling her hairband out, Molly shook her hair before bundling it back up into a messy bun. She hadn't even put any make-up on this morning. Shaking her head, she guessed it didn't matter. They'd only be quick. Hopefully, they could get back before Trevor came. Even though her love for him had disappeared years ago, she still didn't want him seeing her in this state. She still liked to pretend she was in control of her life.

'Mum, she's not coming. She said to tell you, she'll stay here and pack her stuff for Dad's.'

'Mind the mop!' Gently pulling the sleeve of Ellis' jumper, she guided him around the bucket. 'Right, come on then.'

* * *

'Are you happy with them?' Looking in the rear-view mirror, Molly watched as Ellis pulled the bright orange and black checked trunks out of the bag before putting the car into reverse.

'They're okay, I guess.'

'I think they're nice. I know there wasn't much choice there, but at such short notice I think you were very lucky we found any at all.'

'Yes, they're nice. Can I get some other ones if we do swimming at school though, please? I think they'll be a bit bright for school.'

'Yes, okay.' Molly smiled. She knew he didn't really like them but it was sweet of him to make do. Pausing at the exit to the car park, Molly glanced at the clock on the dashboard. They'd been pretty quick in town, quicker than she'd thought they would be, so they still had fifteen minutes to make the journey home before Trevor showed up.

'Thanks.' Grinning, he put his new trunks back into the bag on his lap.

Her phone vibrated from her handbag on the passenger seat. Keeping her foot on the brake, she rummaged inside it and pulled out her mobile, holding it out towards Ellis. 'It's Lauren, can you answer it, please?'

Leaning forward, Ellis grab the mobile. 'Hello?'

Pulling out into the road, Molly put her hand up to thank the driver who had let her out. 'What does she want? Is she okay?'

'All right then. Bye.'

'Is she okay?'

'Yes, she said Dad's got there early and is wondering where we are.'

'Really?' Clenching her jaw, Molly cursed under her breath. What was the point in arranging a time if he just showed up whenever he wanted?

'Yes. He needs to get going so wants us to hurry.' Shifting in his seat, Ellis ducked his head and began playing on Molly's mobile.

'Okay.' No, it wasn't okay, actually. It was far from okay. Trevor needed to understand that they had things to do, places to go as well, and that she and the kids' lives didn't revolve around him. Yes, the children enjoyed going to his and wanted to go but that didn't mean that her time with them should be compromised because he was seemingly incapable of telling the time. Taking a deep breath, she indicated onto the country lane connecting the town to their little village and accelerated.

A ping from the back seat interrupted Molly's thoughts. Twisting around, she quickly glanced back at Ellis. 'Is that my phone again? Can you see what the message says, please?'

'Aww, I've just got to level 101 on Puzzle Mania.'

'You can go back on it after, can you just check what it says, please? It might be Lauren.'

'It says Dad really has to go so can we hurry up.'

'Of course, it does.' Turning the corner, Molly slammed her brakes on as two horses came into view. Great, now they really would be late. Tapping the steering wheel, Molly inched past them, the riders raising their hands in thanks.

Leaving enough distance between the horses and the car, Molly accelerated again. It wasn't as though they'd popped out for her, they'd gone for Ellis, his son. And they'd only had to go out because Trevor was insisting the kids had their swim stuff with them. If he had planned an activity like going in the hot tub, it should really be his responsibility to make sure his children had the proper equipment.

Picking up speed, Molly wriggled her fingers on the steering wheel and loosened her grip. Even just thinking about him and how he acted annoyed her. She should really have learnt by now to accept the way he acted and live with the consequences. Her life would be a lot easier if she didn't let his actions bother her so much.

'Mum!'

Shaking her head, she focused on Ellis' voice from the back seat. 'Has she messaged again?'

'No, but there's a police car behind us.'

'Drat.' Looking in the rear-view mirror, Molly checked her speedometer before hitting the brakes and slowing down to a more reasonable and legal speed limit. Checking the rear mirror again, Molly held her breath.

'Mum, they've put their blue lights on now.'

Biting down on her bottom lip, Molly slowed down again and indicated, pulling to the side. Please go past. Please go past.

'Does that mean we're in trouble?'

'Hopefully it just means they need to get past, that's all. They've probably got an emergency to go to or something.'

'Oh okay. Why aren't they overtaking us then?'

Slowing to a stop, Molly closed her eyes. This was all she needed. To be pulled over for speeding.

'Mum?'

'It's all right, sweetheart. Everything will be fine.' Rubbing her eyes, she watched as a policeman sauntered towards them. What would happen if she just bolted? She could write an email and apologise. Waiting for the inevitable tap-tap on the window, she turned and wound it down.

'Madam, I'm Officer Duffey.' Bending down, Officer Duffey flashed his ID. 'Could you please step out of the car?'

It wasn't really a question; she knew that. She also knew that any thoughts of driving off and taking a plane out of the country would have to remain unspoken. 'I'm so sorry. I didn't realise I was speeding, not until I saw you behind us. It won't happen again.'

'Please step out of the vehicle.' Placing his hand over the radio strapped to his jacket, he flared his nostrils.

'Yes, of course. Sorry.' Twisting around in her seat, Molly reached behind and tapped Ellis on the knee. 'Don't worry. It will all be fine. You stay here.'

'Please, madam.'

Yes, okay, okay. Couldn't he see that she was comforting her child? Not that Ellis looked anything but excited at the prospect of her getting into trouble with the law. Opening the door, she slipped out. 'I'm so so sorry. We're just in a bit of a hurry and the road was clear, and I just got distracted. You know thinking about the time and that we had to hurry, and I forgot to look at my speedometer. I don't usually speed and it honestly wasn't intentional.'

Tapping his pen against the small notepad in his hand, he looked at her, his clear blue eyes peeking from underneath his sandy coloured hair. 'You are admitting you were travelling above the speed limit then?'

'Yes, no, I don't know. I wasn't really concentrating on my speed.' Biting her lip, she shook her head. Why had she said that? 'I don't mean I wasn't concentrating on driving, because I was. I could see the road was clear and so I guess I was just concentrating on that. I didn't realise I was speeding.'

'So you weren't checking your speedometer?'

'No, I mean I was, but just not right then.' Tucking her hair behind her ears, Molly turned to look at Ellis whose attention had returned to her mobile before turning back to the policeman in front of her. 'I was just looking at the road. I didn't realise I had been speeding.'

'Do you know how much over the speed limit you were going?'

Blinking, Molly shook her head. She'd already told him she hadn't looked at the speedometer. He knew she didn't know.

'You were going seven miles per hour above the limit. Do you realise how much of a difference that could make in an impact with another car? Or a pedestrian for that matter?'

Frowning, Molly automatically glanced up and down the desolate country lane.

Shaking his head, Officer Duffey tapped his notepad again. 'I know it's a quiet road but if you had met another car or been on a busier road, I might actually be assisting you after an accident right now.'

He wasn't going to let her off, was he? 'I'm sorry, it won't happen again.'

'I should hope not. Do you have your driving licence on you?'

'Yes, I do. Oh, umm, we've only just moved yesterday, so it doesn't have my new address on.' Was that a crime too? No, surely they couldn't expect you to update the details on moving day, could they? Turning around, Molly reached inside the car and pulled out her handbag. 'Here it is.'

Nodding, Officer Duffey took the licence. Narrowing his eyes, he stared at it.

'As I said, we only moved yesterday so I haven't got round to changing my address, but we're in Payton-on-the-Water at...'

'That won't be necessary, I know where you've moved in to.' Holding up his hand, palm facing outwards, he turned her licence over in his other hand.

Frowning, Molly laced her fingers together in front of her. How did he know where they lived?

Glancing up, Officer Duffey looked across at her and shook his head. 'I'm the local police officer around here, I keep an eye on things.'

'Right. Of course.' Looking down at the ground in front of her, she looked back up. Maybe he'd let her off? He must know how stressful moving was and he could clearly see she had Ellis in the back. He must know that she wouldn't do anything to intentionally put him at risk. It wasn't as though she'd sped deliberately.

Looking down, he scribbled in his notepad. 'I'm afraid at the speed you were going and having a child in the car, I have no choice but to issue you with a ticket.'

'Really? I...' Blinking her eyes, she tried to keep the tears stinging the back of her eyes from spilling over. She'd never had a ticket before. Her insurance premiums would skyrocket now, wouldn't they? That was all she needed – not only to have to conjure up the fine money from thin air but also to have to find extra money each month to pay a higher insurance premium. And it was due to renew next month. What with the mortgage and bills on Bramble Patch and the extra fuel needed to travel that bit further to everywhere they needed to go, money was going to be tight already. Until she could start making a decent profit from the business, anyway.

Passing her licence back to her, Officer Duffey crossed his arms.

Biting her bottom lip, Molly nodded before turning around and opening her car door. With her hands shaking, she dropped her keys. 'Drat.'

'Here, let me.' Bending down, Officer Duffey fished her keys from the puddle at their feet.

'Thank you.' Taking them from him, Molly glanced at his face. His features had softened a little. In fact, if he hadn't just given her a ticket, she would have said his eyes looked kind.

'I don't like giving tickets, you know.' A small sympathetic smile flashed across his face before he again wiped it of all emotion.

Nodding, Molly slipped into the driver's seat and shook her head. Sure, he didn't like giving out tickets, that's why she'd now been fined for barely crossing the speed limit.

'Mum, are you going to jail?' Ellis' voice, quiet and small floated through from the back seat.

Turning around, Molly reached backwards and clasped his hand. 'No, of course not. I've just got to pay a bit of money to say sorry for speeding, that's all. I'm not going anywhere.'

'Really?'

'Yes, really, really. Now, have you still got my phone?'

'Yes, do you need it?'

'No, you keep hold of it. We'd better get a wriggle on or Lauren and your dad will wonder where we are.' Turning back around, Molly clipped her seatbelt in, wiped the few tears that had managed to escape and turned the ignition.

3

Running ahead of her, Ellis threw the shop door open. 'Daddy!'

'Hey, buddy!' Looking from Ellis to Molly, Trevor pointedly fiddled with the ridiculously large and expensive watch strapped to his wrist.

'Sorry, we're late. We had to pop out to get Ellis some swimming trunks. He said he needed to take some to yours and you wouldn't have time to get him a pair.' Of course, if you'd given me a little bit of notice I wouldn't have had to have made a quick dash to the shops at the last minute. There was no point saying anything, she knew that. The number of times he'd changed his mind over pick-up and drop-off times or expected them to suddenly have this, that or the other to take with them to his, it wasn't worth telling him they wouldn't have had to go out if it hadn't been for him.

'Yes! And then Mum got pulled over for speeding!' With his eyes wide open and an enormous grin spreading across his face, Ellis looked from his dad to his sister to make sure they were suitably thrilled. 'The police car had its lights on and everything!'

Frowning, Trevor looked across to Molly. 'Is this true?'

'Well, yes, I was pulled over, but I wasn't really speeding.'

'With Ellis in the car?'

Pursing her lips, Molly stared back at him. He'd always thought himself better than her. She knew he sped with the kids in the car, and not by accident either. Many a time, Ellis had come back from his relaying some story or other where Trevor had 'made the car go really really fast' to show off to them. She didn't need his looks of disgust, not when she hadn't realised she'd been speeding and she'd only been hurrying because he had been getting Lauren to text to rush them home. 'I did not mean to speed and, if I had been at all, I would only have been going a few miles above the speed limit. Besides, we were only in a hurry because we'd had to go out at the last minute to get the trunks Ellis needed.'

'Are you seriously blaming me for you breaking the law?' Folding his arms, Trevor cocked his head to the side.

'Don't look at me like that, Trevor. It's my first driving offence ever. How many points do you currently hold on your licence for speeding?'

Shaking his head, Trevor flared his nostrils. 'Don't turn it around on me. It was you who did it.'

'Yes, it was and I'm not turning it around on you, I'm just saying don't get on your high horse and moan at me for something you've done numerous times in the past. Yes, I sped but, no, I didn't mean to and I certainly wouldn't have intentionally with Ellis in the car. You know that.' Trying to calm her breathing, Molly took a deep breath. 'Besides, if you had actually given me notice about the kids needing to take their swimming things today then I wouldn't have been rushing back from town in the first place.'

Shaking his head, Trevor glanced at the children. 'Right, kids, are you all packed and ready to go? Go and jump in the car and I'll be out in a moment. I just need a quiet word with your mum, okay?'

'Okay.' Pushing her leg back, Lauren pushed herself away from the shelf she'd been leaning on and stood next to Molly.

'It's all right, sweetheart. You can go out, but first, come here.' Holding her arms out, Molly waited until Lauren's head was resting against her shoulder before wrapping her arms around her and kissing the top of her head. 'Love you. Have a lovely time at your dad's.'

'Love you too, Mum.' Pulling herself away, Lauren picked up her rucksack.

'You too, kid.' Pulling Ellis towards her, she buried her nose in his shock of blonde hair and inhaled the scent of the men's shower gel he insisted on washing with mixed with the flowery perfume from the fabric conditioner his pillowcase had been washed with. 'Love you, kid. Have fun at Daddy's.'

'Will do.'

'Pardon?' Gripping him tighter and tickling him under the arms, Ellis squealed with laughter.

'Love you too, Mum.'

'That's better. Right, I'll see you in a couple of days, okay?'

'Go on then. Jessica's in the car with Ruby.'

Damn, she hadn't even spotted his car. She must have walked right past Trevor's new wife and their four-year-old, Ruby. Loosening her hair from its messy bun, Molly shook it out before tying it back up. Tearing her eyes away from the door as it swung shut behind Lauren and Ellis, she looked across at Trevor. 'If you want to have another go at me about speeding, then please don't bother. Don't you think I regret it enough?'

'No, it's not that. Before you came back I was speaking to Lauren, and she was telling me how you were hoping to open this place on Monday?'

'That's right.' What did it have to do with him? Yes, opening two days after moving in might seem crazy but she needed to start making some money, more so now than ever.

'It's just that with it being the half term holidays and you clearly have an awful lot of work to do to prepare this place for opening, I thought I'd take the kids off your hands for a few extra days. To give you a bit of a break and time to get opened without them under your feet.'

Opening her mouth, Molly closed it again. From anyone else, she'd think it was a nice gesture, but from the way he was speaking to her and looking pointedly at the empty shelves and mop bucket which she realised had been knocked again, dirty water puddling beside it and mucky footprints trailing out of the door, she couldn't help but feel he was being condescending. 'I can cope, you know. I wouldn't have bought this place if I didn't think I could cope.'

'I didn't mean that, I just thought it would help you out not having the kids under your feet while you were trying to sort it all out. Plus, Jessica's parents have invited us to stay for the week rather than just the weekend now.'

'Right.' Molly nodded. That was why then. He wanted to take the kids with him to Jessica's parents'. It had absolutely nothing to do with helping her out.

'Well? It just makes more sense than us having to cut our visit short or me having to drive all the way down here and then back up to theirs again.'

'I don't know. I thought you were just having them for the weekend as usual. They haven't packed enough things.' She had wanted them back for the opening of the shop. It was their new adventure – not just hers. She wanted the children to be involved too. 'Do you mind if we just leave it? It's the opening day on Monday and I wanted the children here.'

'Really? They'd just get in the way.' Chuckling to himself, Trevor shook his head, dismissing her idea as if it was ridiculous.

Straightening her back, Molly narrowed her eyes. He always made her feel a lesser person than him, as though her ideas were just silly and whimsical. 'I'm trying to make a home for them here, and, yes, I'd like them to be here for the opening of the shop.'

'Dad, are you coming?' Bounding in through the door, Ellis stopped in his tracks and looked from his mum to his dad. 'I thought we were in a hurry?'

'One moment, buddy. I was just asking your mum if I could have you a bit longer so we could spend some more time up at Grandma and Grandpa Hills' house.'

'Really? Do you mean we'll be able to go in the hot tub every day? And could we go to that theme park? You promised us we could when we went up again, remember?'

Keeping his eyes fixed on Molly, Trevor nodded. 'Maybe. I'm just waiting to see what your mum says.'

'Mum? Can we? Can we go?'

'I...'

'It's okay if we can't though. I don't mind.'

Looking at Ellis, Molly sighed. He did mind, really. He wanted to go to the theme park and spend more time in the hot tub. Now that Trevor had suggested they could stay longer in front of him, she couldn't very well say no, could she?

Shaking her head, she looked at Trevor and narrowed her eyes. He always did this, always put her in impossible positions. It wasn't fair. It wasn't damn fair to play with his kids as he did. Not that they realised what he was doing. Lauren had mentioned a couple of things, such as asking why her dad moved his days around with them or had to cancel seeing them at all at short notice. It wouldn't be long until they both cottoned on to what he was like, to his games, but until then she couldn't win. She either said no and was made out to be the bad person or she did what Trevor had set the trap for her to do and gave in.

'It's completely up to your mum.'

Of course, it was. Of course. Closing her eyes momentarily, Molly nodded. 'Okay.'

'Really? Thanks, Mum. I'm going to go and tell Lauren we're going to the theme park!' Running outside, the door slammed behind him.

'Please don't ever put me in a position like that again.'

'I don't know what you mean. I gave you the choice. It was entirely your decision.'

Molly shook her head. He'd never change. 'You know exactly what you did. Now, what are you going to do about the fact they haven't packed enough clothes?'

'Jessica's parents have a washing machine and if they need anything else, I'm sure we can find a shop nearby.'

Right, a shop. So now he was getting his way, he could manage to pop to a shop to pick extra bits up for the children, but barely an hour earlier, he had made it clear to Ellis that he wouldn't have time to pop out to buy him some new trunks.

'Thanks for this. I'll drop them back on Thursday or Friday.'

Molly watched as he slipped out of the door, letting it slam behind him. She'd have to get a doorstop to put there. It wouldn't take much force for one of the small panes of glass to pop out or crack. Walking towards the window, she stood slightly to the side. She didn't like to wave and blow kisses when she knew Jessica was in the car. It felt too weird. Even though she'd been in their lives for almost six years, Molly still felt like an intruder when she was about. Shaking her head, she tried to push the feeling aside. After all, it was she, Molly, who was Lauren and Ellis' mum. She shouldn't be made to feel as though it was her who didn't belong.

Watching their four-by-four disappear around the corner, Molly made her way towards the back kitchen. She hadn't touched this part of the shop. It was relatively tidy, a few broken coat hangers and plastic bags discarded in the back corner and a couple of mugs abandoned in the sink. It wouldn't take long to clean the dust from the work surfaces, wash the floor and scrub the cupboards out. Walking over to the work surface, Molly gingerly picked up a small plastic kettle which lay on its side. Lifting the lid, she looked inside; it looked okay.

Rinsing the kettle out under the tap, Molly watched the limescale escape down the plughole. It'd be okay to use after a couple of boils and would save a few quid getting a new one.

Leaning back against the grubby work surface, Molly looked out into the small courtyard area and crossed her arms. Why did she let Trevor speak to her like that? Why did she still let him dictate her life? She should have stood her ground. She should have said no, told him that she had wanted the children to be with her when the shop opened. That it was a big deal to her. That she was doing this for them, for her children, to give them the future they deserved and that she had wanted to celebrate the beginning of their adventure with Lauren and Ellis by her side.

Pressing the heels of her hands to her eyes, Molly tried to block out the feelings of worthlessness from her mind. Trevor could make her feel inferior and rubbish with a single look. It was a skill he had always had. She knew it was her, though. Her fault. She knew she was the rubbish one because he obviously didn't make Jessica feel the same. Whenever she saw them together, they always appeared so in love and so happy. It must just be her that brought out the worst in him.

Wiping the tears rolling down her cheeks, she reminded herself that he was wrong, and she was wrong for thinking it. She was worthy. She wasn't inferior to him, or to Jessica, or to anyone for that matter. She was Molly; she was Lauren and Ellis' mum and she deserved to be happy just like everyone else. For years she'd pandered to his needs, wanted to make him feel loved and needed and let him do what he wished with no nagging on her part. She never complained when he spent evening after evening at the pub or round his mate's house.

Looking back she knew that for years before he had announced he was leaving her, their marriage had ended, in his head anyway. And if she was honest, that was why she'd never complained about his selfish behaviour. She hadn't moaned at him for missing bath times or not being there to help with bedtimes with the children. She hadn't mentioned that she was finding juggling work and being a mum with next to no support really difficult. She supposed she had let him distance himself to try to support him, to make him realise he was lucky to have her when his mates' wives and girl-friends all nagged them to come home. She had been so desperate to keep him, she'd let him go. Maybe he had ended up feeling unloved or not wanted or something and that was why he had left. By trying to keep him happy, she had ended up pushing him away.

Tipping the newly boiled water down the plughole, she took a step back, watching the steam rise from the cold metal sink. It didn't matter. She'd never know if she'd pushed him away or when he had stopped loving her. The end result was the same – he'd found happiness with Jessica, and she was left a single mum.

It wasn't as though she still loved him or wanted him back or anything, anyway. After the initial shock, she'd found that life was actually a lot easier. She didn't have any of the false expectations that he would help her or listen to her worries or discuss her dreams and aspirations. She knew she was on her own. She knew she was the only one who she could rely on to sort her life out. And that was fine. Life was a lot easier this way. Jessica could deal with his moods and funny ways.

Refilling the kettle, she flicked the switch and went to get her mug from the counter on the shop floor. She'd never get away from his mind games, though. She was stuck with him in her life forever.

Even when the children had grown up and left home, there

would always be reasons they'd have to see each other – weddings, christenings, birthday parties. Any family get-together and she'd have to see him, but then at least he'd have less of a hold over her. He wouldn't be able to make her feel like an unfit mother when they were older. Well, okay, he probably would be able to but it wouldn't be on a fortnightly basis.

Pouring the water into her mug, she rummaged in one of the boxes she'd dumped on the work surface and pulled out a half-empty jar of coffee. Tipping a little of the brown powder into the scalding water, she watched as it slowly dissolved, turning the water a muddy, dull brown. Picking up the mug, she gently turned it, watching the coffee inside swirl around the mug. She really didn't have the energy to run upstairs for a spoon or milk so black unmixed coffee would have to do. It would probably wake her up.

Wincing as the hot water burned her tongue, she swallowed before grimacing as the bitter taste filled her mouth. The happy ringtone from her mobile filled the room. Looking around, she located it and answered. 'Hello?'

'Good morning, could I speak to Mrs Wilson, please?'

'Miss. It's Miss, not Mrs.'

'Sorry, Miss Wilson?'

'Yes, speaking.'

'I'm just ringing to confirm that your order will be with you between four and half-past five today.'

'Order? Oh, yes, of course. Okay, thank you.' Drat, the order. It was Saturday, wasn't it?

Lowering her mobile from her ear, she looked at the time. It was twelve forty already. She had, what, just over three hours until the stock arrived. Three hours to get the shop floor sorted and ready to stock the shelves, or at least to make enough space to stack the boxes that were due to arrive.

Placing her thumb and middle finger against her temples, she squeezed, relieving some of the pressure she could feel building. She could do it. There wasn't that much left that needed doing. Most of the shelves were in place. Yes, they needed wiping down, but that was it. And the floor needed mopping again where Ellis had knocked the bucket over, but this back kitchen could wait. Heck, even if it was in this state on Monday when they opened, it wouldn't matter. No one needed to come behind the counter apart from her. And she had Bea coming over this evening. Yes, she was coming for a catch-up and a nose at the place but Molly was sure she wouldn't mind helping put the stock out, or in the least chatting whilst Molly did it.

Shaking her arms out, she took a deep breath in. She could do this. She could make this place look like a craft shop. She'd put some music on and get on with it.

* * *

Standing up on the chair, Molly wiped the top of the shelf clean. Spraying a bit more polish onto the wood she turned her cloth in on itself and wiped again. She loved this song. When Lauren had been about two-and-a-half, she'd had to have it playing on repeat to get her to sleep. Lauren had always liked music, almost as much as Molly did.

Stepping down from the chair, Molly turned the volume up and pulled the large baskets into position. Standing with her hands on her hips, she looked around her. She'd managed to get the majority of the work done in just a couple of short hours. Going into the back kitchen, she rinsed her cloth underneath the tap. She could do this. She really could. It had been the right decision. They could make a life for themselves down here.

'Hello?'

Jumping, Molly twisted her neck around. Who was that? It

wasn't four o'clock already, surely? Drying her hands on the front of her jeans, Molly made her way into the shop before coming to an abrupt stop behind the counter. It was the police officer. The same one who had pulled her over and given her a ticket. What did he want? Why had he come here? She had updated her car insurance with the new address; she knew she had because she'd done it at the service station on the way here worried that their call centre would close if she'd waited, and the car had miraculously passed its MOT a few weeks ago. 'Officer Duffey? Is there a problem?'

Standing in the doorway, Officer Duffey crossed his arms and nodded towards the radio on the counter.

'Sorry.' Molly switched it off. Was she in some sort of trouble? She definitely hadn't sped again on the rest of the way back. In fact, she'd made sure she was at least five miles under the speed limit much to Ellis' annoyance.

What if something had happened to Lauren and Ellis? Why hadn't she thought of that before? She'd been so fixated on the speeding ticket and the car. What if Trevor had had an accident? Clasping her hands in front of her, Molly blinked. 'Has something happened to Lauren and Ellis? My children? Have they had an accident? Are they all right?'

Frowning, Officer Duffey's face softened. 'Not that I am aware of. I just wanted to ask you to turn your music down.'

'My music?'

'Yes. My mother lives in the bungalow next door, and I can hear your music blaring through the walls.'

'Oh, right?' The bungalow wasn't even attached to the shop. Yes, it was close, but could music really travel that far? She'd had it up loud, but not that loud, surely? 'I hadn't realised it was that loud.'

'I'd appreciate it if you turned it down. She's quite elderly, and it's not right to impose on someone else's environment like that.'

Swallowing hard, Molly didn't know whether to laugh or cry.

Was there anything else he wanted to berate her for? This was supposed to be her fresh start and yet all she'd managed to do was get in trouble with the local law enforcement, which was not quite the fresh start she'd been hoping for. 'I'll make sure I turn it down when I have it on next.'

'Thank you.' Nodding, Officer Duffey glanced around the shop before shaking his head and making his way out again.

Great. Now she couldn't even play her music. Pinching the bridge of her nose, Molly pulled the plug on the radio and turned on her heels. She still had half an hour before the delivery was due, maybe she just needed a proper coffee with milk and something to eat.

4

———

'This is amazing, Molly! It looks so quaint and sweet.' Pushing her sunglasses up on her head, Bea looked around the shop.

'Thanks.' Quaint and sweet? Trust Bea to come out with a description like that. Quaint and sweet wasn't exactly the vibe she was going for.

'So, I brought us a bottle of red.' Placing the wine bottle on the counter, Bea hugged Molly before pecking her on the cheeks. 'Great to see you, hun. I'm missing you already.'

'We only moved yesterday.'

'I know, but it's not the same without you. I've already had Kelsey on the phone panicking about who's going to take your place on the PTA.'

'I hardly did anything anyway. What with overtime at work, I wasn't even there for half the events that were run.' Molly laughed, she very much doubted Kelsey would miss her from the PTA. Whatever Molly had suggested had always been shot down anyway. In the end, she'd given up bothering to turn up to the meetings.

'Oh, you did. You did more than you thought you did.'

'Umm, I doubt that. Anyway, thanks so much for coming. I really appreciate it.'

'You wouldn't have been able to keep me away. You're my oldest and dearest friend, I needed to know where you'd moved to.'

Molly smiled. They'd been friends since secondary school and even though their lives had turned out completely differently, they were always there for each other, through the tears and the happiness. 'Well, it means a lot.'

'Have you got wine glasses?'

'Somewhere, but I haven't unpacked much of the flat yet, I've been sorting out down here. Give me a moment and I'll grab a couple.'

'Okay, great. After the week I've had at work, I need to let my hair down.'

'Are you sure you don't want to stay over? I feel bad you paying out for a hotel.'

'No, it's fine. I deserve a bit of luxury, besides the one I'm staying at has a spa so I'll get my nails done in the morning. I've got a big meeting on Monday so I need to be on top form.' Looking down at her hands, Bea inspected the already perfect red nail varnish and frowned.

Pouring the wine, Molly passed one of the glasses across the counter to Bea.

'Am I all right leaving my car here tonight and grabbing a taxi to the hotel? I'm assuming you do have taxi's even in a village this small?'

'Yes, it'll be fine. And yes, I'm sure we do.'

'Great. In that case...' Sliding her large designer weekend bag from her shoulder, Bea pulled out another bottle and placed it on the counter in front of her.

'I can always rely on you.' Grinning, Molly lined the two bottles up. 'I don't suppose you fancy helping me unpack that lot, do you? Or talking to me while I unpack them?'

'Yeah sure, I'll help. What is it? Stuff to go in the flat?'

'No, it's stock for this place. It was delivered a couple of hours ago.'

'Ooh, that's exciting. It'll be just like Christmas!' Rubbing her hands together, Bea turned towards the boxes.

'Thanks.' Walking over to the boxes, Molly pulled one from the stack and sliced through the tape with her scissors. 'Right, this one is jars of buttons so they need to go... over there on the shelf closest to the counter. Are you okay with that one?'

'Yes, of course.'

Sliding the box towards Bea, Molly pulled the next one towards her. Ribbons, rolls and rolls of ribbons.

'So have you decided when you're opening up then?'

'Monday. We're opening on Monday.' Molly placed her box on the floor next to Bea's and began filling the shelf with rolls of ribbon.

'Next Monday? Do you think you can get it all ready in a week?'

'No, this Monday. We're opening this Monday.' Molly grimaced.

'As in not tomorrow but the next day?' Holding a jar of buttons up, Bea stared at her.

'Yes.' Molly swallowed. 'I put a post on social media before we left our old place so I've got to stick to it. Plus, I need to start bringing money in as soon as possible or this whole thing's not going to work.'

'I guess so. Wow, do you think you can get it all ready in time?'

'I think so. I've only got to stock the shelves in here. I'm going to pop to the car boot in the morning and hopefully pick up some comfy chairs for the middle of the shop floor and then I think it'll be pretty much ready.'

'I guess you'll have the kids back tomorrow to help anyway,

won't you? And then you can all go for a celebratory meal or something when the shop shuts Monday.'

'That was the plan but Trevor has decided he wants to have them for the week. He's taken them up to Jessica's parents' place today, and he wants to keep them longer.'

'Oh right, I thought you wanted them here for when you opened?'

'I did, but you know what he's like. He tried to make it sound as though he was doing me a favour by having them so I could sort this place out, and then when I said I'd wanted them here for the opening, he said it in front of Ellis. Ellis was naturally excited about staying there for longer because they have a hot tub and a theme park close by.' Molly shrugged.

'He's always been like that, hasn't he? Underhand?'

'He certainly has. Anyway, I guess in a way it'll be good. It'll mean that I can get the flat sorted too so that when they do come back, it'll feel a bit more like home.'

'I guess so.' Standing up, Bea flattened her now empty box. 'Right, what's next?'

* * *

'So, what do you think?' Tapping the notebook in front of her, Molly looked across at Bea.

'Looks great. Wait, what? Knit and Natter? You're doing a Knit and Natter here?' Placing her glass of wine on the floor in front of her, Bea took the notebook.

'Yes, what's wrong with that?' From her position next to Bea on the floor, Molly reached across and pushed a roll of fabric which was sitting precariously close to the edge of the nearest shelf.

'Nothing. No, nothing. Actually, I think it's a genius idea, you get people into the shop on the promise of free refreshments and they buy your products.' Tilting her head, Bea passed the notebook back to Molly. 'And, I think the fact that the posters are hand-drawn adds to the charm.'

'You mean they're rubbish.' Pointing with her wine glass, Molly laughed as the red liquid sloshed over the rim, dripping across the notebook in her hand. 'Umm, maybe I'll redo that one.'

'I don't know, the promise of red wine might entice more people in.'

'Yes, you could just imagine that, couldn't you? A gang of knitters getting drunk in charge of their knitting needles!' Hearing her mobile ping, Molly pulled it from the back pocket of her jeans before discarding it on the floor next to her.

'Aren't you going to read it?'

'Nah, it's nothing.'

'It's not nothing. I'd know the sound of that notification anywhere. Let's have a look then.'

Grimacing, Molly shook her head. 'No.'

'Go on. It's DateToday.com, isn't it? You've got a message.' Leaning forward, Bea picked up Molly's phone. 'Go on, read out what they said. Who is it you're talking to?'

'I'm not at the moment and I've got no interest in meeting anyone for the time being. I was speaking to one bloke, but he's just disappeared so whether he's met someone and deleted his account or he's blocked me for some reason. I have no idea, I thought we were getting on all right. We'd even spoken about meeting up – he'd asked me, not the other way around, so I don't get why he's suddenly disappeared.' Molly shrugged.

'There could be loads of different reasons, he might have got back with an ex, or moved elsewhere. Don't let one bloke put you off.'

'No, that's it now. I'm deleting it tonight.'

'What? Because of one bloke?'

'Not just because of him. Because of all of them. I mean, think about the other people I've met on there – one who got together with an old friend and ghosted me, one who didn't want a relationship but as soon as I told him I didn't want to see him for fun any more got a girlfriend less than a month later. No, there's been loads of them.' Shaking her head, Molly picked up her phone.

'Hey, they're not all bad on there, I met Stuart through the site, remember?'

'I know, but that was just a complete fluke. It doesn't happen any more. That, or I'm just so completely horrible that men don't like the look of me on my photos enough to actually want to get in touch, let alone want to meet up with me.'

'Don't be silly. You've had relationships since you and Trevor broke up. Actually, I think this is the longest stint you've not been in a relationship.'

'Not real ones though, not any I've felt serious enough to introduce to the kids. I mean, there's obviously something wrong with me, everyone else seems to break up and fall into another relationship straight away.'

'Yes, but you've got the kids. '

'That's no excuse, I'm in enough single parent groups on social media to know that even single parents manage to jump into a relationship not long after their last one. It's just me. There must be something wrong with me.'

'Don't be daft, there's nothing wrong with you.' Topping up their wine glasses, Bea took a gulp.

'Yeah right. Look at me. I'm fat, frumpy and almost forty.'

'You are not fat, or frumpy for that matter. Yes, you're nearing forty but you certainly don't look it.'

'Oh, I do. I even found a white hair the other day. Obviously, I yanked it straight out, but how harsh is that? Going straight to white rather than transitioning from grey to white?' Laughing,

Molly looked down into her wine glass. Gently circling her wrist, she watched as the red liquid sloshed upwards towards the rim and back down. Bea would tell her she wasn't fat or frumpy – she was her best mate, that was her job. But the mirror didn't lie.

'You're too hard on yourself. You need to start seeing yourself how other people see you. You're beautiful. You have amazing eyes and your hair is always gorgeous.'

'Yeah right. I haven't even brushed it today.' Unleashing it from its messy bun, she raked her fingers through her unruly curls and grimaced.

'Well, it always looks as though you've spent hours doing it every day.'

'Umm, you have to say that. Anyway, I've decided to have a break. I don't want anything to do with men again. At least while I get this place up and running. Maybe I'll go back on there in a few months or something, but I need a break. I want to be able to be one of those confident, happy single women. You know, the ones you see and you think yeah, she's got it? She doesn't need a man?'

'I know the ones you mean.' Nodding, Bea pointed to Molly's mobile. 'But aren't you even a tiny bit curious to find out who's messaged you and what he's said?'

'Have a look if you're that bothered.' Picking her phone up, Molly threw it into Bea's lap.

'Okay, I will.' Holding it in her free hand, Bea punched Molly's pin in and scrolled through. 'Oh, okay. Never mind.'

'Tell me then.'

'No, I wouldn't worry. It's a rubbish site. Maybe you could try a different one though instead of giving up completely? Someone at my work has recently got engaged to someone she met on Linked-Love.com. Why don't you get an account on there?'

'What did the message say?' It must have been something awful for Bea not to have shown her or even to have told her straight away. 'Go on, let me see.'

Bea passed Molly's mobile back to her and took another gulp of wine.

Squinting at the screen, Molly read the short message from someone called DanTheMan105. Yep, online dating really wasn't for her. Half the men were only after one thing and the other half were still pining for their exes. 'See what I mean now? There's no point.'

'Okay, maybe not on that one but, like I said, give Linked-Love.com a go. It sounds as though it might be better. You both have to have liked each other's profile in order to be able to message, I think, so at least you won't have to put up with sleazy comments like that.'

'Nope, I'm done. I am officially done. Let's face it, I haven't found a decent man in the past seven years since me and Trevor split and, to be honest, we both know he's miles away from being anything close to decent. I'm destined to be on my own.' Molly took a gulp from her glass, missed her mouth and quickly wiped the red liquid dribbling down her chin before trying again. 'I'm happy. I'm happy to be on my own. I'm going to focus on settling the kids at their new schools and getting this place up and running. I haven't got time for a relationship.'

'There'll be someone out there for you.'

'I think we both know that's probably a lie.'

'No, it's not.'

'Anyway, let's change the subject. Now the stocks in, what do you think?' Molly waved her glass around to encompass the shop floor. 'I know there's still a lot of empty shelf space but I'll order some more things soon. I just hadn't realised how much I could actually fit in here. But on the whole, what do you think? If I pick up some chairs tomorrow, do you think it'll look like a proper shop enough to open on Monday?'

'Yes, definitely.'

'Okay, cool. I'll pop those posters up in the morning then, try to get some knitters and natters to come in.'

'Good idea.' Staring at the wall opposite, Bea laughed. 'Just think a couple of weeks ago on a Monday morning you'd have been in some stuffy meeting and now, this Monday morning you'll be chatting to a load of people knitting and drinking tea!'

'Yeah, very weird. I still can't believe it's happening. I'm so glad to be out of the corporate world though.' Looking across at Bea, Molly frowned. 'Oh, I didn't mean there's anything wrong with the corporate world, there isn't, not with what you're doing. Your job sounds interesting and exciting, mine really wasn't. I was being paid minimum wage to be available to put up with whatever rubbish my egotistical boss decided to throw my way.'

'I do love my job but I'm glad you've got this place. I can really see you making a go of it and enjoying it at the same time.'

'I hope so.' Jerking her head, Molly stared at the front door. 'Surely that can't be someone knocking at the door at this time?'

Bea checked her watch. 'It is only half nine. Remember, we started early.'

'Yes, but I don't know anyone around here.'

'Probably the delivery guy, he might have realised he'd missed something off when he got back to the depo.'

'Yes, you're right.' Gripping the shelf behind her, Molly pushed herself to standing and smoothed down her top. Walking towards the door, she realised that she'd probably have to make the next drink a coffee if she wanted to get up and go to a car boot in the morning. Pulling the front door open, she let her eyes adjust to the dim light from the moon outside and focused on the person in front of her.

'Evening.'

'Oh, hello, Officer Duffey.' Frowning, Molly looked down at the wine glass in her hand. Was he going to tell her there was a law about drinking in your own home in this quaint little village? Surely not? 'I'm not driving.'

'No, I can see you'd be in no fit state to drive anywhere.'

What? Did he really just insult her? He'd come to *her* home, not the other way around.

'Did you say Officer? Are you a policeman?' Sidling up next to Molly, Bea beamed at Officer Duffey.

'I'm a police officer, yes, but I'm not on duty at the moment.' Pulling his coat sleeve up slightly, he looked at his watch.

Bea looked him up and down. Not very discreetly either. 'So, Officer Duffey, how can we help you? Would you like to come in for a drink?'

'It's Richie when I'm not on duty, and, no thank you.'

'Come on. Have you got another glass?' Putting her hand on Richie's arm, Bea gently guided him into the doorway.

'Honestly, I'm fine. Thank you.'

'Oh, go on, I bet you need a good drink or two to unwind after catching all of those dangerous criminals?'

Molly coughed. 'Me, he caught me. I was speeding.'

'Oh, really?' Pausing, Bea lowered her hand before shaking her head. 'Well, what's a speeding ticket between friends? I'll get you a glass.'

Watching Bea disappear up the stairs towards the flat to find another glass, Molly looked at Richie. 'Why did you really come round? We haven't had any music up loud. In fact, we haven't had it on at all.' Not that it's really any of your business. Yes, you may be a police officer but you can't dictate my life.

'No, it wasn't about the music. There's a car blocking me in, is it anything to do with you?'

'A car? Nothing to do with me, I'm afraid. My car's in one of the parking bays.' There were enough parking bays in front of the shop. Did he really think she'd park across his driveway?

'Do you mind taking a look and checking? I need to get home.'

'Okay.' Sighing, Molly walked past him out into the night air and glanced across at his mum's bungalow. In the dim light from the moon and the lonely streetlamp halfway down the road, she could just about make out a silver-coloured car. Drat, was that Bea's? It looked like hers.

'Everything okay?' Running back into the shop carrying an extra glass, Bea frowned. 'How come you're outside?'

'Bea, is that your car?'

'Where? Mine's the silver one.' Pouring the wine, she made her way back over to them.

Rolling her eyes, Molly stepped back into the warmth of the shop. 'You've parked across Richie's mum's driveway. How come you didn't use one of the parking bays?'

'Oh, hardly. I didn't know they were for the shop. I thought you might have to have one of those silly permits or something and I didn't want to get a fine.'

'Could you move it, please?' Richie crossed his arms.

'Really, Officer? I will if you promise not to arrest me.' Looking down at the wine glasses in her hand, Bea laughed. 'I'm hardly blocking the driveway, anyway. It might be a smidge over, but that's all. Here, have a drink.'

Taking the glass forced into his hand, Richie shuffled his feet. 'The thing is, there's a gate post the other side and I really don't want to end up scratching my car.'

'Okay, no worries. I'll move it.' Retreating back towards the counter, Bea pulled her car keys from her weekend bag before teetering back towards them.

'If you don't mind, I'll move it.' Holding his hand out, Richie frowned.

'Of course, that was what I was going to suggest. As you can see, I'm probably in no fit state to drive anywhere.'

'Exactly.' Taking the keys, Richie passed his glass to Molly and made his way towards the car.

'He's cute, isn't he?' Nudging Molly's arm, Bea blinked.

'Cute? No, he's anything but cute! He's already pulled me over and given me a speeding ticket, making me late for Trevor and allowing Trevor to feel superior about yet something else, and then he knocked earlier and complained at me for having my music turned up. I mean, his mother's bungalow is almost three feet away from my boundary wall. I'm starting to realise why the previous owners upped and left.'

'I'm sure he's okay really. Anyway, with muscles like that, I'm sure we can forgive quite a lot! He's probably just having a bad day or something.'

'Maybe, but it doesn't really make me feel very welcomed into the village.'

'Plus, the music thing was probably his mother complaining and making him do the dirty work.'

'Maybe.'

'Ooh, look here he comes. Why don't you ask him in? Offer him a coffee. Maybe for some reason, he doesn't like wine.'

Molly shook her head. She really didn't want to have to entertain him of all people, not that he'd want to spend time with them, anyway. 'No, you heard him, he's going home.'

'Ahh, but the night is young!'

'Bea, stop it! Let him get back to his wife and two-point-four children.'

'Fine.' Taking another gulp of wine, she held out her hand as Richie returned with her keys. 'Thank you.'

'You're welcome. We have a great taxi service in this village. I can ring one for you, if you like?'

'All booked, thank you!'

'Great. Bye.' Turning on his heels, Richie disappeared back into the dark night.

'See, he's helpful as well.'

'He was being condescending, he was making sure you weren't going to drive.'

'Well, of course I'm not going to drive. I've been drinking.' Frowning, Bea looked at her wine glass.

Shrugging, Molly locked the front door. 'I think I'm going to grab a coffee. Do you want one?'

'No, I'm good thanks. I'd better have Richie's drink.' Grinning, Bea took the full glass from Molly's hand.

5

Rolling over in bed, Molly hit her alarm. How could it be morning already? She was sure she'd only just got into bed. Yawning, she slipped out from underneath the duvet, quickly grabbing her dressing gown from the foot of her bed. She really must try to decipher the timer on the boiler.

Rubbing her eyes, she made her way down the hallway into the small galley kitchen and switched the kettle on.

Reaching into the pocket of her dressing gown, she pulled out her mobile as it pinged at her. Looking at the screen, she opened the message from Bea.

Bea – Good luck for the launch day!!!!!!!!!!!!!!!!!!

Biting her bottom lip, Molly scooped an extra spoonful of sugar into her coffee mug. That was why she felt like she hadn't slept. She probably hadn't. Even though she'd come up to bed early, she'd probably had a really light sleep. She always did when she was worried about something.

Wrapping her hands around her hot mug, she padded down the

stairs and into the shop. Looking around, she smiled. The chairs she'd found yesterday had added a really homely touch to the place. Even if it had taken her all morning to source them from various car boots and a house clearance. It made it look a bit different to the chain craft stores. There was a reason people would choose to come here, hopefully anyway.

She'd brought cupcakes for the Knit and Natter group today, not that she would every week. She'd try to bake her own. Home-made cakes would add a certain touch, and maybe she could even offer vegan ones too.

Taking a sip of coffee, she lowered her mug. What if there was a vegan knitter who came today? She hadn't bought any soya or oat milk or anything. Why hadn't she thought of that? More and more people were turning vegan, even Lauren who a few short weeks ago had been the most prolific chocoholic ever was trying to transition. She really would have to remember to get some oat milk in before the kids got back, Lauren had been nagging her for ages now. She shook her head; it wasn't worth worrying about. She was due to open the shop at nine and the local corner shop opened at the same time, she'd just have to offer juice or squash if needed. It would be fine.

Putting her coffee down on the counter, Molly plumped up the cushions on the assortment of chairs. Each one had been a good find. Yes, they were worn, but they still had a lot of life left in them and each fray and bald patch kind of added to the shabby chic feel.

She had two and a half hours until opening. Plenty of time to grab a shower, breakfast and venture into the courtyard to see if she could find some fresh flowers to pick and bring inside.

* * *

'Ooh, this looks lovely.'

'I love what you've done to the place!'

'Look, Susan, is this the wool you were looking for?'

'Yes, that's it. Just the shade of blue I need too.'

Making her way around the front of the counter, Molly clasped her hands in front of her and smiled, hoping no one could see the fear in her eyes. She hadn't thought she would be this nervous to welcome a group of potential customers into the shop. She tried to remind herself that they were coming for a nice, relaxed Knit and Natter, they weren't here to judge her or what she'd done with the shop.

Clearing her throat, she stepped forward. 'Hi, my name's Molly and I'm the owner of Bramble Patch. Thank you for coming.'

'Morning, lovely to meet you too, Molly. Come on, ladies. Let's take a seat.' An elderly lady with a purple wash in her short hair, stepped forward and took the first seat.

Smiling, Molly watched as the chairs quickly filled.

'Right, now, Molly, I'll begin with the introductions. I'm Gladys and I live just down the road, in fact, the next but one to your immediate neighbour.' The lady with the purple rinse grinned and looked to her left.

'Morning, I'm Susan. I live just outside the village but Gladys told me about your group and so I thought I'd join you. I hope you don't mind?'

'Of course not. Thank you for coming.' Molly smiled. Susan reminded her of her mum in some way. Possibly the quiet manner.

'I'm Lucy, and this little one is Frankie. This is usually his nap time so I'm hoping for a break.' Lucy grinned and shrugged out of her coat, revealing baby Frankie asleep in a sling strapped to her chest.

'Oh, he's lovely. How old is he?' Molly perched on the arm of an empty chair.

'He's seven weeks now. So still a newborn and not quite in a routine yet, but I'm hopeful.'

'Hey, I'm Eva. I have never knitted before in my life. Actually, I lie, my grandmother spent a painstaking four hours trying to teach me when I was about seven and she was babysitting me. She never tried again so I'm a little concerned I'm just not meant to knit but, hey, I saw your poster and thought I'd give it a go.' Eva grinned and patted her swollen belly. 'And of course, if by some miracle I can produce something not too embarrassingly rubbish, it would be nice to have something for when this one arrives.'

'I'm sure you'll soon pick it up. When are you due?' Molly tucked a loose strand of hair behind her ear.

'Not for another couple of months yet, so I've plenty of time to learn!'

'I'm Pat, myself and my husband, Bill, here, retired a few months ago and so we're looking for new hobbies to fill our time.'

'That's right. My mum always knitted and Pat here was interested in learning so I thought I'd come along too.' Crossing his legs, Bill grinned.

'Great. Well, I've got to be honest and say I'm overwhelmed by how many people have come along today so thank you, everyone, for coming along.' Looking around, Molly smiled. It really was great that so many people had turned up, even if it was nerve-wracking. 'Eva, Pat and Bill would you like to choose a ball of wool while I make the teas and coffees and then I'll come and help you choose the knitting needles?'

* * *

Patting a small notepad with the list of people's choices of tea and coffee, Molly stood in the doorway to the small back kitchen and smiled. Eva, Pat and Bill were sorting through the small basket of balls of wool Molly had placed on a coffee table she'd found at the car boot. Gladys and Susan had pulled their knitting from bags by their feet and were now chatting and cooing over baby Frankie.

Turning away, Molly went and switched the kettle on. She could do this. She could make friends and make this village their home. Plus, if this small group was anything to go by and the people around here were nice, their children must be as well. Lauren and Ellis would be fine, they'd settle into school. They'd enjoy it here. They just needed time to get used to everything.

Pouring the water into the mugs, Molly smiled. She knew it was all a big move, a huge deal, for the children especially, but they could do this. They could put roots down here. Eva and Lucy might have older children. Maybe they could set up a playdate for Ellis or organise a meet-up at the local coffee shop for Lauren. If the kids joined school even knowing one person, they'd find it easier, less daunting.

Placing the mugs on the tray, Molly put the plate of cupcakes on too and carried it through to the shop floor.

'Ooh cupcakes, lovely. There goes my diet this week!' Gladys chuckled before reaching out and grabbing one. 'Thank you, love.'

'You're welcome.'

Making her way around the group. Molly placed mugs in front of everybody before positioning herself between Eva, Pat and Bill.

* * *

'Can I get anyone another tea or coffee?' Standing up, Molly patted Eva on the arm. 'That's it, you've got it. Another six rows and I'll come back and show you what to do next.'

'Thanks.'

'I'll have another coffee, please?' Lowering his knitting needles, Bill raised his mug.

'Certainly.' Making her way through to the back kitchen, Molly lowered the tray full of empty mugs onto the work surface. Things were going well. Checking the time on the wall clock, Molly grinned. They'd been here for just over an hour already and she'd only expected people to hang around for an hour at the most. She must be doing something right. They must feel welcome at least.

Filling the mugs with boiling water, Molly stirred in the sugar before checking her phone. No messages or missed calls. She'd half expected Lauren or Ellis to have messaged to wish her luck. Well, Lauren anyway. Molly shook her head. Since splitting with Trevor, she'd always worked on the assumption that if she didn't hear anything from them, then she knew they were okay and happy. They never really called or messaged when they were at their dad's. Lauren had once confided that she found it more upsetting when Molly texted her, she'd said it reminded her of how much she was missing her, so since then Molly had told them she didn't mind if they didn't contact her as long as they knew they could, day or night, whatever the time. As long as they knew she was always there for them, they didn't have to make contact and Molly tried not to message them. However unnatural it felt, she needed to do what was best for Lauren and Ellis and for whatever reason they felt uncomfortable with it so she had to respect their wishes.

Grabbing the dishcloth, Molly wiped up a splash of tea from the work surface. Friday seemed so far away.

Shaking her head, she tried to put the fact that she was missing out on them being here for the opening week out of her mind. Lauren and Ellis would be having a far better time staying at Jessica's parents' house with the hot tub, large garden and theme park on the doorstep. However much Molly had wanted them here to open up their little family business, she knew they'd be enjoying themselves probably far more than if they were here, cooped up in the shop.

Molly picked up the tray, careful to keep it balanced as she made her way back through to the shop floor.

* * *

'... and then he took one look at my bump and said he'd let me off this time. I was so relieved. You can just imagine me having to explain to the midwife that I was late for the appointment because I'd been caught speeding. Thank you.' Eva took her coffee from Molly and turned back to Lucy.

'Aw, he's so lovely. I think we're really lucky here to have a police officer like him. You hear horror stories from other places where they've got officers who are just on an ego trip. You know the ones I mean? Who give out parking tickets just for fun?'

'I know the ones you mean, I got caught speeding yesterday just coming along the country road from the town and I must have literally only been doing a couple of miles over the limit, if I was doing that!' Placing Lucy's coffee on the coffee table in front of her, Molly grimaced at Eva. 'I wish it'd been the officer that pulled you over.'

'Yes, Officer Duffey is lovely.' Eva sipped her drink.

'Not to mention absolutely gorgeous!'

'Lucy!' Spluttering into her mug, Eva placed it on the table and took up her knitting again.

'Officer Duffey?' Frowning, Molly looked from Eva to Lucy. He was the officer they were speaking so highly of? How?

'Yes, he's always been very good. When the farm up the road was broken into last spring and half their farming equipment was stolen, he went above and beyond to get their stuff back.' Lucy patted baby Frankie on the back.

'I often think how difficult it must be for him to see this place every time he visits his mother. You can't imagine it, can you?' Eva wrapped her wool around her needle.

'Molly, love, could you just help me with this bit? I think I've gone wrong somewhere, this stitch looks really loose, doesn't it?' Pat held up her knitting.

Glancing back at Eva and Lucy who were again in deep conversation, Molly made her way towards Pat. What had they meant when they'd said he must find it difficult seeing this place? What did Bramble Patch have to do with him? Molly shook her head, it didn't matter anyway. It was none of her business.

* * *

Locking the door, Molly twisted the sign around to 'closed' and pulled the blind down to cover the glass panes in the door. Going back to the counter, she opened the till. The takings weren't too bad, not for a first day, anyway. Yes, she'd have to make more each day to keep afloat, but for a first day, she was happy.

Closing the till again, Molly ran her fingers through her hair and yawned. A nice warm bath and a good old cuppa were calling her. She just needed to switch off for a bit. Maybe after a bit of downtime, she'd find the energy to unpack some boxes upstairs.

Closing the door to the shop, she made her way up the narrow staircase towards the flat and reached into her back pocket as her mobile pinged. It was Lauren.

Lauren – Hey, Mum. How did the opening go?

Sinking down onto the top stair, Molly replied.

Molly – It was good thanks. Had quite a few people to the Knit and Natter and had a few customers xxx
Lauren – That's good then x
Molly – Yes. How's your day been? Xxx

Lauren – OK I guess. Ellis is annoying me x
Molly – Oh no, how come? Xxx
Lauren – Just being him. He's OK really. Miss you x

Pinching the bridge of her nose, Molly blinked back the tears stinging her eyes.

Molly – Miss you too. You'll be home soon though xxx
Lauren – Dad's on about us staying til Saturday now x

What? He'd said Thursday or Friday. Why did he have to keep changing the goalposts? He was quick to pick them up late and drop them off early when they were just going to their house, but when something like taking them to Jessica's parents' or something came up, he wanted to have them for longer. Taking a deep breath, Molly reminded herself that as long as he was seeing the kids and spending time with them, it didn't matter what the motivation behind it was. It didn't matter if he only wanted them when it was convenient for him. As long as Lauren and Ellis felt wanted and as long as they didn't realise what game he was playing, it didn't really matter.

Molly – How come? Xxx
Lauren – Jessica's brother is coming with his kids and Dad's said we can all go to the park Friday if we stay x

Molly swallowed.

Molly – I thought they were going the same time as you? xxx
Lauren – No that's Freya and Max's parents, this is another brother. Max and Freya are here already.
Molly – That'll be good then xxx

Lauren – I guess so x
Molly – Can I ring you? xxx

Shifting on the step, Molly crossed her legs and leant her back against the wall.

Lauren – Can we just text? I'm in the living room and everyone is here x
Molly – OK that's fine. We can text xxx
Lauren – Actually I need to go. I'll message later x
Molly – OK. I love you and can you tell Ellis I love him too, please? xxx

Clasping her mobile in her hand, Molly wiped her eyes. He'd done it again. He'd asked the kids if they wanted to stay before asking her if it was okay. For all he knew, she could have had something planned for Saturday. But, hey. It was all about him, wasn't it? She didn't matter. She never had.

Reaching behind her, she rubbed her neck. She certainly didn't matter now, but the kids did and she didn't want them being used as trophies he could flaunt when he wanted to and then not bother with until the next time something came up.

She wasn't going to message back, was she? It was probably dinnertime or something. Standing up, Molly picked her way through the towers of boxes to the bathroom.

6

Turning her music up to full volume, Molly switched her headlights to full beam. She could get used to this. Being the only person for miles around. Beyond the hedgerows lining the road, fields stretched for miles into the distance, their crops standing tall and proud against the moonlit backdrop of the evening.

Molly smiled, she'd treated herself to a bottle of wine and a frozen pizza from the supermarket which she was looking forward to opening. A nice TV night was calling for her today. Yes, she should probably spend the evening unpacking but, thanks to Trevor, she now had all week to do that and after moving things around to make room for another delivery, she needed a soak in the bath and then an evening binge-watching her favourite series. And she deserved it.

A loud 'pop' vibrated through the car and she gripped the steering wheel, trying to pull the car back towards the left as it shuddered and veered across the lines in the middle of the road.

Damn, what had happened? Slowing down, Molly could feel something was wrong. What was it? Had her tyre blown? Bringing the car to a stop at the side of the road, Molly was careful not to pull over too far onto the grass verge, she was sure a ditch ran the entire length of the road next to the hedgerow. The last thing she needed was to have to call someone to pull her out. Flicking her full-beam off, she clicked on her hazard warning lights and slipped out of the car.

Using the torch on her phone, she walked around the outside of the car, shining it on the tyres. The front ones were fine. Maybe she'd been imagining things.

Nope, the back right tyre had blown. A gasping gash seared its way through to the metal of the wheel. How had that happened? She'd only recently had the MOT done before they'd moved. Wasn't the garage supposed to check the tyres?

Shaking her head, she took a deep breath. Who was she kidding? She had no idea what was involved in a MOT apart from that it was supposed to give the car the all clear of being road-worthy and safe. Maybe they didn't check the tyres, or maybe it couldn't be predicted if a tyre was going to blow or not.

Turning around, she glanced up and down the road. There was no one to be seen, no car headlights in the distance and she was too far out for anyone but the most serious dog walkers, and it was too dark and late for them. Nope, she was definitely on her own.

Okay, she could do this. Well, no, she couldn't change a tyre, she never had. She'd never tried. She'd never needed to. The only time she'd got a flat tyre had been shortly after she'd passed her test and she'd driven one of her old friends to the City to go shopping. They'd noticed they had a flat and had rung her breakdown cover. She could remember as clear as if it was yesterday, that the mechanic who had come out had told her she wouldn't have been able to have changed it on her own anyway because she wouldn't have been strong enough. She remembered she'd felt more than ever so slightly miffed at that remark.

Well, she'd put on enough weight since then to have the power behind her to undo the wheel nuts now. She was sure of that. She just wished she'd learnt how to do it.

Shrugging her shoulders, she sighed. She paid enough money for breakdown cover, she might as well use it. Turning her phone over in her hand, the torch pointing downwards and illuminating the tarmac; she scrolled through her contacts. What would she have saved the number under? Something generic like 'Breakdown' or under the name of the company she was with?

Here, pressing the green button, Molly held the phone to her ear and listened to the rings.

What? The mobile went silent, the ringing stopped and the torch went out, the darkness suddenly engulfing her, only the hazard warning lights flickering on and off punctured the night. The pale shimmer from the moon up above barely illuminated the trees and hedges enveloping her.

Holding her phone in front of her, Molly stared at it, rapidly pressing the power button. Damn, the battery had run out.

Looking around her, the dark shadows of branches danced on the road in the glow of orange from the intermittent hazard warning lights. Rubbing her temples, she reminded herself that was all they were. They were just trees; it was just nature. There was nothing to worry about. She'd just charge her phone and ring them again. It wouldn't take long to get a bit of power.

Slipping back behind the steering wheel, Molly switched the little light on above the rear-view mirror and rummaged through the empty mint wrappers and old receipts in the small space beside the gear stick. She'd bought a new in-car phone charger only the other week after her old one had stopped working, which had probably been something to do with the fact that Lauren had yanked it out of the cigarette lighter in a panic to answer her phone to one of her friends.

Umm, that was strange. It wasn't there. Replacing the wrappers, she reached down into the side pocket on her door before leaning across the passenger seat and checking the one on the passenger's door.

Nope, it wasn't there either. Where on earth was it? She knew she'd definitely had the new one in here, she'd used it on the way when they'd moved. Leaning back against her chair, she closed her eyes. Lauren had taken it. She remembered now. She'd said something about Trevor not having the same phone as hers and needing to take it with her to charge her phone on the way to Jessica's parents' house.

Damn. Opening her eyes, she hit the palm of her hands against the steering wheel. What now? She was stuck in the middle of nowhere. Okay, not the middle of nowhere. She was probably only a few miles from home, but without a torch, Bramble Patch may as well have been twenty miles away.

Taking a deep breath, she breathed out slowly through her nostrils. She was being daft. All she needed to do was change the tyre and then she could get back. It couldn't be too hard, could it? And she basically knew how to do it, she'd just never tried to before.

Yes, she could do it. She vaguely remembered that cars normally had a jack hidden somewhere in the boot. And she knew that she'd have to be careful where she placed the jack. In a certain position, it would go through the bottom of the car. She was sure of that. It couldn't be too hard to work out, could it?

Slipping back out, she made her way to the back of the car and opened the boot. With the orange light from the hazards, she felt with her fingertips around the inside of the boot, and carefully pulled back the carpet covering the bottom. There it was, the little compartment. She'd known there'd be one. Putting her hand in, she felt around until she felt the cold of metal under her fingers. Pulling out the contraption, she slipped back into her seat to have a proper look at it in the light.

Okay, it looked as though it would be easy enough to work out. If she twisted this bit, that bit extended. She could do this. She'd get the jack in place and raise the car and then get the spare tyre out. Switching her headlights back on, she stood up and closed the driver's door.

Back around the back next to the blown tyre, Molly knelt down. Even with the glow from the headlights, it was still difficult to see. Resting back on her ankles, she ducked her head under, trying to see where to place the jack. Feeling along the underside of the car, she found a place which felt as though it might be a bit stronger than the rest.

Positioning the jack in place, she began twisting the small handle.

She felt the slow rumble of tyres on the tarmac before she saw the headlights swinging around the corner. Jumping up, Molly breathed a sigh of relief. Maybe they could help her. Or if they couldn't, they were bound to have a mobile she could borrow. Standing behind her car, out of the way of the oncoming vehicle, Molly waved her arms in the air.

Please stop. Please stop. Yes! As the car indicated and pulled to the side of the narrow country lane, Molly squinted against the bright headlights and tried to focus on the person who was getting out and coming towards her.

'Thank you so much for stopping.' Holding her hand up, Molly shielded her eyes from the bright headlights and cursed. 'Richie.'

'Miss Wilson. What's happened?'

'My tyre's blown.' Lowering her hand as he came and stood in front of his car, she could see he was on duty, he was wearing his uniform and although he hadn't put on the blue lights, the white of the car stood out in the dark night. Before moving here, she'd had literally nothing to do with the police; now she almost felt like a fugitive.

'How long will your breakdown recovery mechanic be?'

Looking down at the floor, Molly sighed. 'My mobile's out of battery so I haven't been able to ring them.'

'I see.' Crossing his arms, Richie strode towards the car, spotting the blown tyre. Whistling under his breath, he kicked it with the toe of his boot. 'That could have been quite nasty, you'll want to get it checked at a garage when you can, make sure it's not caused any other damage.'

'Yes, I will.' Nodding, Molly narrowed her eyes. All she needed was to borrow his phone. 'Could I borrow your phone to ring my breakdown cover, please?'

'Ah, it's okay. I can change it for you.' Rolling up his sleeves, he stepped towards the boot. 'Is the spare in here?'

'Yes.' Had the spare been in there? She hadn't noticed it when she was getting the jack out but then she hadn't been able to see much. They were normally kept in the boot, weren't they?

Turning on the torch on his phone, he pulled back the carpet again. 'There's nothing in here.'

'I've got the jack. Maybe the spares underneath.' That was a common place for them to be kept too. She remembered that's where the spare had been when she'd got a flat all those years ago.

Kneeling down, Richie shone the torch underneath the car before reaching underneath with his hand. Standing up, he wiped his hand down the leg of his trousers. 'Not there. You do have one, don't you?'

'Yes. Well, I assume I do. Every car has a spare, doesn't it? I've never had to use it, but I'm sure there must be one.'

'Actually, not every car has a spare, some just have repair kits.' He glanced at the jack which still stood underneath the car next to

Molly. 'But if you have a jack, I would assume you should have a spare.'

'Right. Well, I don't know.' Molly shrugged, it wasn't anything she'd ever looked for before. Why would she?

Shaking his head, Richie sighed. 'You'll have to wait until morning now, anyway.'

'No, if I could just borrow your phone please, I'll give the breakdown service a call.'

'And you think they carry around spares? Enough different sizes to fit any car?'

Opening her mouth, Molly closed it again. Right, that had told her, hadn't it? Who did he think he was, talking to her like that? Okay, maybe she hadn't thought about it properly, but would the breakdown service really not be able to fit a new tyre? Surely they must come across this problem all the time?

'And before you say they'll be able to tow you, garages around here close for the night. It's not like where you're from, where everything probably stays open all night. This is the countryside.'

Seriously? He didn't even know where she'd moved from. Shaking her head, Molly reached inside, turned the lights off and pulled the key from the ignition. Shutting the door quietly but firmly behind her, she turned on her heels and began walking.

'Where are you going?'

Glancing behind her, she could see him still standing in the middle of the road. 'Thanks for the help, but I'm going to find somewhere I can ring from.'

'We're miles from the village.'

Shrugging her shoulders, Molly clenched her jaw. Yes, she knew that, but what was the alternative? Stay on the side of the road until morning or have him possibly offer her a lift home? Not a chance that she'd be getting in the car with him. She had no idea what problem he had with her apart from the fact that he'd caught her

speeding, but even then, as she'd overheard, he'd caught other
people from the village speeding and let them off, so she'd obviously unintentionally annoyed him from even before that meeting.
She shrugged, maybe he didn't like the model of her car, who knew.
She certainly wasn't going to hang around and let him make her
feel worse, she was sure of that.

'Miss Wilson. Please, it's dangerous to walk that far in the pitch
black.'

Molly grimaced, she hated people referring to her with her
surname. She hadn't changed it back to her maiden name after the
divorce – she'd wanted to stick with the same name as Ellis and
Lauren – and every time someone used it out loud like that she was
reminded she would always be Trevor's ex. Whatever she did,
however much she changed as a person in her own right, she would
always be his ex-wife. Nothing would change that. 'It's Molly, my
name's Molly.'

'Okay, Molly, please get in the car and I'll give you a lift back to
yours. You'll only get knocked down or cause an accident. This road
is treacherous in the dark.'

Great, so he wasn't really worried about her, he was worried
about her causing an accident. Thanks, Richie. Molly blinked back
the tears stinging her eyes. Where had they even come from? She
didn't even need to think about it. She knew why she felt like
crying. She knew why she'd had the icy-cold feeling of despair in
the pit of her stomach ever since they'd moved. Even before, once
she'd made the decision, if she was honest. It just hadn't felt as
overwhelming when they'd still been living in the marital home,
back in the town she knew, back where she felt safe and had
people around her she knew. Back where she'd had a support
network.

Now, it was all gone, the friendly neighbours popping around
for a cuppa and a catch-up, her parents living a couple of miles out

of town. Heck, even the ex-in-laws. Everyone she'd relied on to feel safe and secure, to have as a backup were gone.

Lauren and Ellis must be feeling the exact same. No, worse, because let's face it, they hadn't chosen this. They hadn't wanted to leave their home, their friends, their family. They'd wanted to stay.

Curling her fingers up, Molly dug her nails into the palms of her hands. It wasn't her fault. Yes, she'd chosen to move here, to move this far away. She'd ultimately made the final decision. But it had been Trevor who had pushed for the sale of the house. It had been Ellis and Lauren's own father's fault that they had been kicked out of their home, that he had fought for just enough of the equity to force them to leave. To make sure that she had been priced out of all the suitable housing in their old town and surrounding villages.

But, maybe she hadn't needed to move them quite as far. There had been places closer, but not close enough to stay at their old schools. And if they had to move schools anyway then she'd thought why not give them a better life? And that's what she'd wanted, she'd wanted to give them the stability of being in control of their income, of having a family business, of at least being there for them after school. She had visions of them drinking milkshakes and eating biscuits stood around the shop counter after school, chatting about their day and taking it in turns to serve customers.

It wasn't going to be like that, was it? What had she actually done? Lowering herself to the grass verge, Molly put her head in her hands, the tears fresh and rapid against her cheeks. She shouldn't have moved them so far. Lauren was right, she'd chosen this new life, not them. What had she done?

Taking deep rasping breaths, Molly was grateful for the darkness encompassing her. She'd had to be so strong, had to have been 'the strong one' ever since the solicitor's letter had been pushed through the letter box. Throughout the whole court proceedings Molly hadn't let herself cry, hadn't let herself admit how she was feeling. She hadn't told anyone how much it hurt, again and again and again, to know that Trevor, the person she had thought she'd spend the rest of her life with, showed such indifference towards her, such loathing that he couldn't care less if he pushed her out of her home.

Car headlights penetrated the darkness, getting brighter and brighter as they neared. Lifting her head up, she pushed the heels of her hands against her eyes, trying to stop the flow of tears.

They'd pass. If she just kept sitting here, they wouldn't even notice her.

Sighing, Molly realised that the car was slowing until it came to a stop just in front of her.

'Molly? Get in the car.' Richie's voice, with its unmistakable twang, filtered out from the window.

Pulling the sleeves of her jumper down over her hands, Molly wiped her eyes, drying her tears. Biting her bottom lip, she watched as he got out and walked towards her. Why couldn't he just leave her alone?

'Please, just get in and I'll give you a lift.' Kneeling down in front of her, Richie looked her in the eye. 'Are you crying?'

Shaking her head, Molly looked away.

Running his fingers through his hair, he looked down at the floor before looking back at her. 'Look, I'm sorry if I was a bit harsh. I certainly didn't mean to upset you.'

'Please, just leave me alone.' Pushing her hands against the cool grass, Molly stood up and began walking again.

'Molly, please? I know I've upset you. I shouldn't have spoken to you the way I did. I...' Jogging to catch her up, he gently touched her elbow.

'You haven't upset me.' Looking away into what she assumed was another field of corn standing proud in the dark night, Molly lowered her voice. 'I just... it's not you. It's everything.'

'Let me give you a lift. Please?'

Nodding, Molly followed him back to the police car, waited until he had opened the passenger door for her and slipped in. At least if she had a lift, she'd be home quicker. He would only keep following and nagging her otherwise. This way would be quicker.

Sitting in silence, Richie turned the ignition, the low rumble of the engine firing to life. She'd never ridden in a police car before. She glanced behind her into the back seats. At least she wasn't sitting in there. The way Richie seemed to have something in for her, she was quite surprised she wasn't.

The radio crackled into life, drawing Richie's attention.

'Sorry, I just need to get this.' Picking it up, he spoke into the radio, a woman's voice on the other end directing him. Lowering the radio back into its holder, Richie tapped the steering wheel with his thumbs. 'I'm really sorry, but I'm going to have to take that job. I just need to make a quick stop and then I'll get you back.'

'Okay.' Looking out of the side window, Molly clasped her hands in her lap. She might as well just give up on any idea of rescuing her car tonight. She'd ring the breakdown service in the morning. Richie was probably right, and if he was, the car would end up getting towed to the nearest garage where no doubt she'd be charged a small fortune to get a new tyre fitted. She shook her head. That could be a problem she faced tomorrow.

Pressing a button on the dash in front of him, they were suddenly surrounded by an aura of blue as the lights from the siren whirred into action. 'Really sorry about this. It's a little all-night truck stop café, they've rung in. It's probably nothing but...' Richie shrugged.

'It's fine.' Keeping her eyes focused on the hedgerow beside her, Molly watched as trees and road signs momentarily appeared and disappeared as they sped past. As they took corners at speed and drove through another small village, the few cars on the road moved out of the way for them, bumping up kerbs and pausing at roundabouts. It was all new to Molly, since moving they'd barely had time to explore their village let alone venture any further. She'd have to take the kids on a drive one day, check out the local environment.

Passing through a village, Richie took a sharp left turn. 'It's just up here.'

Molly nodded, she could see it now, a fairly large illuminated greasy spoon café surrounded by a large car park half filled with lorries and trucks.

Pulling into the car park, the police car came to an abrupt stop outside the café and Richie turned to her. 'Lock the doors and stay here.'

Molly watched as he jogged inside, the glass door swinging shut behind him. Squinting her eyes, she tried to make out what was happening inside. There didn't seem to be any commotion. A group of three drivers sat hunched over their meals in the far corner of the café, but apart from them, Molly could only see the woman behind the counter.

Peering out of the window, she watched as Richie spoke to the woman before coming back outside.

Opening the driver's door, Richie leant his head in. 'False alarm. Some wiring issue with their alarm system or something. Did you want to grab a bite to eat? They said we could have something on the house for our troubles.'

Go in? Running the pads of her thumbs across her cheeks, she wiped the dried tears. She must look a complete state and it would be obvious she'd been crying. Going in and getting something to eat with Richie was the last thing she wanted to do, but she couldn't very well say that, could she? Thank him for giving her a lift but deny him the chance to get a freebie dinner? She knew she was being unfair. Nodding, she opened the passenger door and slipped out. She hadn't eaten, and her stomach was beginning to rumble, she should eat.

Holding the door open for her, Richie smiled as she pulled her hair over her shoulder hoping it would cover her pale, tear-stained face.

Leaning in, he whispered, 'Don't worry. You look great. You don't look like you've been crying.'

Feeling her face burn with the blush creeping across her cheeks, she looked at the floor. How had he known what she'd been thinking?

'Where do you want to sit?' Standing inside the doorway, Richie looked over at Molly.

'Umm, over there?' Molly pointed to a table by the window overlooking the car park. She didn't really care where they sat, she just wanted to get this over and done with and go home to her sofa and TV.

'Choose anything you want on the menu, all on the house.' The woman from behind the counter came over to them, pulling a pen from behind her ear and a notebook from her apron pocket before she got to them. 'Anything at all. I can only apologise again for the misunderstanding. The boss is on the phone to the alarm service as we speak. Although what luck he'll have at this time of the night, I don't know.'

'Like I said, no need to apologise. I'm just glad you're safe. I'd much rather a false alarm than the other.'

'That's true. Do you want a drink before you choose?'

'Yes, that'd be great, please? Molly?'

'Umm.' Scouring the laminated menu on the tabletop, Molly shook her head. 'I'll have a coffee, please?'

'Fat white, latte or cappuccino?'

'Flat white, please?' Looking up, Molly smiled. She noticed that pinned on her blouse the woman had a badge telling the world that her name was Majorie. With tight black ringlets framing her face, the name Majorie suited her. Not that Molly had ever met a Majorie before or had ever really wondered what a Majorie would look like, but it did, it suited her.

'Me too, please?' Tapping the menu against the top of the plastic white table, Richie stretched his arms above his head and yawned.

'Coming right up.' Turning on her heels, Majorie made her way back behind the counter.

'Are you tired? Has it been a long shift?'

'Not especially, but I didn't get much sleep and I'm definitely feeling it today. Coffee was just what the doctor ordered. Thanks for coming in with me.'

Molly shook her head. 'Thanks for the lift.'

'Well, the half lift anyway.' Richie chuckled under his breath. 'I will get you home though, I promise.'

'Thanks.'

'You're welcome.' Putting his hands down on the table in front of him, he looked her in the eye. 'Are you all right?'

'I'm fine, thanks. Although I have just realised, I left my shopping in the boot of the car.'

'Oops! Anything frozen in there?'

'Only the pizza I was going to have for dinner tonight.' Molly laughed.

'Good job we're eating here now then.'

'I guess so.' Nodding, Molly looked at him. His eyes looked kind and the lines around his eyes suggested he was certainly capable of laughing. What was it with her that wound him up so much?

'Here you go. Two flat whites. Are you ready to order?' Majorie placed the two mugs on the table between them.

'Thank you.' Pulling her mug towards her, Molly looked at the menu and ran her finger down the selection.

'There's so much to choose from.'

'The all-day breakfast is good. I highly recommend it. In fact, that's what I'll go with, please?'

'Could I have the same please, but the veggie option?' An all-day breakfast sounded good. She couldn't actually remember the last time she'd had a cooked breakfast. Last year, maybe? When she'd taken Lauren and Ellis to the caravan park for a week in the summer holidays.

'Coming right up.' Scribbling in her notepad, Majorie left the table.

Lacing her fingers around her coffee mug, Molly shifted in her seat. 'So, have you been here long then? At the village, I mean.'

'Yes, I was born and bred there. Moved away to the City for a bit, but the draw of village life soon pulled me back.'

Nodding, Molly stared into the pale froth of her coffee.

'How about you? What brought you here?'

'Oh, umm.' Looking up, Molly shook her head. 'I was just looking for something different.' He didn't want to hear the whole sorry affair of the events that had led them to move.

'Nice.'

Crossing her legs under the table, Molly took a sip from her coffee.

Slipping the laminated menu back into its holder, Richie looked across at her. 'Look, I know I've said this before, but I am sorry if it seemed like I was having a go at you back there.'

'It's okay.'

'No. No, it's not. I shouldn't have been so...' Pulling a sachet of sugar from the ceramic pot perched at the edge of the table, he shook it before emptying its contents into his mug.

'Flippant, cold-hearted?' Molly laughed. 'Sorry, I didn't mean to say that.'

Pausing, Richie looked at her before laughing. 'No, you're right,

I probably have come across as quite cold. Which obviously isn't great for my reputation as being the caring local copper.'

'Nope, it's not.' Taking another sip of her coffee, she looked over the rim at Richie. Stirring the sugar in, he looked quite sad, lost. 'Sorry, I didn't mean to offend you.'

Laying the spoon down on the table next to his mug, he blinked and looked at her. 'No, you haven't offended me. You're right though, I haven't been especially welcoming to you. You see, the shop you've bought has stood empty for a couple of years now. Ever since...'

'Here you go. Two all-day breakfasts. One veggie, one meat. Enjoy!' Sliding two large plates across the table, Majorie grinned at them. 'Just shout if you want anything else.'

'Thank you.' Looking down at the plate in front of her, Molly inhaled the steam, the aroma of mushrooms, hash browns and beans filling her nostrils. Nothing could beat a cooked breakfast. Looking back over at Richie, she tilted her head. 'What were you saying?'

'Oh, nothing. It doesn't matter.'

'Yes, it does. You were going to tell me something about my shop. About it being left empty for a couple of years.'

'Oh, I'll tell you another time.' Waving off Molly's question, he picked up his cutlery. 'This looks amazing, doesn't it?'

Frowning, Molly looked down at her plate. 'Yes, it does.'

7

Pushing back the duvet, Molly grimaced as her feet touched the cold floorboards. She really did need to invest in a rug. The kids' bedrooms already had carpet laid but hers for some reason didn't. Padding to the window, she inched the curtain aside and peeked out. It had been the door that woke her then, Richie was stood on the threshold to Bramble Patch.

Ducking back behind the curtain, Molly bit down on her bottom lip. What was the time? Had she overslept? She needed to open the shop at nine, but she was sure she'd set an alarm.

'Molly!'

Damn, he must have seen her. Pulling her dressing gown from the back of her door, she wrapped it around her and pulled the belt tight, knotting it as she ran down the stairs. She must have overslept, she should have opened up already. Her second day of trading and she'd failed already.

Hurrying through the shop, she pulled open the front door. 'Sorry, I must have overslept. I just need to get dressed and I'll open up.'

'Open up? It's only half past seven. Sorry, have I woken you?'

'Half seven?' So she hadn't overslept then. She'd planned to have a bit of a lie-in and had set the alarm for eight.

'Yes, I thought I'd give you a lift to the garage and we can get a new tyre for your car. I thought it would save you the hassle of calling out the breakdown service and having to wait around for them.'

'Oh right. Thank you. That would be great, if you really don't mind?'

'That's why I'm here.' Grinning, Richie held out his arms.

'Right, of course. Well, I just need to get dressed. Come in, I won't be long.' Holding the door open for him, Molly stood to the side.

'I'm okay here, thanks. I'll wait outside.'

Molly shrugged. 'Okay.'

* * *

Pulling the door to the shop closed behind her, Molly locked it. Turning around, she took a deep breath, letting the cool spring air fill her lungs, and made her way towards Richie who had perched on a small wall surrounding a raised planter in front of the shop.

'Ready?' Standing up, Richie wiped his hands down his jeans.

'Yes, thanks for waiting.' Tucking a loose strand of hair behind her ear, Molly gave up and pulled the hairband out, bundling her hair back into a messy bun. She hated having her hair up, but she hadn't wanted to make Richie wait while she straightened it and if she'd left it down as it was, she'd resemble someone who had recently stuck their fingers in a plug socket. Shrugging, she wrapped the hairband around again. It would have to do.

'You're welcome. My car's at mine. I felt lazy driving the few metres to yours.'

Molly nodded. He wasn't on duty today then, at least not yet.

His jeans and brown jumper suited him. Not that he didn't look good in uniform, but he definitely looked more relaxed in his normal clothes. Molly shook her head. 'Looked good' where had that come from? Matching his pace, she followed him to the end of the road and turned left.

'It's the one with the blue car at the end.' Pulling his keys from his pocket, he jangled them in his hand.

'Lovely.' The end of terrace small chocolate box cottage was beautiful. Sunshine yellow shutters framed the windows and a blossom tree, just beginning to flower, filled up most of the small front garden.

'Thanks. Unfortunately, the inside doesn't quite match up to the outside yet. The previous owners had stripped it of all its period features, trying to modernise it apparently, so I've still got quite a lot of work to do to get it back to its former glory.'

'Have you moved in recently then?'

'A couple of years ago now. There's really no excuse for me not to have finished it by now. But, I've got someone coming to make the chimney usable again next week and then I have a beautiful vintage cast iron fireplace I'm going to install.'

'It all takes time, doesn't it?' Molly slipped into the passenger seat and pulled the seatbelt across.

'Yes, it does. It just takes some people longer than others.' Grimacing, Richie looked in his rear-view mirror and pulled away from the kerb.

* * *

Sitting on a low wall in front of a garage in the town, Richie checked his watch again. 'Sorry, I just assumed they'd open up at eight.'

'Don't worry.'

'You'll be late opening the shop though, won't you? Have you got your group today?'

Molly shook her head. 'Not today, I think I'm going to officially run it three times a week but have the option for people to come in to sit and knit whenever really. I probably won't have any customers today so I doubt it matters what time I get back. Why don't you ask your mum if she wants to come along tomorrow? The people who came yesterday were really lovely and we have a few beginners too, so it doesn't matter if she can knit or not.'

Looking down at his feet, Richie bent down and tucked in a loose shoelace. 'I don't really think it's her thing.'

'Oh, okay.' Molly shifted her position on the wall before clearing her throat. 'Is it because of the music?'

'What music?'

'Because I had my music up loud the other evening after my kids had gone to their dad's and you came to say it was too loud for her?'

Shaking his head, Richie wiped his hand across his face. 'I'd forgotten about that. No, she doesn't mind music and, to be honest, she's losing her hearing so wouldn't have been able to hear it anyway.'

Narrowing her eyes, Molly frowned. 'So why did you come and complain then?'

'I... Sorry, like I said last night, I haven't made you feel particularly welcome here, have I?' Glancing across at the garage, he stood up as someone came out and pulled the shutters up revealing the door to the reception area. 'Great, we might just be able to get your car back on the road by half nine.'

Looking down at her fingers clasped in her lap, Molly bit her bottom lip. 'Hadn't made her feel particularly welcome'? That was an understatement if ever she'd heard one. A speeding ticket, a complaint about her music and moaning about parking all in the space of twenty-four hours? What was really going on? Standing up, she placed her arm on his forearm, waiting for him to turn around. 'You're right, you've not made me feel particularly welcome. In fact, you seem to have gone out of your way to make my life more difficult.'

'I wouldn't put it quite like that.'

'Really? Let me see, you gave me a speeding ticket, complained about my music, which for your information I had only put up so loud because I was trying to drown out the thoughts swirling around in my mind about my kids going up to spend a week with their new step-mum's parents. Oh, and then you had to come and complain about my friend's car because it was overhanging your mum's driveway by, what? An inch?' Shoving her hands in the pockets of her light jacket, Molly could feel the heat rising to her face. He had been awkward, rude. It wasn't just her imagination.

Looking down at his shoes, Richie rubbed the back of his neck.

She'd made him feel uncomfortable. She should stop. Just let it all go. He had brought her here and was helping her get her car back on the road and he'd been uncharacteristically pleasant at the café last night. Maybe she'd just caught him on a bad day? But no, it still wasn't right. She'd been having a bad time of it lately too. In fact, she'd been having a pretty rubbish year by all accounts and she hadn't gone out of her way to treat anyone with the same distaste he had shown her. 'Then, just to top it off, last night when you saw my tyre had blown, which I may add wasn't my fault, you were really rude to me.'

Glancing towards the garage behind him, Richie looked back at her and held out his arms. 'I'm sorry. As the local police officer, I should have been more welcoming.'

'As a normal human being, you should have been more welcoming.' Shaking her head, she tried to flick loose hair from her eyes as the slight morning breeze picked up before looking him in the eye.

She'd gone too far. He looked upset, his eyes had glistened over. She was the one being rude now. He was doing her a favour, and this was how she was repaying him. What was the matter with her? 'I'm sorry. I'm being rude, I just... I don't know. I guess it's been playing on my mind. I've obviously done something to annoy you and I don't know what.'

Taking a step towards her, Richie reached out and tucked a loose strand of hair behind her ear before letting his hand drop in front of him. 'It's not you. It's a lot of things. But not you.'

'What is it then? Have you had a bad experience with newcomers before or something?'

'No. Look, I used to own the shop.'

'Bramble Patch?'

'Diane's Dresses as it was called back when I owned it. Well, when my ex-wife owned it. I bought it for her as a gift on our wedding day. My grandparents had recently passed away and left me some money, I ploughed it all into that shop to give to her. She'd always dreamt about opening up a clothes shop.'

'Oh right. That's nice then.' Molly frowned. What did that have to do with her though?

'Yes, it was. It was lovely. She loved running the place. Obviously, it being right next to my mum's place was the icing on the cake. It meant that when our daughter was born, my mum could help with childcare when my ex had to go into the shop.'

'I didn't know you had a daughter.'

'Yep, she's fourteen now.'

Molly nodded. 'The same age as my daughter, Lauren,'

'It's a good age.'

'Yes, apart from the teenage mood swings, I guess. So you're annoyed that I bought the place then?'

'No, not annoyed.' Sitting back down on the low wall, Richie looked down at the floor. 'I don't know. It just dredged up a lot of emotions, if I'm honest. The fact that someone else was moving into the place that had meant so much to Diane, I guess.'

'Do you still see your daughter?' Sitting down next to him, Molly laid her hand gently on his arm.

Smiling sadly, Richie nodded. 'Yes, I do. She comes to stay every other weekend and then she stays over sometimes during the week too. Not as often as I'd like, mind. I'm sorry, I can't even explain why it was such a big deal to me. I guess, when I finally put it on the market just over a year ago I was all ready and prepared for it to sell. Then when it didn't sell, I just kind of put it out of my head. I'd just got over my relationship with Diane and what she'd done and then, you came, and it all came back.'

'What happened? Sorry, I shouldn't have asked. You don't have to answer that.'

'No, it's fine. She left me for another bloke. Ran off to Spain to begin with until that relationship broke down and she came back, tail between her legs, wanting me to take her back. The worst part though, which I hadn't known about, was that she'd been using the flat above the shop to spend time with him. She'd practically had him living there for a good six months before she left me.'

'That's awful.'

Richie nodded before looking at her. 'It is, but it's also in the past. I've moved on from her now. If she walked up to me now and said she wanted to get back with me, there'd be no chance.'

'I know what you mean, though. I don't love Trevor, my ex, any more and, to be honest, the whole idea of getting back with him turns me cold, but it's still weird when he comes to pick the kids up or drops them off. He was still the person who I was convinced that I'd live with and love until I died, and now, he treats me like a complete stranger. Actually, he almost treats me with contempt which I don't understand because I don't think I've ever done anything wrong to him.'

'I'm sure you haven't done anything. It says more about him than you.'

'Maybe. But that's what hurts, the fact that it's all gone, everything. That feeling of him being my home and caring for me, gone. I just don't understand how anyone can switch their feelings off so completely that they don't hold any feelings for the other person whatsoever. He has this whole other life now that doesn't include me. And that's fine, like I said, I don't love him any more, probably stopped loving him before we divorced even, but it's the way I've gone from supposedly being the love of his life to be not worthy for a civil "hello, how are you?" type thing.'

'It is strange how you can be the centre of someone's universe one moment and then not mean anything to them the next. I mean, I still care about Diane, and I probably always will, she's the mother of my daughter and we've so many memories together.' Sitting up straighter, Richie put his hand on her arm.

'Exactly.' Shaking her head, Molly looked down at his hand and then across at the garage. 'I don't think I'll ever understand. Anyway, I suppose we'd better go and get the tyre or any potential customers of mine will be left standing outside.'

'Yes, we should.' Standing up, he held his hand out towards her, waiting until she'd grasped it, and pulled her to standing.

8

'Good morning, I don't think we've met.'

Looking up from where she'd been kneeling helping Eva with her knitting, Molly stood up. 'Oh, hello. No, I don't think we have.'

'I'm Wendy Thomas, the mayoress. Pleased to meet you.'

'Pleased to meet you too.' Slipping her hand into Wendy's, Molly shook hands and smiled. 'Have you come to join our Knit and Natter?'

Smiling, Wendy shook her head. 'No, sorry, I wish I had the time. I've come to sign you up as a participant to the Spring Village Food and Drink Fete.'

'Oh right.' Molly frowned. 'I'm afraid apart from offering tea and coffee, I don't really serve food.'

'Oh no, I don't mean for a stall, I mean as a shop.'

'Right.' Molly glanced across at Gladys who looked as though she was busy winding some loose wool into a tight ball, but Molly knew she was probably eavesdropping.

'No one's told you about the Spring Fete, have they, love?' Lowering her ball of wool, Gladys smiled kindly.

Thank you, Gladys. 'No, I'm afraid I don't know anything about it.'

'Ah, that's okay, love. We get a ton of stalls selling food and drink, some stalls from local cafes and some who travel that bit further. The village shops all stay open late and normally have demonstrations or activities going on to entice the shoppers. It's normally a good day.'

'Yes, it's quite the event. One of the local tour companies puts on coaches to ferry people from the local towns, so we get up to close a thousand people visiting the village.' Wendy clasped her clipboard to her chest.

'Wow, that's a lot.' Molly looked around the small shop.

'Don't worry, that's throughout the day. It doesn't feel like too much at the time.' Lowering his knitting needles, Bill looked across at them.

'So, what can I put you down for? What activity or demonstration will you be offering? And what type of discount or offer can I put you in for? I'll be sending out the village newsletter in the next couple of days and I also need to let the organisers know for the programmes they'll be printing.'

'Give the poor girl a bit of time. She's only just moved in, haven't you, love?' Gladys chimed up.

'No, it's fine.' Molly smiled, she certainly didn't want to miss out on any free advertising. 'Umm, I'll put on a knitting demonstration, and for the offer, I don't know, a twenty per cent discount on anything bought that day?'

'Great, great. I'll write you down for that. Thank you.' Scribbling on her clipboard, Wendy turned on her heels and disappeared out of the door.

'She's a funny one, she is.' Bill nodded after her.

'No, she's not. She's just focused, that's all.'

'Is that what you call it? In that case, she's so focused she doesn't give anyone any time to think. It's all just jump, I'm here type of attitude.'

'Oh, do stop moaning, Bill. We all know the only reason you don't get on with her is because you wanted to be mayor.' Pat tapped him on the arm with her knitting needle.

'Did you run to be mayor?' Perching on the edge of an empty chair, Molly looked across the circle at him.

'This was years ago which makes it even harder to fathom why he's got a problem with her.'

'Yes, but you've got to admit, she is a tad abrupt.'

'Maybe.' Pat shook her head before looking across at Molly. 'So, love, do you need any help with the knitting group? We're free the Saturday after next, aren't we, Bill? We could come over and give you a hand for a bit, if you like? We'll have our grandchildren at some point, no doubt, but we could come for a few hours. I know we're beginners ourselves but we could help with the tea and coffee or something?'

'Did you say the Saturday after next?' Rubbing the back of her neck, Molly grimaced. Why hadn't she asked when it was? How had she forgotten to ask about the details? She didn't know anything about it and yet she'd just agreed to run a group and offer a discount. She should have just told Wendy that she'd get back to her. She should have worked everything out first. Would she even make much of a profit if she gave a discount of twenty per cent? But then anything lower might not be enough to entice the shoppers. Biting her bottom lip, Molly looked down. She should have given this more thought.

'Yes, don't look so worried, love. It'll be fine. I can come across to help too if you want?' Lowering her knitting to her lap, Gladys smiled at her.

'Thanks. That'd be great if you guys really don't mind?'

'Of course, we don't.' Pat grinned.

'I'm happy to come too.' Taking a sip of her coffee, Susan patted Molly's knee. 'The shop is ready anyway and if we all come, we can help with the knitting groups and with the refreshments. Between us, we should be able to cover most of the day I should think, can't we?' Looking across at Pat, Bill and Gladys, Susan picked her knitting back up.

'Count me in too, I'll have to bring my brood but I'm sure we can put them to good use helping.' Lucy rubbed Frankie's back.

'And me. I've got work in the afternoon, but will be able to help in the morning, if that's any good?'

'Thanks, Eva. Thanks all of you. It would really be amazing to have some help and some moral support.' Molly had never done anything like this before. After working in an office for years, her interaction with the general public had always been quite limited.

'You're very welcome. By offering these Knit and Natter groups, you've done us a good deed, now it's our turn to repay the favour.' Gladys nodded and hooked a strand of wool over her needle.

'Thank you. Do you think there'll be many people who actually come in here? I'm not sure if I need to put an extra order in.' Tapping her fingers against her knee, Molly tilted her head.

'You and your husband used to run the old toy shop, didn't you, Susan?' Pat used her knitting needle to point across the circle. 'Did you find that you had more sales on the day of the fete?'

'Yes, we did. Oh, I remember those days used to be crazy. We'd have hundreds of visitors through the door. Yes, we used to be rushed off our feet and then when we did eventually close – the mess! You've never seen anything like it! Toys put back in the wrong places, mud traipsed through on the carpet. I remember one year we found a missing piece of a puzzle two weeks later which had somehow got kicked under one of the shelves.' Smiling, Susan shook her head. 'The hard work was always worth it though, some years we made as much in that one day as we did in a month.'

'Really? Wow, it does sound as though I need to get an extra order in then!' Did she have enough money in the business account to buy extra stock in the hope that it sold on the day of the fete? Molly shook her head. She'd have to make sure there was. She couldn't miss out on the opportunity. Plus, if she made a good impression then hopefully some of the visitors would become regular customers. She could only try her best and hope.

'It really will be a good day. Always is.' Bill grinned and looked at Pat.

* * *

Balancing on the small stool, Molly reached up and Blu-tacked the poster above the shelf.

'Careful you don't fall.'

Gripping the edge of the shelf, Molly twisted her neck. It was Richie. 'Hi. Everything okay?'

'Yes, thanks. Just thought I'd pop in and check to see if your car's all right after yesterday.'

Turning around, Molly stepped down from the stool, holding the Blu-tack in her hand. 'I'm sure it is, I've not used it since yesterday but I'm assuming it's fine. Have you just finished work?' Molly indicated to his uniform.

'Nope, just on a break. Did you get back in time for your customers?'

'Ah, yes, nobody was waiting anyway. Thanks again for sorting the tyre yesterday.'

'It was nothing.' Waving his hand, Richie looked up at the poster.

'It's not straight, is it?' Turning back, Molly laughed. 'Yep, it's definitely not straight. In fact, I don't think I could have got it any more crooked.'

Tilting his head, Richie grinned. 'Possibly not. You might actually have a talent for putting up the most crooked posters.'

'Oi! Thanks!' Turning back to him, Molly shrugged. 'I'll have another go later. Do you have time for a coffee?'

'Yes, that'd be lovely, please?'

'Coming right up. Do you have sugar? Milk?'

'One sugar and a dash of milk, please?'

Nodding, Molly made her way into the kitchen, placing the small ball of Blu-tack on the counter as she went.

* * *

'Here you go.' Carrying the two mugs of coffee, Molly tried not to spill them. She knew she'd filled them up too much. She should have tipped a bit down the sink.

'Thank you, that's just what I need.' Taking the mug, Richie held it to his lips.

Glancing over the rim of her mug, Molly looked at him. He seemed to be okay, a little on edge maybe, but if this was the first time he'd properly come into the shop in such a long time, it was to be expected that he'd feel a bit strange being back in the place. Especially after what he'd said about their break-up. 'Are you okay?'

Nodding, Richie lowered his mug and looked around. 'I'm all right. Thanks for asking, though. It's weird being back in here, thinking about what she did and everything.' He cleared his throat. 'I love what you've done with the place, though. It's amazing how completely different it is to when it was Diane's.'

'Thanks. There's still so much that needs doing.' Molly glanced around, a blush colouring her cheeks.

Richie nodded. 'There can't be much more you want to do, surely? It looks great the way it is. I think having the comfy chairs is a great idea.'

'Thanks. I wanted to make it more inviting. I don't know, it probably sounds stupid, but I want to get to a point where people want to come in and sit and chat. Like a low-key coffee shop, I guess. Where people can meet up and talk about all things crafty.'

'That's what you're doing with the Knit and Natter though, isn't it?'

'Yes, and that seems to be working.' Molly wrapped her hands around her mug. 'In the long term, I'd love to set up other craft sessions.'

'That's a good idea. What would you do?'

'I don't know. Felting maybe? I did a course on that a couple of years ago. Then there's crochet, needlecraft... there are loads. I think running other sessions like the Knit and Natter and maybe even focusing on teaching new skills too would bring in customers who would then hopefully buy things too and come back for all their craft supplies.'

'It sounds like you've got a great business plan. Something a little bit different too. Out of the few people who came to view this place, I'm glad you bought it.' Richie looked her in the eye.

'Thanks.' Looking across her mug at him, she pulled her hair over her shoulder, shielding her face. 'I'm glad I did too.'

Richie cleared his throat. 'Right, I'd better get back to work.' Passing his mug towards Molly, his hand brushed against hers, warm and confident.

Turning around, she placed his mug on the counter and gulped the rest of her coffee. Looking up at the poster, she smiled. He'd straightened it. He must have done that whilst she had been in the kitchen making the drinks.

9

Turning the Open sign to Closed, Molly checked the time on the wall clock above the button shelf. The kids should be back by now. Trevor had said afternoon. Surely half past five was fast approaching evening?

They'd be back soon. Anytime now. They'd be travelling back from Jessica's parents' house and Trevor would have probably taken the motorway, any roadworks or an accident and traffic would have tailed back quickly.

Straightening the cushions on the chairs, Molly flopped down into the one facing the door. Pulling the cushion onto her lap, she hugged it to her chest. She couldn't wait to see Lauren and Ellis' reaction to what she'd done with the shop, and with their rooms. Lauren had always wanted fairy lights in her room, so she should like what Molly had done when she'd unpacked, and Ellis would love his new football rug. She shrugged, if they helped them feel a little more at home, the local shop prices would have been worth it.

Checking her mobile for messages, Molly balanced it on the arm of the chair and let her eyes drift close. She'd just have a quick rest before they came back. Both the flat and the shop were tidy, and there was no point starting on dinner. If she did, they'd come home and tell her they'd eaten, if she didn't then they'd be starving but she had oven chips in the freezer which wouldn't take long to cook.

* * *

Jolting awake, Molly flung her eyes open and pushed herself to standing. They were back. Walking the few short steps towards the front door, Molly grinned and pulled it open. 'Lauren, Ellis. You guys okay?' Hugging them in turn as they walked into the shop, Molly kissed them on the heads. 'Did you have a good time?'

'Yeah, it was great. We went to the theme park yesterday and the...'

Stepping inside, Trevor cut Ellis off mid-sentence. 'Molly, do you mind if Jessica brings Ruby in for a wee? We've been stuck in a traffic jam for at least three hours.'

Great. In other words, Jessica wants a nose around, but not just being content with making up an excuse to come and look around the shop, she has to go that one step further and make sure she gets to poke around upstairs too. But what could she say? She couldn't very well deny the toilet to a four-year-old, could she? 'Yes, of course.'

'Thanks. Ellis run back to the car and tell Jessica they can come in.'

Why did he always have to make everything such a big deal? Why hadn't Jessica just come to the door with them? Yes, it wouldn't have been nice to open the door ready to bring Ellis and Lauren into her arms only to be faced with her ex-husband's wife and their perfect little daughter stood there, but it would have been better than this fiasco. Jessica either knew it was all a game or else Trevor made up some lie or other about Molly not being very hospitable towards her. She shook her head, Jessica didn't need to worry. She didn't hold anything against her. Jessica was welcome to Trevor.

Gripping the door handle, Molly smiled as Jessica teetered towards her on her high heels, Ruby walking obediently next to her, her small hand in Jessica's. 'Hello, Jessica. Hello, Ruby. Wow, look how much you've grown!'

'Lovely to see you again, Molly.' Ushering Ruby through the door, Jessica looked around the shop. 'Ooh, I love what you've done. You've completely transformed the place. It's beautiful.'

Transformed the place? What did she mean? For all Jessica knew, Molly might have bought it like this. Unless... unless they had looked at the estate agent's photos. That's what they'd probably done. Slowly shutting the front door, Molly momentarily closed her eyes. Nothing she did was her own business any more, was it? She'd always have Trevor, and Jessica, monitoring her moves, judging her. 'Thank you.'

'Look at this, Trevor. How adorable.' Picking up a roll of pale pink fabric emblazoned with glittery unicorns, Jessica turned towards Trevor. 'How perfect would this be made into curtains for Ruby's room?'

'Great.' Nodding, Trevor drew his mobile out from his jacket pocket and studied it.

'Do you offer a sewing service? Do you make curtains to fit?'

Molly shifted her feet. 'I'm afraid I don't, no. Not at this moment in time, anyway.' She wasn't going to offer to make them for her. She had enough on with the shop and the kids. She didn't want to be devoting her time to making Jessica's perfect house even more perfect. Plus, she'd no doubt do something wrong because she'd be worried about getting them right. No, it wasn't worth it, no matter how much Trevor's current affluent wife offered his pauper of an ex. Nope. 'Did you need the toilet still, Ruby?'

'The toilet? Oh yes, of course. Come along, Ruby, darling, let's get you upstairs.' Carefully slipping the roll of fabric back into its spot, Jessica held her hand out for her daughter before glancing across at Molly. 'It's upstairs, right?'

'Yes, the first on the left.' Jessica had definitely snooped on the estate agent's website before she'd come, and Ruby definitely wasn't acting like a four-year-old desperate for the toilet. Molly shook her head. Let them play their games. 'So, Ellis, you were telling me about this theme park. Was it good?'

'Yes, it was great. It had the most amazing rides ever. Like, literally, the rollercoaster was a hundred miles tall and...'

'Don't be stupid, Ellis, Mum knows it's impossible for a rubbish old rollercoaster to be a hundred miles tall.'

'It was so, wasn't it, Dad?' Looking towards his father, Ellis' lip wobbled.

'What?' Glancing up from his phone, Trevor looked at his son. 'The rollercoaster? Yes, it was tall. Very tall.'

'See, I told you.' Sticking his tongue out at Lauren, Ellis turned back to Molly.

'He doesn't mean it was a hundred miles tall, Dad just said it was tall.' Slumping into one of the chairs, Lauren leant her leg over the arm.

'It doesn't matter how tall it was. I can imagine it would be super tall.' Molly patted Lauren on the shoulder. 'How many loops did it have? Were you brave enough to go on it?'

'About twenty. Like, it had twenty loops. Yes, I went on it! Twice! Lauren didn't though, she was too scared.'

'I wasn't scared. It just looked too lame. Too boring.'

'It wasn't. It wasn't boring or lame. It was awesome. It really was, Mum. It was the most awesome rollercoaster in the whole world and I was brave enough to go on twice!'

'That sounds great. What else did they have there?' What was taking Jessica so long? Surely she wasn't snooping around the

whole flat? The sooner Trevor took his new family and left, the
sooner Molly could actually spend some quality time with Lauren
and Ellis.

'There was a ghost train, which was super scary, and a huge
slide you had to sit on mats to go down. There was a really cool
thing you had to walk through and try to shoot the aliens and...'

'It's adorable, Molly. I can see why you fell in love with it. Very
cosy and full of character.' With Ruby dutifully walking in front of
her, Jessica pushed through the door adjoining the shop with the
stairs up to the flat.

Really? Was that supposed to be a compliment? 'Thank you.'

Tearing his eyes away from his mobile, Trevor looked up
towards Jessica and nodded before turning to Molly. 'Do you mind
if I have a quiet word while Jessica says bye to the kids?'

'Right, okay.' A quiet word? The last time he'd had 'a quiet word'
with her, he'd told Molly that Jessica was pregnant. What now? Was
she expecting again? Well, she certainly looked good on it if she
was. She looked as though she'd lost weight rather than put any on.
Pregnancy obviously suited Jessica, not like Molly. When she had
been expecting Lauren and Ellis, she'd ballooned to the size of a
whale. Turning, she led the way through around the counter and
into the back kitchen.

'Thanks for this.' Closing the door quietly behind him, Trevor
looked down at his feet before crossing his arms and staring her in
the eye.

'What is it? Was everything okay at Jessica's parents' house?'

'Yes fine. As you heard, the kids really enjoyed it.'

Molly nodded, all she'd heard was that Ellis had loved going to
the theme park, nothing else.

'I'm just going to come straight out and say it. I'm worried about
Lauren. She's confided in Jessica's mum, Joanna.'

Molly bit down on her bottom lip. Confided in Joanna? What had she confided?

'She's really upset about being forced to move out here and away from her school friends. It's a difficult year for her, what with beginning to study for her exams and having to navigate the social life of a teenager.'

Navigate the social life of a teenager? How had he come up with that one? Jessica's mother, she must have said that. Taking a low breath in, Molly gripped her hands on the edge of the work surface behind her. 'She's only just begun her exam options, she's still got two and a bit years until she actually takes the exams.'

Looking down at his feet, Trevor rolled his shoulders before looking back up at her. 'It's still an important time in a young girl's life.'

Seriously? Was he literally just going to repeat whatever had come out of Jessica's mother's mouth? Or was it Jessica who had put him up to this? She'd known when to distract the kids so Trevor could get her in here on her own. She must have known what he was going to talk to her about. Feeling a blush creep across her cheeks, she bit down on her bottom lip, the taste of fresh blood filling her mouth. They'd been speaking about her behind her back. They'd no doubt all been crowing about what a bad mother she was, tearing her children away from their home and school. Shaking her head, she looked down at the floor. 'It's not like it's my fault.'

'What did you say?' Crossing his arms, he stared at her.

Looking back up, Molly cleared her throat. 'I said, it's not like it's my fault we had to move. I didn't make the decision to go back on what we had agreed.'

'Oh, that's it. Pass the blame to me. It was you who decided to drag them halfway across the country. That wasn't me.'

Narrowing her eyes, Molly mirrored his stance and folded her arms. 'You knew what you were doing when you took me to court and forced me to sell the house. You knew you were pricing me out of the town. Of anywhere remotely near our old place.'

'It didn't mean you had to drag them this far away though. You could easily have got a place closer.'

Molly shook her head. 'You know what the house prices are like in and around Tipston. You knew I wouldn't have been able to afford anywhere, not even on the dodgy estates.'

Snorting, Trevor sneered. 'As if that was my first thought, to price you out of the town. They're my kids too, you know.'

'Well, maybe you should have remembered that when you were pushing them out of their home.'

'Look, Molly, I did it for them. Me and Jessica needed a bigger house, needed somewhere where Lauren, Ellis and Ruby could have their own bedrooms. They were my main focus and always will be.'

Blinking, Molly opened her mouth, closed it again and swallowed. Glancing at the kitchen door, she kept her voice low and level. 'You made us sell, forced your own children out of their home, forced them to leave their schools and friends so that they could have a bedroom each for four days a month?'

'Now that they are getting older, they need their own space. Lauren's fourteen for goodness' sake, she doesn't want to be sharing a bedroom with her younger brother.'

Uncrossing her arms, she flung them around, encompassing the small kitchen. 'And you think she has space now? You think us living upstairs in a pokey little flat gives them the space they need?'

'As I said, this was your choice. You could have got a place closer. Even if you couldn't get one in our old town, you damn sure could have got one a heck of a lot closer than this.'

'Right, okay, and then I suppose I could have stuck Lauren on a bus to school, right? As if I have the spare hundred or two sitting in my back pocket to pay for the privilege. And what about Ellis, should I have made him walk? Because you do realise that primary school children can't take the normal school buses, don't you? Or should I have stuck him on public transport? At his age? On his own?'

'There's no need to be melodramatic. You could have just driven them.'

Rolling her eyes, Molly slapped her forehead. 'Why hadn't I thought of that myself? I could have driven them. I suppose you would have offered to up the child maintenance to replace my wage because, you know, I can't be sat at my desk in the office as well as doing the school runs.'

Shaking his head, Trevor scoffed. 'Other people do it.'

'Other people's exes don't chuck their own children out of their home. You know I came here because property is cheaper out here, and you know I bought the shop so I could work around the kids, so I could do the school runs.'

'So you're closing up the shop to take the kids to school and pick them up? Well, that makes good business sense.'

'Actually, yes it does. I'll be back in time to reopen for the people popping in on the way home.' Momentarily closing her eyes, she shook her head. Why did she always feel as though she had to justify herself to him? They'd been split for years now. When was she actually going to feel independent? As though she didn't need his approval? Because she didn't, she knew that. She had her life, and he had his.

'Molly, I...'

'Mum, when are...' Pushing the door open, Ellis stood still, looking from one parent to the other. 'Are you having an argument?'

'What? No, of course not. We're just talking, that's all.' Stepping forward, Molly laid her hand on his arm.

'As if I'm going to believe that.'

'It's true, buddy. Me and your mum were just having a chat.'

Narrowing his eyes, Ellis shook his head. 'I'm hungry. What can I have to eat?'

Turning back to the cupboard, Molly pulled a tin of biscuits down from the shelf. 'We can take these upstairs and go and watch a film if you like? There should be some left.'

'What? With Dad?'

'No, he's just going now.'

'Yes, I've got to get Ruby back before her bedtime.' Turning his head as he followed Ellis out of the kitchen, he whispered, 'Speak to her, to Lauren, would you?'

Nodding, Molly blinked back the tears stinging her eyes. What if he was right? What if there had been a way she could have bought somewhere closer and made it work so Lauren and Ellis could have stayed in their schools? She shook her head, she'd spent many sleepless nights writing lists and going over budgets, this was the best solution. It had to be.

* * *

Leaning against the doorframe, Molly watched as Ellis rocked from side to side in unison with the bright blue car on the TV screen. With a controller in his hand and his tongue poking out in concentration, he manoeuvred his car around sharp turns and jumped over fallen tree trunks in a bid to win the race.

'Ten more minutes and then we'll put the film on, okay?'

'Uh-huh.'

Shaking her head, she smiled. At least he seemed content with his new surroundings. Turning on her heels, she made her way to Lauren's room. She knew she should be grateful to Jessica's mother for speaking to her about her worries over the move, but it still stung that they all thought Molly was the one in the wrong.

'Hey, Lauren, can I come in for a bit?' Pushing the door ajar, Molly peered inside. Lauren had only been back for half an hour or so and yet she'd certainly managed to make her room look like home again, regardless of the fact that Molly had cleaned and unpacked her things when she'd been at her dad's. If home meant clothes strewn on the floor, wardrobe doors left open and the distinctive musty smell of an incense stick filling the air.

'Suppose.' Leaning up on her elbows, Lauren squashed her pillow with her feet and lowered her mobile to the maroon duvet cover.

'Thanks.' Stepping around the clothes, Molly bit her tongue. Perching on the edge of the bed, she indicated the floor. 'I see you've made yourself at home then?'

Pushing herself to sitting, Lauren shrugged. 'I was looking for these pyjamas. I couldn't find them.'

'Oh sorry, I probably put them at the bottom of your drawer because of the holes.'

'I like the holes.' Hooking her fingers through the broken material in the cuffs, Lauren flashed a brief grin. 'Are you putting the film on now? Not that Ellis will actually watch anything we choose together, anyway.'

'He might do. And, anyway, I thought we could let him choose something first and then we could choose a girly film for after? Judging by the dark circles under his eyes, he'll probably be asleep before his choice of film finishes.'

'Probably. He didn't go to bed until gone midnight last night.'

Molly nodded. And this was why she could never manage to get Ellis into any kind of decent sleep pattern – every time he went to Trevor's he had to be the 'cool dad' and let him stay up until all hours.

'What did you want then? If it's not to get me to go into the living room?'

Shuffling on the bed, Molly twisted to look at her daughter. 'I wanted to talk to you about the move. Your dad mentioned you'd got quite upset with Jessica's mum about it?'

'So that's what you two were arguing about then.'

'What? No, me and your dad weren't arguing.'

'Yes, you were. Whenever you argue you always go into a different room, shut the door and don't think we can hear the hushed voices behind. It was completely obvious you were arguing.' Looking down at her duvet cover, she traced the golden moons and stars with her index finger.

'We weren't arguing, we were having a discussion.'

'About me? I happened to mention something to Nanny Joanna, and that causes an argument.'

Frowning, Molly watched as Lauren's face turned from ashen to a deep crimson and back again. 'No, no. He told me he was worried about you, yes, but that wasn't what we were arguing about.'

'I didn't even tell Nanny Joanna that I was upset about moving. I just told her how two-faced Hayley and Olivia are.'

'What do you mean? You've always been good friends.'

'Not any more. That horrible snitch Davina has muscled in now. I knew she would. You should have seen her face when I told everyone we were moving. She almost grinned. Literally, like, it was so obvious she couldn't wait to get rid of me so she could take my place in the group.'

'I'm sure it wasn't like that.'

'You didn't see, Mum. It was. And now all Hayley and Olivia can talk about on video chat is Davina. It's all Davina, Davina, Davina. They're glad to be rid of me.' Hooking her thumbs through the holes in her top, Lauren wiped her eyes, the light blue fabric darkening with tears.

'Oh, sweetheart. I'm positive Hayley and Olivia are not glad you've moved. You've known them for years, you're practically sisters with Olivia, the amount of time you both spent together. I bet they're missing you like mad.'

Sniffing, Lauren shook her head. 'They're really not. You should have seen the videos they were uploading on Hayley's sleepover. They don't care I've moved away. They probably don't even notice, not now they're so pally with Davina.'

Leaning across the bed, Molly took Lauren's hand in hers. 'I know for a fact, they're hurting just as much as you. Hey, why don't we drive back there tomorrow? You can arrange to meet up with them in town?'

'No way. I don't want anything to do with either of them any more. I don't ever want to see them again.'

'You will do. Give it time and things will settle down.'

'It doesn't really matter though, does it? I've got to go to that stupid new school on Monday. I don't need them. I don't need Hayley or Olivia any more. I don't need any friends.'

'You'll soon meet some other people to hang around with.'

'No, I won't.'

'Yes, you will. Remember what Grannie used to say? Strangers are just friends you haven't gotten to know yet.'

Pulling her hand away, Lauren went back to tracing the pictures on her duvet cover. 'What did she know? It's not like she was dragged halfway across the country and torn away from her friends.'

Halfway across the country? So Trevor *had* been talking about her then. That's the exact phrase he'd used when they were arguing. She was sure it was. 'Umm, she did when she was younger, a bit younger than Ellis I believe.'

'There you go then, it's not the same as leaving mates behind when you're my age and you've known them your whole life.'

'Maybe not, but she does have a point. You're bound to meet

some people you want to become friends with when you start school on Monday.'

'No, I won't and I'm not even going to try. I'll keep myself to myself and then when we move again I won't be leaving loads of mates.'

'Oh, Lauren. Why don't we go back and see Hayley and Olivia tomorrow?'

Picking her pillow up and hugging it to her chest, Lauren flared her nostrils. 'I've already told you I don't want to. I don't want to stay friends with people who just go and replace me.'

'They haven't. They've known you too long. They won't be able to replace you and they won't want to.' Looking down, Molly picked at a cuticle. 'I'm sorry, sweetheart. I really am. I thought I was doing the right thing. I still think I have. If we just give ourselves a bit of time I really do think we can build a life for ourselves here. A good life rather than me working outside of the home and always rushing around and trying to sort childcare for Ellis. This way we get to spend more time together.'

Lauren scoffed. 'You'll always be in the shop though.'

'Yes, during opening hours I will be, but you'll be able to come downstairs too and spend time in the shop with me and then come five o'clock I'll be free as soon as I've closed up, they'll be no commuting or messing around picking Ellis up from the childminders and everything. You know the only other option would have been for us to stay as close as possible to yours and Ellis' schools and that would have meant at least a half hour's bus ride for you, a childminder for Ellis and an hour or so commute for me to get to work and back. It would have been such a long day. It wouldn't have been fair on either of you.'

'I guess.' Looking up at her mum, Lauren leant her head against Molly's shoulder. 'I'm sorry. I know we couldn't have afforded a house close to our old place. I know you're doing what you think is best for us. It's just difficult and I'm scared about starting school on Monday.'

'Lauren, sweetheart, it will all work out, I promise you.' Twisting around, Molly wrapped her arms around Lauren and pulled her close. 'You're amazing, you'll be inundated with people wanting to be your friend.'

'Yeah right.'

'You will be. Now, shall we go and have a film night? I've got popcorn.'

'The stuff you put in the microwave?'

'Yep. Come on.' Standing up, Molly held out her hand and pulled Lauren up. 'Do you want sweet or salted?'

'Sweet.'

10

'All sorted? Are you not going to put your boots on, Lauren?' Pulling her jumper over her head, Molly looked down at Lauren's white trainers.

'No, I'll be fine. It's not winter now.'

'Yes, but it rained during the night and if we wander off the paths, you'll find the fields a bit muddy I should think.'

'These will be okay. I don't want people seeing me wearing those.' Indicating her pale pink wellies, Lauren scrunched up her face in disgust.

'Fair enough. Maybe we can have a look online later and order you some new ones?' Molly smiled at her. She was growing up too fast.

Nodding, Lauren looked in the mirror and tucked a piece of hair which had come loose from her ponytail behind her ear.

'Right let's go.' Holding the front door open, Molly watched Ellis and Lauren file out before stepping into the sharp cool spring air. Turning her face up towards the low sun, she took a deep breath, filling her lungs with the scent of the orange blossom growing between the shop and Richie's mum's front garden. Its distinctive sweet smell reminded her of her grandmother, who had always been a proud gardener. She remembered playing hide and seek between the trees and bushes with her grandfather.

'Which way are we going?' Stopping at the road, Ellis looked left and right, pointing his finger in each direction.

'Shall we have a look around the centre of the village? See what the other shops are like?'

'Yes! Can I get an ice cream from the newsagents?'

'No! If you're going that way I'm going back.' Lauren turned towards her mum and held her hand open, palm up. 'Can I have the keys?'

'What? Why?'

'I don't want to go traipsing through the village with my mother and weird younger brother, there'll be people I'll see at school tomorrow.'

'I'm not weird!' Walking over to Lauren, Ellis pouted.

'Look, see what I mean? Mum, you said we would be walking through fields. You said nothing about going to the shops.'

'Okay, okay. We'll go right then, the road will lead us out of the village and, hopefully, we'll come across a bridleway we can go down.'

'But what about my ice cream?'

'Me and you will pop to the newsagents after our walk, okay, Ellis?'

'Okay.' Grinning, Ellis led the way along the narrow path leading out of the village.

* * *

'Are you sure we can go this way? I think that's a farmer's field.' Looking back at his mum, his eyes wide, Ellis pointed over the wooden stile.

'Yes, look, the sign is pointing this way. There's a public right of way through the field, that's why there's this stile so people can get over the fence.'

'Are you sure?' Tilting his head, Ellis chewed his bottom lip.

'Positive. Come on, up and over you go.' Holding out her hand, Molly helped Ellis across the stile. 'Your turn, Lauren.'

Rolling her eyes, Lauren ignored Molly's hand and climbed over. 'What now? We're in the middle of a field.'

'Now, we walk. We walk and talk about things. Take in the country air and the sights. Look, can you see the sheep in the next field? We never had anything like this on our doorstep back in town.'

'Umm, we also didn't have all the mud and gross stuff either.' Looking down, Lauren lifted her feet, checking the soles of her trainers.

'It's only a bit of mud, it won't hurt. We can clean it off when we get back.'

'Can I go on ahead? See what's in the next field?' Pausing, Ellis turned back to them.

'Yes, okay, as long as you don't wander too far. Remember, if you can't see me...'

'Then you can't see me. Yes, I know.'

'This is nice, isn't it?' Linking her arm through Lauren's, Molly grinned as Ellis ran along the narrow walkway between the crops growing in the field. Every so often he jumped and spun, practising his 360 turn, no doubt.

'I guess.'

'How are you feeling about starting school tomorrow now?'

Scrunching up her nose, Lauren looked across at her mum. 'Better I guess. Hayley messaged me earlier and said good luck for tomorrow, and me, Hayley and Olivia are going to do a group call this evening.'

'That's good then. Really good. Do you feel better now you know they haven't forgotten about you?'

Nodding, Lauren looked out across the field. 'Now I know they will still be friends with me, it doesn't matter if I make any new friends or not. I'll be able to go back to Tipston to see Hayley and Olivia on my weekends with you anyway, won't I? So I don't need to make friends here.'

'It would still be nice to make friends here and get to know people though, wouldn't it? Otherwise, school is going to be a very boring place. Why don't you just go in tomorrow with an open mind and try to get to know people?'

'Umm, I guess.'

'Good, I'm glad you're feeling a bit better about it all.' Looking over at Lauren, she squeezed her arm. 'I'm proud of you, you know that, don't you?'

'I've not done anything yet.' Pulling her arm out from Molly's, Lauren chewed her fingernail. 'Look, Ellis has found a dog.'

Shielding her eyes with her hand, Molly focused in on Ellis, who was now kneeling down and stroking what looked like a golden Labrador. 'Oh, so he has. However many times I tell him to ask the owners before petting a dog, he doesn't listen.'

'That one looks friendly enough, and I don't know if there's an owner around. He might be lost.' Picking up her pace, Lauren jogged towards Ellis, bending down next to him and fussing over the dog.

Hanging back, Molly watched as Ellis and Lauren fussed over the dog, who by the looks of it was in his element, wagging his tail and circling them both. Maybe they should get a one? They'd always wanted a dog. Especially Ellis. And now with the country-side just outside their front door and her not going out to work, it could be perfect. She could get a baby gate on the shop's kitchen door and have the back door open into the courtyard for it to roam in the courtyard and kitchen. It wasn't as though she was selling food or anything. Yes, she was making tea and coffee for the Knit and Natter group but surely that would be fine. Yes, maybe a dog would complete their little family and make this place feel like home.

'Rocco!'

Walking towards Lauren and Ellis, Molly watched as a man holding a lead ran towards them. Pausing in her tracks, she realised it was Richie. Richie must be the dog's owner. Walking slowly up to them, she hoped the blush she could feel creeping across her cheeks wasn't noticeable and cleared her throat. 'Richie, hi.'

'Molly!' Clipping Rocco's lead onto his collar, Richie straightened his back and indicated Rocco. 'Hi, I'm so sorry that Rocco ran up like that. He's not learnt to respect people's personal space yet, have you, Rocco?'

'It's okay, Lauren and Ellis love dogs.'

'Even so, he needs to learn. He's my daughter's dog, really. We got him from a rescue a couple of months back so I'm trying to complete his training but, unfortunately, when he's off the lead and sees someone interesting he tends to go deaf. Hence why I take him out here rather than letting him off at the park with the other dogs.'

'He's lovely.' Bending down, Molly patted Rocco as he put his front paws on her knees.

'We think so. Even if he can be a bit of a pest.'

'Aw, he's not a pest, are you, Rocco?' Ellis looked up at Richie. 'Is that his ball?'

'Yes, yes, it is. Do you want to throw it for him?' Richie looked across at Molly. 'If that's okay with you, of course?'

Molly nodded. 'Yes, that's fine.'

'Right, let me take his lead back off then and you can throw the ball for him. I'll warn you though, he's quite fast, you won't get much rest between throws!'

'That's okay.' Grinning, Ellis took the ball and waited for Richie to unclip Rocco's lead.

'There you go then.'

'Ready, Rocco?' Bringing his arm back, Ellis propelled the ball forwards, watching as Rocco chased it. Running ahead, Ellis took the ball again as Rocco retrieved it.

'Take turns with Lauren, please.' Molly grinned as Lauren jogged forwards and took the ball from Ellis.

Matching Molly's pace, Richie walked alongside her. 'You okay, then?'

'Yes, thanks and thanks for sorting out that poster. I only noticed after you'd gone.' Pulling her hair over her shoulder, she glanced at him.

'You're very welcome.' Grinning, Richie touched her briefly on the elbow. 'If you ever need anything, just shout.'

'Thank you. That means a lot.' Looking down at the ground in front of her, she felt the heat rising to her cheeks again.

'So, are the kids looking forward to starting their new schools tomorrow?'

'Ellis seems okay about the whole thing. I think he sees it as a bit of an adventure now. Lauren, on the other hand, isn't looking forward to it one bit.'

'I suppose it's probably a bit more intimidating being the new kid in a secondary than it is a primary. Plus, I guess at that age, friends are a massive part of her life.'

'You're right. That's what has upset her most, I think. It hasn't helped that another girl has seemed to just take her place in the group she used to hang around in. It just makes me feel so guilty for taking her out of a school she loved, but I just couldn't have made everything work back in Tipston.'

'I'm sure she'll be fine. My daughter goes there, and she loves it.'

'I hope so.' Swallowing, she tried to stop imagining everything that could go wrong tomorrow. It was such a big day for both Lauren and Ellis. 'I really do hope we can make a life for ourselves here. A happy life. One that'll make all the upheaval worth it.'

'As parents, we have to make some tough calls, don't we?' Pulling a plastic boomerang out of his back pocket, he threw it to Lauren. 'Hey, Lauren, Rocco likes to play with this too.'

'Okay, cool. Thanks.' Catching it deftly in her right hand, Lauren immediately threw it in front of her and watched as Rocco bounded forwards, jumped and caught it between his teeth.

'We sure do.'

'My daughter has decided she wants to come and live with me and now I have to decide whether to say yes and annoy her mother or say no and break both her heart and mine. I want to say yes, and, of course, I will. I've always wanted her to live with me anyway and want her to know I'm always there for her, but I'm not looking forward to the fallout from my ex.'

'Ah, you're in a bit of a tricky position then.'

'I sure am. She's coming to stay with me this week anyway because Diane, my ex, is off to Spain with a couple of friends until Friday but I don't think Diane has a clue that she might not be going back to live with her.'

'What do you think she'll say?'

'I'm not sure. It will be the best thing for our daughter because Diane spends most evenings out with her mates or latest bloke. So it makes sense for her to come and live with me. It will mean that she won't be spending the evenings on her own and, in truth, it will make Diane's life easier, but I don't think she's going to take it well and I think it's me that's going to get the blame.'

'I can understand how devastated she'll be. It's every divorced parent's worst nightmare, but it's not your fault. Ultimately, it's your daughter's decision.'

'She'll be hurt, sure, but I don't think she'll be devastated. She's never had much patience with our daughter. Diane's always treated her more of an inconvenience than anything else. Obviously, I've never, and would never, say that to Diane or our daughter, but this has been coming for years now.'

'Will she go to her mum's at the weekends?'

'Yes, she'll probably go every weekend, to begin with at least. And, to be honest, that'll probably suit Diane quite well.'

'That's something then. I'm sure it will all work out.' Looking across at him, Molly could see he was frowning. Even though he never spoke very highly of his ex, he obviously still cared about her. Cared enough that he was worried about upsetting her by letting their daughter move in with him.

'The things we go through for our kids, hey?'

'Umm.' Had she done enough to fight for what Lauren and Ellis had wanted? Had she done enough to try to stay in their old home? She'd certainly tried. Yes, the solicitor she'd hired to fight Trevor in court hadn't been great, but he'd been the best Molly had been able to afford at the time. Pinching the top of her nose, Molly watched Lauren and Ellis as they walked ahead of them, running to pick up Rocco's ball and boomerang while the dog darted in and out of the crops, probably chasing birds. She'd done what she could have at the time and she'd made the best decision available to her. They'd had to move, and that had been out of her control. What she could do now, though, was to make sure she built a happy home and life for them here.

'Mum, watch how fast he can go!' Running back to them, Ellis raised his right arm and threw the ball, watching as it propelled through the air before bouncing across the ground. 'Rocco! Come and fetch the ball!'

'He's disappeared!' Laughing, Molly held her hand to her face, shielding her eyes from the sun.

'He'll come. Keep watching, Mum! Rocco!'

Pausing, Molly turned her head as the corn to the side of her waved from side to side. She watched as Rocco bounded out from the crops and, in a flash, ran to grab the ball before carrying it back to Ellis.

'See!'

'Well done, mate. You've got him better trained than me already.' Laughing, Richie gave him the thumbs up. 'Now, just to get him to realise that not all farmers appreciate a big lump like him racing through their crops and flattening them.'

'Oh, that's a point.'

'Yep, it's just a good job I happened to retrieve some farm equipment for Dave, the bloke who owns the farm, last summer, so I hope he's not going to chase me and Rocco off his land.'

Smiling, Molly looked across at Richie. 'I see it pays to be a police officer then!'

'Sometimes, yes.'

'Right, kids, we'd better get a wriggle on and turn back for home now.'

'Oh, can we come for a walk with Rocco again another time?' Ellis dragged his feet as he walked back towards them.

Molly looked across at Richie. 'You'll have to ask Richie.'

'Can we, please?'

'Yes, of course, you can. Anyone who likes to play fetch with Rocco is always welcome to come for a walk with us.'

'Yay! Thanks, Richie. When? When can we come on a walk again?'

'Ellis, give Richie a break.' Lauren walked back towards them, pulling her mobile out from her back pocket.

'It's okay. It would be lovely to go on another walk with you all.' Richie grinned and winked at Molly. 'Look, I'm going to pop into the pub for a quick pint on the way back. Did you want to join us? They do a mean fruit smoothie for the kids.'

'We'd better not, thanks though, but we've still got quite a bit to do to get ready for school tomorrow.' Avoiding eye contact with Ellis, Molly tucked a piece of hair behind her ear.

'Maybe another time then. I'm going to keep heading forwards to the pub then. I'll hopefully see you soon. Bye, kids. I hope you both have a great day at school tomorrow.'

'Thanks. Bye.' Turning around, Molly led the way back along the bridleway.

'Why did you say no? Why couldn't we go and get a smoothie?' Running to keep up with his mum, Ellis' lip wobbled.

'We've just got a lot to do when we get back, that's all.' Why had she turned him down? It might have been nice to meet some other people from the village and it would have been nice to spend some more time getting to know Richie. Molly shook her head. She still had the dinner to make, the school uniforms to iron. It would no doubt take a long time to get the creases out of them after being shoved in a box for the move.

'Oh.' Looking down, Ellis kicked at a stone.

'We'll go another time. I promise.' Ruffling Ellis' hair, Molly bit down on her bottom lip.

11

'Have you got your bottle?' Grabbing the car keys from the hook, Molly glanced behind her.

'I'll buy one there.' Looking in the mirror, Lauren brushed her hair for the fiftieth time that morning.

'Why? Please take your bottle, Lauren. I can't afford to give you money to buy a bottle of water every day, especially being as we have perfectly good water here. Plus, think about all the plastic you'll be saving by taking your own bottle.'

'Okay, okay. I'll take the thing if it means so much to you.' Slamming the hairbrush down on the shelf, Lauren stomped up the stairs towards the flat.

'Hurry up, Lauren. You're going to make me late for school.' Pulling his shoes on, Ellis looked up. 'Mum, she's going to make me late. I don't want to be late, not on my first day.'

'No, she won't. We've got ages yet.' Looking at her watch, Molly grimaced. As long as they left in the next three minutes, they'd be fine.

* * *

Leaning across, Molly patted Lauren on the arm. 'You'll be fine. Remember, keep your head up and your shoulders back and smile!'

'Whatever.' Shrugging her mum's hand from her arm, Lauren opened the car door and slipped out.

'Are we going now?'

'Yes, one moment, Ellis. I just want to make sure she gets in okay.' Peering across the lay-by, Molly watched as Lauren weaved through the groups of teenagers loitering on the path, through the tall green gates and into the waiting crowds on the playground. Head up, Lauren, keep your head up. Fake the confidence.

'Mum, can we now, please? I really don't want to have to walk into my new class late.'

Molly shook her head and clicked the indicator on before pulling out into the road. 'Are you excited?'

'A bit. I want to see if they have art clubs. Do you think they have clubs I can go to? I really liked the art club at my old school. Do you think there'll be an art club I can join?'

'They might do, do you want me to ask at the office?'

'No, it's okay. They might tell us in assembly or something. If not, I'll ask the teacher.'

'Good idea.' When had he grown up so much? As the traffic slowed down, Molly indicated and pulled onto a side road. 'Here we go, this is the closest I can get so we'll have to walk the rest of the way.'

'Oh, but I'll be late.'

'We would have been if we'd stayed in that traffic jam. Look, it's hardly moving. It looks as though everyone's trying to get as close to the school door as possible. We'll be much quicker walking from here.' Pulling the sun visor down, Molly checked her reflection in the small mirror. Damn, she'd forgotten to put her make-up on. She rolled her eyes. Of all the days to forget. 'Right, come on then.'

* * *

Back in the car, Molly ran her fingers through her hair. They'd be fine. She knew they would be. Loads of children moved schools. It wasn't really as big of a deal as she'd made it up in her head to be, was it? Children were resilient, that's what everyone said. They'd be fine.

Turning the ignition, Molly swallowed the bile rising to the back of her throat. They'd make friends. They'd enjoy it. They'd both always been quite sociable children. They'd always enjoyed school and clubs they'd been to. They'd be fine. Now, to get through the next six hours until she could pick them up and find out how their days had gone.

* * *

Looking up, Molly checked the time on the clock above the button shelf. It was half twelve – lunchtime would be starting. Tapping her pen against the top of the counter, Molly picked up her mobile. There were no messages. She hadn't had even one text from Lauren to say school was going okay. She'd text her now, though, wouldn't she? Now it was lunchtime, she would let Molly know how it was going.

Scrolling through to Lauren's name, Molly rolled her eyes. No, she would not call her. She couldn't. If she was with people, Lauren would never forgive her, not for embarrassing her on her first day at her new school. It wasn't worth the risk.

'Afternoon, Molly.'

'Hello again, Gladys.' Looking up, Molly smiled. 'How are you today?'

'I'm just fine, thank you. I've just popped in for a couple of crochet hooks. I've got my two grandkids coming for dinner tonight and I thought I'd teach them crocheting but I can't for the life of me find my crochet hooks. I know I have some because I remember putting them somewhere thinking they'd enjoy learning how to make something but...' Shrugging her shoulders, Gladys tutted to herself.

'Let's have a look. I'm sure there's some over there by the window. If you find the ones you've lost, you can always bring these ones back.' Slipping her mobile into the back pocket of her jeans, Molly came around from the back of the counter.

'Thanks, love. Although I'll probably just keep them, even if I find the others today, there'll only be another day when I lose them.'

Laughing, Molly led the way to the shelf holding the crochet hooks and numerous sizes of knitting needles. 'Here they are.'

'Thanks, love. How's business been today?' Taking the crochet hooks, Gladys patted them against her other hand.

'Quiet, to be honest. Very quiet. I definitely haven't had even half the number of people through the door as I did last Monday. I guess the novelty of checking out a new shop in the village must have worn off.' Frowning, Molly rearranged a display of cotton reels on the next shelf.

'You had a couple of customers this morning during the Knit and Natter group.'

'Yes, they've been the only ones though.'

'Don't worry, love. You wait until Saturday, the Spring Fete will bring a lot of curious folk into the shop and you're bound to collect some loyal customers.'

'I hope so.' The last thing she wanted was to have to sell up and try and find a full-time job somewhere. She wouldn't ever be able to face Trevor again. Not that she really cared what he thought, but after him and Jessica belittling the place, she didn't want to fail. Plus, Lauren and Ellis really didn't need another upheaval.

'Good afternoon, Gladys. Hi, Molly.'

Jerking her head up, Molly looked towards the door as Richie closed it behind him. 'Hi, Richie.'

'Are you on your break, love?' Gladys patted Richie on the arm.

'Yes, just thought I'd take ten minutes before I go off into town to talk about some more farm thefts.'

'The world needs more people like you, fighting to make the world a safer place.'

Richie chuckled and loosened the shirt collar of his uniform. 'I try my best.'

Gladys looked from Richie to Molly and back again. 'Right, I'd better get some wool to go with these crochet hooks.'

'Okay, give me a shout if you need anything.' Tucking a loose strand of hair behind her ear, Molly looked down. She could feel the heat rising to her face. Gladys had brought a whole bagful of wool on Saturday. Surely she hadn't run out already?

'I just thought I'd pop in and see how this morning went? Were Lauren and Ellis okay going into school today?'

'They were good, thanks. A bit nervous obviously, but they went in okay. I haven't heard anything from Lauren though, and she'd said she'd give me a ring or at least message at break and lunchtime.' Pulling her mobile from her back pocket, Molly checked it again. Still nothing.

'That could well be a good sign. It might mean she's been busy getting to know people and just hasn't had the chance.'

'Yes, you're probably right.' Molly shook her head. She'd find out in a few short hours. 'Did you want a drink?'

'A coffee would be great, thanks.'

'Okay, a coffee coming up.' Molly looked over towards Gladys who was busy looking through the giant baskets of wool. 'Gladys, I'm going to put the kettle on, did you want a tea or coffee?'

'No thanks, love. I'll be just fine.'

* * *

'Here you go. One sugar, right?' Placing Richie's mug on the counter, Molly wrapped her hands around hers.

'Perfect. Thanks.'

'So, what brings you in here then? Not that it's not nice to see you. It is.' Why had she said that? Shuffling her feet, she looked down into her coffee. She should have given it a better stir. Hopefully, Richie's didn't have bits of coffee granules floating on the top too.

'Thank you. It's nice to see you too. I just popped in because I knew you'd offer me a coffee.' Richie grinned, raised his mug to his lips and took a sip.

Molly laughed. 'Your mum lives next door. I'm sure she would have offered you a coffee too.'

'Yes, you're right. Okay, there was a reason I wanted to pop in.' Lowering his mug, he looked across at Gladys, who was still searching through the baskets of wool. 'I wanted to ask you if you were going to the Spring Dance on Saturday?'

'Spring Dance? I've heard about the Spring Fete but haven't heard anything about a dance. What is it?' Molly scrunched up her nose.

'Ah, well, the name gives it away a little, I believe.' Tilting his head, Richie grinned.

'Haha, very funny. I kind of assumed it was a dance.'

'Sorry, I couldn't resist!' Richie laughed. 'It's a village tradition. After the Spring Fete finishes the villagers and a few visiting stragglers from the fete meet at the village hall for a dance and BBQ.'

'Ah okay. Sounds nice.'

'So, are you going to go?'

'Umm, I don't know to be honest. I'll probably just see how

things go, see how long it takes me to clear up this place after the fete.'

'Oh, okay.' Richie looked down into his mug. 'Anyway, I'd better be off. I don't want to be late for this meeting.'

'Okay, hope it goes well.'

'Thanks. Bye, Gladys.'

Holding her mug in her hands, Molly watched as Richie got to the door, pulled his car keys from his pocket and threw them in the air before deftly catching them again.

'You do know he was asking you to accompany him to the dance, don't you?' Bustling up to the counter, Gladys rolled the balls of wool from her arms.

'What? No, he wasn't, he just asked if I was going.' Putting her mug down, Molly straightened the balls of wool.

'One thing you need to remember about Richie, is that he's been single ever since Diane cheated on him. Oh, must be at least three years now. So, he's a bit out of practice, love.' Gladys briefly patted Molly's arm.

'Oh, I really don't think he meant anything by it. He was literally just asking me if I was going.' Feeling the heat of a blush flush across her cheeks, Molly looked down. He hadn't been asking her, had he? He had literally just asked if she was going. He would have asked her directly to go *with* him if that's what he'd meant.

'When you see him again, tell him you're going. You'll be good for each other, any fool can see that and when you get to my age you'll wish you'd grabbed love with both hands.' Gladys cleared her throat.

Nodding, Molly smiled.

'Honestly, love, if you have any feelings for him, and anyone can see the spark between you both, then don't waste a minute. I wished I'd listened to my heart the first time I saw my Stan.'

'Why? What happened? Sorry, you don't have to tell me.'

'It's fine, love. Me and Stan met when I first started work at the old shoe factory. We could both feel there was something special between us. A special connection, if you like. But he was my boss, and I was just fresh from school, and when I got onto my apprenticeship in the offices, we decided to go our separate ways.'

'Oh, that's a shame.'

'It was. It really was. I ended up marrying someone I really didn't feel anything for and knew he didn't for me either, but back in those days it was the done thing to get married and neither of us wanted to be left on the shelf. He was a kind man, mind, but things didn't work out. He ended up going off with another woman, someone he'd fallen for when he was a teenager, just like me and Stan. Anyway, that gave me the kick to go searching for my Stan again.'

'I take it you found him?'

'I did, yes. But, unfortunately, we didn't get as long together as we would have if we'd acted on our feelings all those years ago. He passed away four years ago, ten years after we'd met up again.'

'That's awful. I'm so sorry.'

'It is, it is awful, but I'm forever grateful we had the time together that we did have, and it acts as a constant reminder how important it is to follow your heart and your dreams. Just as you have with this place, I'm assuming?'

'Yes, yes. It has always been a dream of mine to own a craft shop. I just hope I can pull it off.'

'You will do, love. This village needs a decent craft shop like this.'

Molly smiled. 'I hope so.'

* * *

Tapping her fingers against the steering wheel, Molly peered out of the side window, trying to see Lauren through the crowds of teenagers racing through the school gates and across the road.

'... and then this boy, I think his name is Charlie, yes, it's definitely Charlie. And then Charlie shows us what he's made at home, and it was amazing! It was a volcano that erupted! Not a real one, but a little model one and he had made it out of a bottle and decorated it to make it look like a volcano and then he poured coke into the bottle and put some mints or something in there and it exploded. I mean, erupted. It erupted.'

'Wow. That sounds amazing.' Twisting her head towards where Ellis sat in the back seat, Molly smiled at his infectious grin. 'You've had a good day, then?'

'Yes, the best! Hillside Primary is sooo much better than my old school and I've made some really good friends there. And at break time they do football and dodgeball matches, and anyone can join in. I played dodgeball with Charlie and our team won!'

'That does sound fun.' Turning back to the side, Molly squinted her eyes. Was that Lauren walking out of the school gates? Yes, it was. She was sure it was. 'Are you pleased you started there then?'

'Completely, one hundred per cent definitely! And we're going on a school trip in a few weeks! Mr Zac wouldn't tell us where to though, which I thought was a bit mean. I mean, we're going to find out soon anyway, and we all begged and begged him to tell us but he said it was top secret until next week. Why do you think it would be top secret? Why do you think he wouldn't tell us?'

'I don't know. Maybe it's not been confirmed yet, and he doesn't want to get everyone's hopes up.'

'Oh, I hope they confirm it. I hope we can go. It's going to be so cool. I can go, can't I, Mum?'

Molly glanced at him. 'Yes, of course you can go.'

'Awesome! Thanks, Mum. I'm going to tell Charlie I can definitely go then tomorrow.'

'Okay. Look, here's Lauren coming over now.'

'Who's she with? Is that her new friend?'

Molly looked at the girl Lauren was linking arms with as they crossed the road and breathed a sigh of relief. 'It looks like it.'

'We've both made friends today then!'

'Hopefully.' Leaning across the handbrake, Molly pushed open the passenger door. 'Hi, Lauren. How's your day been?'

Slipping into the passenger seat, Lauren squashed her bag into the footwell. 'Okay, I guess.'

'Did you make some new friends?'

Shrugging, Lauren looked out of the window.

Clearing her throat, Molly turned the ignition. 'Was that girl you came out of school with one of your new friends?'

Looking across at her mum, Lauren rolled her eyes. 'Yes, she's a mate. Do we really have to have this interrogation now, or can it wait until we get home? I'm starving.'

'Wasn't there anything nice for lunch? I thought they had two canteens?'

'Yes, they do, but I don't have an account yet. They don't take money, it's all done online and then we use our fingerprints to pay for the food.'

'Really? They should have told me. Have you not had anything to eat since your measly piece of toast this morning then?' Molly had told her to have something more substantial, but Lauren had insisted one piece of toast was enough to fill her up. Molly bit down on her bottom lip, she'd messed up already. She should have sent Lauren in with something, just in case. Even a cereal bar would have been better than nothing.

'I did. Marissa bought me some pizza.'

'That's a relief then. Was that Marissa who you were walking with? When are they going to sort an account out for you?'

'I don't know. Yes, that was Marissa.'

'What do you mean, you don't know? Haven't they told you?'

Yanking her bag up from the footwell, Lauren unzipped it and pulled out her reading book. 'I don't know. They didn't say anything about it.'

'Well, did you ask?'

'No.'

'Lauren, how come you didn't ask?'

'I'll ask tomorrow, it's no big deal.'

'It is if you can't get food.'

'I'll just grab something from home for tomorrow and ask my tutor.'

Nodding, Molly indicated and turned left out of the town. 'So, you had a good day today? It wasn't as bad as you thought?'

'I guess not. It seems okay.'

'Good.' Molly grinned. She couldn't ask for more than that. 'Okay', they could work on. In fact, 'okay' was high praise when it came to Lauren. 'You all right there, Ellis? When we get back you can help me in the shop, if you like? We'll open up again and see if we get any more customers.'

'Cool. Can I use the till?'

'You sure can.' Maybe things were going to work out for the best. It sounded as though they'd both had a good first day and they both seemed happy enough. Maybe things had turned a corner.

12

Reaching into the box, Molly pulled out yet another wad of fabric squares and piled them on top of the display on the counter. With their beautiful colours and the contrasting ribbon tied around them, she hoped they'd be a good little on-the-spot purchase. Moving the A4 cardboard picture forwards, she stood back. Yes, that looked nice and quilting was popular at the moment so, hopefully, some of them would shift at least.

A banging on the window pulled her from her thoughts. Jumping and turning around, Molly hurried to the door. It was only eight o'clock. Who on earth could it be?

Pulling the blind up, Molly peered out and unlocked it.

'Morning, Molly! The cavalry's here!' Bustling in, Gladys was followed by Susan and Eva.

'Hi.' Grinning, Molly shut the door behind them. 'You didn't need to come. And definitely not this early.'

'Don't be silly. It's nice to have something to do. Plus, us oldies wake up early so this is more like lunchtime to us.' Laughing Gladys indicated Susan. 'Isn't that right?'

'It sure is.'

'And I don't sleep very well anyway, any more. This little foot-baller in here keeps waking me up at all hours.' Rubbing her belly, Eva yawned.

'Well, thank you.' Molly blinked back tears. It felt good to have people who wanted to help.

'Right, first things first, I'll pop the kettle on. Is it coffees all round?' Shaking out of her coat, Susan made her way into the back kitchen.

'Could I have a peppermint tea, please, Susan? I've brought some tea bags with me.' Rummaging in her bag, Eva followed her.

'What do you want me to do?' Rubbing her hands together, Gladys grinned.

'Umm, I'm not sure, to be honest. My head's all over the place.' What needed doing? She'd made a list at about two o'clock in the morning after waking up in a cold sweat, but couldn't for the life of her remember where she'd put it.

'Let's have a look.' Glancing around the shop, Gladys looked back at Molly. 'Right, so we need to set up the activity. You're demonstrating knitting, right?'

Nodding, Molly bit down on her bottom lip.

'So we need a collection of knitting needles and wools set out on the coffee table.'

'Yes. I thought about setting up other little stations around the room. Well, not stations, I mean sort of like little displays. I've got some other display stands like the one on the counter with step-by-step instructions on how to do things. I've got some leaflets too, somewhere. I thought we could put them out with the displays. Just to try to show people what they could use things for. To encourage them to try something new.'

'Great idea! We can space those displays around the shop then.'

'Here you go, girls. Three coffees and one peppermint tea. I've popped a sugar in all of the coffees, I thought we could do with a bit of an extra energy kick to start us off.' Lowering the tray onto the counter, Susan picked up the mugs, placing them in front of everyone.

'Wow, have you seen out there? They've got little fairground rides set up in the market square this year and I've just seen a coach arriving already.' Closing the door behind them, Lucy herded two small children in ahead of her. 'I'm sorry, I've got these two munchkins for an hour or so until their dad gets back from the gym. They're under strict orders to be good and not to touch anything.'

'Hi, that's fine. Hello, I'm Molly. What are your names?' Molly smiled at them. It would have been lovely if Lauren and Ellis could have been here too but Trevor had apparently already arranged something so couldn't swap weekends. Still, hopefully they'd be having a nice time at his.

'This is Edward, and this is Hannah.'

'Lovely names.'

'Right, off you two go. Here, take my bag, you can sit in the kitchen and do some drawing. Is that all right?'

'Yes, of course. Do you two want some squash or something?'

'They'll be fine. They've got snacks and drinks in my bag. Right, off you go then, you two.' Lucy looked down and rearranged Frankie as he slept in his baby carrier.

'Thank you for this, but don't you want to go and look around the stalls with them?'

'Oh no, competing with hundreds of people to get a look at some pesky stall selling something made in a factory that I can buy offline? No, thank you!'

'I thought it was supposed to be all food and drink stalls?'

'The majority of them are, love. I think Lucy here has more of a problem with people rather than what stallholders are selling, isn't that right, Lucy?' Stroking Frankie's head, Gladys chuckled.

'You've summed that up perfectly as always, Gladys. Phil will come and get the kids in an hour or so and take them around. No doubt he'll treat them to an abundance of sugar-filled rubbish and armfuls of plastic tat. He's always one to sniff out rubbish anywhere.'

Molly grinned. 'Well, thank you.'

'You're welcome. It gets me out of the house for a few hours with the added bonus that when the kids are out in public they're less likely to tease and kill each other. The joys of having five-year-old twins, hey?'

* * *

Standing by the front door, Molly scanned the room. Susan and Eva were manning the till, Eva perched on a stool next to Susan who was itching to start serving. Gladys was rearranging the balls of wool and knitting needles on the coffee table and Lucy was meandering around the shop floor, rubbing Frankie's back as he slept attached to her front.

Taking a deep breath, Molly pulled the door open and kicked the heavy dog-shaped doorstop into place. Smiling, she greeted the first customers before rushing back to the circle of chairs.

* * *

'That's it, keep going. You've got it.' Smiling, Molly patted the young woman on the shoulder and looked around the circle of chairs, each occupied by someone learning to knit for the first time.

Choosing knitting as their demonstration had been a good idea. It was a skill that could be taught and picked up by any age group. So far today, they'd taught both men and women, boys and girls from the age of seven and up. One lady had said it had been her ninety-fifth birthday last weekend.

'Does anyone want a drink? We've got tea, coffee and squash?' Straightening her back, Molly took out a small notebook from her back pocket, ready to scribble down any orders. With the chatter and bustle from numerous people looking around the shop, she didn't trust herself to be able to correctly remember what people wanted.

'Ooh, a nice cuppa would be lovely, please?'

Weaving in and out of the crowds, Molly slipped behind the counter. 'Susan, Eva, how's it going? Do you both want another drink?'

'That would be lovely please, Molly?' Susan thanked another customer before turning to her. 'It's going great! I've lost count of the number of customers I've served.'

'There's certainly been a lot. And loads of them have commented how nice this place is and how refreshing it is to find a craft shop where you can come in to actually craft and chat.' Eva sat back down on the stool.

'Yes, we've had quite a few people asking if you're going to do classes.'

'We've had a lot of people asking about quilting classes especially. I think having this display here has really got people interested.' Eva indicated the display of fabric squares.

'We've been handing out these business cards here and telling them to check your social media page for updates. I hope that was the right thing to do?' Susan patted the pile of cards next to the till.

'Yes, that's great, thank you. I'd forgotten about those.' That twenty pounds she'd spent when she'd been arranging to buy Bramble Patch had been worth it then.

* * *

Filling the kettle up, Molly looked across at the table. A couple of crayons lay forgotten on the floor, no doubt abandoned when Lucy's husband had come to pick the twins up a couple of hours ago.

Walking across to the table, Molly knelt down and reached under towards the wall to pick them up. Leaning a bit further under, she curled her fingers around a rather used red crayon.

'Hey, Molly.'

'Ouch!' Jerking her head up, she bashed it on the underside of the table. Rubbing her head, she ducked, backed out and stood up. 'Richie, hi.'

'Sorry, I didn't mean to startle you. Are you hurt?'

'It's okay. I'll live.'

'Here, let me take a look.'

'Honestly, don't worry. I'm fine.' Placing the crayons on top of the table, Molly switched the kettle on.

'Let me take a look, just in case. I am First Aid trained, you know.' Grinning, Richie stepped towards her.

'Okay.' She lowered her head and stood still as he ran his fingers across the top of her head, parting her hair to see if it was bleeding. His fingers were warm and reassuring against her scalp.

'You're okay, no blood. I wouldn't be surprised if you get a bit of a bump come up though.'

'Thank you.' Standing this close to him, his face barely an inch away from hers, she could feel his warm breath against her forehead. As she lifted her head back up, she could almost sense the tingle from his lips next to hers.

'Molly, a lady is asking if you've got any green ribbon for sale?'

As Susan pushed the door open, Molly jumped away from Richie and looked away. She could feel the telltale heat of a crimson blush spreading up from her neck. 'Yes, I think so. There should be some with the other ribbons. If there isn't the right shade she's after I can order some in. I'll come and show her the catalogue.'

'Great. I'll go and tell her.' Pulling the door open, Susan slipped back out onto the shop floor.

Biting her bottom lip, Molly smiled at Richie. 'Sorry, I'd better get out there.'

Nodding, Richie ran his fingers through his hair.

Stepping out of the kitchen, Molly was met with a hubbub of noise and bustle. Bramble Patch was full of people of all ages. Some had clearly just come in for a nose around and lapped the shop relatively quickly, pausing every so often to touch a super soft ball of wool or to run their fingers through a furry stretch of fabric. Others had clearly come in on a mission and beelined straight towards their chosen item, picking it up and walking straight towards the till, ignoring every other craft item on display. A fair number of people weaved in and out of the other customers, meandering through the shop and filling their arms with a mismatch of goodies before waiting patiently in line to be served whilst chatting to the person in front of them.

'Busy, hey?' Balancing a box in her arms, Lucy bustled past her. 'I was just going to fill up the display of those patchwork fabric bundles on the counter. Is that okay? They're selling like hot cakes!'

Grinning, Molly nodded. 'Yes, of course. Thank you. I can't believe how busy it's got.'

Grabbing a catalogue from underneath the counter, Molly made her way towards a lady with a pushchair standing in front of the ribbon selection. 'Excuse me, I'm Molly, the owner of Bramble

Patch. Susan mentioned you were looking for a ribbon that was a specific shade of green?'

'Hi, yes. I've got this cardigan that my grandmother made for Verity here, only somehow my washing machine has swallowed the ribbon and I'd like to replace it before she visits next weekend.'

'Ah okay. Can I have a look at the cardigan, please?' Holding out her hand, Molly took the pale green cardigan. 'Wow, this is beautiful. Such a detailed pattern. Your grandmother's very talented.'

'Thanks. Yes, she is. She's always loved knitting for as long as I can remember, so since I've had Verity, her first great-grandchild, she's been in her element. She spends so long on them, I really want to fix it before we see her.'

'I'm sure we can sort something. What shade of green was the ribbon? Was it similar to the wool?' Molly picked up a pale green ribbon. 'This one's very close.'

'No, it was this green, the one on the buttons.'

'Let's have a look.' Picking through the reels of green, Molly bit down on her bottom lip. She couldn't remember seeing any that particular colour. 'No, I don't think we have a good match in stock, I'm afraid. We can find the right colour in this catalogue though and I can order it in for you, if you'd like?'

'I'm not going to be able to come back to the village before next Friday, unfortunately. What with work and childcare.'

Molly smiled. 'I could always post them to you, if that would help?'

'Really? I didn't realise you offered that service?'

'It looks like we do now.' Molly laughed. It was actually a good idea. If she could advertise it properly, it would be another income stream even if it didn't earn them much.

'How much would postage be?'

'Nothing. In fact, you can have the ribbon on the house, you've given me an idea.'

'Are you sure?'

'Absolutely. Now, let's see if we can find the right colour.' Flicking through the catalogue, Molly ran her finger down the index page.

* * *

Slipping the catalogue back under the counter, Molly straightened her back. The lady had seemed happy enough and had promised to tell her friends about Bramble Patch.

Drat, the drinks. She'd promised the group of knitters their drinks. She checked her watch, they'd been waiting twenty minutes now, and each group was only lasting thirty. Rushing back into the kitchen, Molly refilled the kettle and looked around for the tray. Where had she put it?

She must have left on the shop floor. Slipping back onto the shop floor, Molly made her way towards the knitting group.

'All right there, love?' Looking up from a customer's knitting she was trying to untangle, Gladys smiled.

'Yes, sorry, I got waylaid helping a customer. I'll get those drinks now.' Picking up the tray from the coffee table, Molly turned back towards the kitchen.

'Hey, Molly, it's fine. We've had our drinks. Richie brought them out.'

'Did he?' Turning back around, Molly noticed the empty mugs and glasses sat on the coffee table.

'Yes.'

'Oh, right.' Glancing around the shop, she tried to locate him amongst the crowds of people.

'He had to get back to work. He said to tell you he'll catch you later.' Turning back to the teenager sat next to her, Gladys pulled her reading glasses further down her nose and spoke to the girl, indicating the knitting in her hand.

Molly nodded. 'How's everyone getting on? Does anyone need any help?'

* * *

'Thanks again for all your help.' Hugging Susan and Gladys, who had stayed until closing time, she held open the door.

'Now, are you sure you don't need a hand tidying up?' Looking behind her at the shop floor, Susan pulled her handbag further up on her shoulder.

'No, honestly, you've helped me out more than enough today. Thank you, though. To be honest, I'm going to grab something to eat and tackle the mess a bit later.'

'Okay, if you're sure, love. We'll see you at the village hall in a couple of hours then.' Gladys zipped up her lightweight coat.

'Village hall?'

'For the dance, remember?'

'Oh, that. I'll probably sit this one out.' Yawning, Molly shook her head.

'Well, we'll be there if you change your mind.' Patting Molly on the arm, Gladys stepped outside. 'Come on, Susan, time to get our glad rags on!'

Shutting the door behind them, Molly pulled the blind down before turning around and leaning her back against the door. Ribbons had been pulled out and lay strewn across the shelves (she really must get proper storage for them), rolls of fabric had been stretched and left hanging near the shelves and that was just the start of the mess.

Bending down to pick up a button which had somehow found its way to the doormat, Molly grimaced, she'd have to get the hoover out once she'd tidied. The amount of mud, crumbs, and general dirt on the floor was disgusting. Straightening her back, she shrugged. A bit of tidying and cleaning was a small price to pay for the amount of money they had taken today, not to mention all the new customers who had promised to revisit. It had definitely been a success and a great way to get the word out about Bramble Patch. Hopefully, she could really make a go of it and put some roots down for her and the kids.

* * *

Slumping onto the stool behind the counter, Molly circled her shoulders before wrapping her hands around the steaming mug of hot chocolate in front of her. Although most of the tidying and clearing away had been done, the floor was still filthy and after a day on her feet, she really couldn't face dragging the vacuum cleaner out. It would have to wait until tomorrow.

Molly nodded, it wouldn't hurt to leave the dirt until the morning. It wasn't as though anyone was going to be walking across it anyway, so at least it shouldn't get engrained.

Pulling her notebook towards her, she ran her forefinger over the scribbled total Bramble Patch had brought in today, picked up the pen and drew big fat circles around it. Finishing off with some fireworks shooting out of the circle, she lowered the pen and grinned. Not in a million years had she ever thought the shop would earn that much in a week, let alone a day.

Stretching her arms to the ceiling, she yawned. If half of the people who had promised to use Bramble Patch as their go-to craft shop did, she'd be able to afford to decorate Lauren and Ellis' bedrooms soon. She knew Lauren hated the floral purple and white wallpaper she currently had in her bedroom, and although Ellis' room was decorated in the standard magnolia, it would be nice to let him choose how he wanted it.

Folding her arms on the counter in front of her, Molly lowered her head. She would just have a couple of minutes' rest before she jumped in the shower. As the heaviness of sleep made her eyes droop closed, she smiled. She had this. She could do this. She really could make a life here for her little family.

13

Jerking her head up, Molly blinked. There it was again. What had begun as a gentle tapping grew increasingly louder. Straightening her back, she blinked into the dim light. She must have fallen asleep. The evening had crept in, and with the lights off, Bramble Patch had fallen into the gloominess of dusk.

There it was again, still louder this time. Slipping off the stool, Molly made her way to the door and pulled it open. Pausing, she let her eyes adjust. It was Richie.

'Hi, Molly.'

'Hi, is everything okay?'

'Yes, great thanks. Can I come in?'

'Yes, of course, sorry.' Stepping back, she opened the door fully and fumbled to find the light switch. Blinking as the shop floor descended into light, she looked across at Richie as he closed the door behind him. Dressed in dark blue jeans and a checked red and cream shirt, he held two tickets in his hand.

'I just happened to have these two tickets for the dance and wondered if I could change your mind about coming?' A slow grin spread across his face and he reached out to tuck a strand of hair behind Molly's ear.

Bringing her hand to her head, her fingers swept past his as she smoothed down her hair. She must look a right state. Yawning, she rolled her neck from side to side. 'Sorry, I fell asleep at the counter. What time is it?'

'Umm, let's see.' Pulling back his sleeve to check his watch, he looked back up at her. 'Seven thirty-five to be exact.'

'Oh, okay.'

'So?'

'So?'

'So, can I entice you to accompany me to the village hall for the Spring Dance?'

'Right. Sorry, I think I'm still half asleep.' Rubbing the back of her neck, she looked at him. He'd been on duty all day so he must be as shattered as she was, and yet he'd gone to the effort of not only dressing up to go to the dance but also to call around and try to get her to go. Although her sofa was calling her, she knew the dance would be a good chance to meet some new people. She nodded. She'd wanted to become part of the village, to feel at home and the Spring Dance was perfect timing. She'd go. Plus, Gladys and Susan were definitely going to be there and the others from Knit and Natter no doubt would be too. If they could put a whole day's work in and still have the energy to spend the evening socialising and dancing, then she should be able to too.

'Is that a "yes"?'

Taking a deep breath, Molly nodded again. 'Yes, it is. I'll come.'

'Great!'

Looking down at her T-shirt, she tried to wipe off a droplet of hot chocolate only to smudge it into the pale fabric and grinned. 'I think I might have to get changed though. I'm happy meeting you there if you want to get there for when it starts.'

'Don't worry, I'm happy to wait.'

'Okay, thanks. I won't be long.' Turning on her heels, Molly ran up the stairs.

Pulling her black ankle boots on, Molly stood up from the bottom step and pulled her dress down towards her knees. Frowning, she wished she'd unpacked her one pair of strappy heels, but she didn't have the time to go rummaging around in boxes now, so the boots would have to do. Glancing in the full-length mirror Lauren had insisted she had put up on the wall opposite the stairs, she smiled. It didn't look too bad. Yes, the boots were a little clumpy but being as the dress she was wearing was dark in colour and not particularly dressy, she'd probably get away with it.

Pulling the dark floral fabric of her dress down again, she pushed open the door and walked onto the shop floor.

'You look lovely.' Bringing his hands down from where he had been leaning on them behind his head, Richie jumped up from one of the comfy chairs.

'Thanks. You look nice too. Sorry, I should have said that earlier. I thought it, but my head was just muzzy from sleep.' Shaking her head, she bit down on her bottom lip and willed the heat travelling up her neck to subside. Why had she said that?

'Why, thank you. Are you ready?' Holding out his arm, he grinned.

'Yes, let's go and have some fun.' Striding towards him, Molly linked her arm through his and let him lead her out of Bramble Patch. 'By the way, thank you for making the drinks earlier when I got called away.'

'You're very welcome. It was really busy when I popped in, was it like that all day?'

'Yes. I don't know what I'd have done if it hadn't been for my Knit and Natterers coming to help. Great for business, though! And no end of people said they'd be back.'

'That's great. Hopefully, you'll stick around for a while then.' Glancing across at Molly, Richie grinned.

'Hopefully.' Smiling, Molly looked down at her boots.

* * *

As they headed toward the centre of the village, music with a country twist floated out from the hall up ahead. People had set up plastic garden tables and chairs in the car park and on the green in front of the hall and clustered around them talking and drinking. A few teenagers sat drinking fizzy drinks out of cans on the low wall surrounding the car park and a handful of parents walked little ones up and down in buggies trying to get them to sleep so they could return to the celebrations.

'It looks busy.'

'It normally is. The whole village normally comes and quite a few people from the surrounding villages too.' Unlinking her arm, Richie pushed open the heavy wooden door and stepped back, letting Molly go through first.

Pausing just inside, Molly glanced around. Tables and chairs lined the walls and music blared out from large speakers on the stage at the far end. The rest of the hall was full of people dancing in unison up and down the wooden floor.

'Shall we dance or would you like a drink first?'

'Umm, a drink, please? I don't know the moves to this song.' Clasping her hands in front of her, she watched as the couples on the dance floor spread out, twirled and then found a new partner. She hadn't realised it was going to be organised dancing, or what-ever it was called, she'd just assumed if people did dance they'd break out into the usual drink induced moves that were popular in pubs across the country.

'Don't worry. I don't know half of them either, and the ones I do know I've just picked up from coming here each year. But, look, do you see Kevin and Deb at the front?'

Standing on her tiptoes, Molly peered above the crowds of dancers. 'On the stage?'

'That's them. They're showing everyone what the moves are, so I'm afraid there really is no excuse.' Glancing across at her, his eyes crinkled as he grinned. 'But we can get a drink first. I take it you've met Deb already?'

'No.' Molly shook her head, she'd met a lot of people in the past week but she was sure she'd have remembered meeting Deb, with her flamboyant dress sense and bright bleached hair she would have stuck in her mind.

'Oh, that's a surprise, she's a councillor and thinks she runs the village. In a good way, I mean, she heads up all the organising for the village events along with Wendy the mayoress and generally busybodies about. I would have thought she'd have been the first person to check out Bramble Patch.' Richie shook his head. 'No doubt she's been too busy organising this. You wait, I bet she'll be in checking you out on Monday.'

Molly grimaced.

'Don't worry. She's lovely. Nosy, but her heart's in the right place.'

* * *

Squeezing themselves past the dancers as they came waltzing across the hall floor, Molly and Richie found a spot to lean against the wall.

Taking a sip of her drink, Molly felt the sharp flavour of gin hit the back of her throat as the bubbles from the tonic filled her mouth. 'Are there any other village events throughout the year?'

'A fair few. There's normally a monthly village BBQ from June to September, another dance to celebrate Harvest, a Christmas Fete similar to today's one and then a Christmas Eve dance and the same for New Year's Eve. People do seem to like their dancing here.'

'I can't believe so many people are joining in.' Molly watched as Deb took hold of a mic and announced a break.

'Fancy having a go after the break?'

Molly nodded. 'Why not? Although I've got to warn you, I can't dance to save my life.'

'That'll make two of us then. As long as I don't go home with a leg cast it'll be a good evening.' Chuckling, Richie took a swig from his bottle of lager.

'Evening, Richie. Wonderful to see you here.' Deb sidled up to them, Kevin just behind. 'And who's your lovely friend?'

'Hi, Deb, Kevin.' Bending down, Richie accepted Deb's peck on the cheek before shaking Kevin's hand. 'This is Molly. Molly meet Deb and Kevin.'

'Hello.' Smiling, Molly shook hands with Kevin before being pulled into an embrace by Deb.

'Lovely to finally meet you. You've just moved into Diane's old shop, haven't you?' Bringing her hand to her mouth, Deb looked across at Richie and frowned. 'I'm so sorry for bringing her name up, Richie.'

Shrugging his shoulders, Richie smiled. 'It's fine.'

'Yes, I've opened a craft shop there.'

'Yes, yes, Bramble Patch, isn't it? I've been meaning to come across and introduce myself. Please forgive me. Organising this dance has taken up the majority of my time, hasn't it, Kevin?'

'It has indeed.' Kevin nodded.

Shaking her head, Molly smiled. 'That's okay. You've done an amazing job here. It looks as though everyone's having a great time.'

'It does, doesn't it? It's nothing, really. I just like to give something back to the place I've called home all of my life. I really couldn't have done it without that group of wonderful volunteers over there.' Raising her hand, Deb waved at a group of women and men standing at the bar. 'Right, I'd better be off. I need to relieve my bladder before the dancing begins again.'

'Lovely to meet you both.' Smiling, Molly watched as they both weaved their way back through the crowds. 'She seems nice.'

'Yep, and as a bonus she's one of those people you'll never forget.' Richie laughed.

* * *

Tilting his head towards the dance floor as the music began again, Richie grinned at Molly. 'That's our cue. Let's get onto the dance floor.'

'Do we really have to?' Laughing, Molly gritted her teeth, part in jest and part because she didn't actually know if she would remember what having rhythm felt like.

'Yes, I'm afraid we really do. It's a compulsory activity if you live in the village. Besides, if we don't go up there and start the dance off together, it won't be too long before any one of the people around you drag up a beautiful woman like yourself.'

'Haha, very funny.' Tipping her glass back, she took a final swig of gin and tonic and held out her hand. 'Come on, then.'

'Great!'

Smiling back at Richie, Molly led him onto the dance floor just as Deb and Kevin took to the stage again to lead them.

'I promise not to stand on your foot.' Leaning forward, Richie whispered in Molly's ear, his warm breath tingling her skin.

'I'm afraid I can't be as confident as you, but if I do step on your toes, please don't arrest me!'

Throwing his head back, Richie laughed. 'I promise.'

Watching Deb and Kevin swan across the stage, Molly tried her best to copy. Right foot forward, left foot back. Right foot sideways and follow with the left. 'This is impossible!'

'Here, just relax into it.' Placing his hands on her hips, Richie guided her across the dance floor. 'See, you've got it now.'

'And, swap!' Deb hollered through the microphone, her voice echoing through the high-ceilinged hall.

'What does she mean?' Molly knew exactly what she meant, but really? Swap partners? Why would anyone actually do that when they'd gone to a dance with someone? Surely everyone would want to stay dancing with the people they came with?

'You'll be fine.'

Molly watched as another woman took her place, a tall blonde lady, and immediately fell in step with him. Biting down on her bottom lip, Molly wished the floor would open up and swallow her. She hated things like this.

'May I?'

Looking up, Molly smiled. It was Bill. Holding her hand out, she let him envelop hers and began dancing in time with him. 'You may.'

'Sorry we couldn't stay long to help earlier. What with the grandkids...' Bill raised his eyebrows and grimaced.

'It's fine. Thank you for coming and helping for the time you did. It was lovely to meet your grandchildren too.'

'What? Those horrors?' Bill chuckled. 'They do have character, no one can take that away from them.'

'Aw, they were lovely.' And they had been. Yes, they'd been confident, but that was a good thing. She wished she could breathe a little more confidence into hers, especially Lauren. She had so much going for her but struggled to see it sometimes.

'I trust the rest of the day was as busy as it was when we popped in?'

'Yes. Super busy.'

'Good. Me and Pat used to run the hardware store on the corner and found that the Village Fete worked better than any advertising we could ever afford. You wait, now that people know about you, you'll be busier each day now.'

'Hopefully.' Molly looked down at her feet as Bill swept her along in his arms. 'You're really good at this, aren't you?'

'You could say I've had a fair bit of practice. Pat insists I go to dance classes with her in town once a week.'

'Well, it certainly shows.'

* * *

'Bye, loves. Make sure you both get some rest tomorrow.' Hugging them, Gladys gave both Molly and Richie a peck on the cheek.

'Bye. Bye, Susan.' Holding her hand up to wave, Molly turned back to Richie. 'Thank you for making me come tonight. It's been great fun.'

'You're welcome. Thank you for coming with me.'

Nodding, Molly stepped aside as another influx of people streamed out of the village hall, all calling their 'goodbyes' and 'see you laters'. It had been a great night. Really fun. Molly shook her head, she'd have never thought she would ever have described a village dance as fun, but it had been. She'd had the most fun tonight as she'd had in, well, for a long time.

'I'll walk you home.' Holding out his arm, Richie waited until Molly had slipped hers through his and began walking towards Bramble Patch.

'Thank you, but there really is no need.'

'As a police officer I would have to disagree.'

'Oh, you think I can't look after myself?' Looking up at him, Molly frowned.

'I don't think that at all. I just need an excuse to spend a bit more time with you.' Looking sideways at her, Richie cleared his throat.

Blushing, Molly laughed. 'Well, it's nice to spend a bit more time with you too.'

'Do you mean that?'

Nodding, Molly momentarily closed her eyes. She meant it.

Pausing, Richie turned to her. 'I'm glad to hear that.' Leaning towards her, his lips millimetres away from hers, he whispered, 'This okay?'

Nodding, Molly leant forward, the warmth from his lips transferring to hers. Stepping closer, she felt his arms embrace her, warm and strong against her body. Kissing him felt different to the men she had so-called dated since breaking up with Trevor. It felt right; it felt like home. Closing her eyes, she felt the energy flow between them.

Dropping her arms, Molly stepped back as the kiss ended. Looking at the floor, she tucked her hair behind her ear. She could feel the heat of a blush flushing across her face.

'You okay?'

Looking up, Molly watched as Richie frowned and laid his hand gingerly on her arm and smiled. 'Absolutely.'

Smiling back at her, Richie held his arm out again.

Linking her arm through his, Molly led them down the path towards Bramble Patch and fished her keys from her pocket. 'Did you want to come in for a coffee?'

'Yes, that would be nice.' Nodding, Richie stood aside to let her open the door.

Shutting the door behind them, Molly waved to a woman standing across the street. Frowning when she didn't get any response, she locked the door and peeked through the blinds.

'Everything all right?'

'Yes, fine.' Glancing back at Richie, she shook her head. 'I just waved to someone across the road, but I don't think she saw me.'

'Probably not, it's pretty dark out there.' Shrugging out of his jacket, he walked towards her. 'Now, come here.'

Going towards him, Molly circled her arms around his neck and pulled him towards her.

14

Placing the can of polish and the cloth on the counter, Molly put her head in her hands and yawned. Closing her eyes, she gritted her teeth against the sharp pain of a hangover. Turning around, she leant her back against the counter and surveyed the shop floor. The cleaning was done, at least. She'd even managed to haul the vacuum cleaner around, but she did need to stock up. A lot.

Massaging her temples with her index fingers, she reminded herself it was a good thing she had so much stocking up to do. They'd done well yesterday. She glanced at the wall clock. It was eleven o'clock; she had about six hours until Trevor brought the kids back. Plenty of time to get the shelves filled up again and to put an order in of what they had run out of altogether. But also enough time to sit down for ten minutes. Maybe if she grabbed a coffee, she'd wake up a bit.

* * *

Placing her hot coffee mug on the coffee table, she sank into one of the Knit and Natter chairs and drew her legs up underneath her. If she'd gone upstairs to the flat, she would have switched the TV on and been drawn into some fantasy world or other. This way at least, she could still have a break but not relax too much.

Reaching for her coffee, she dipped her head, breathing in the hot bitter aroma and smiled. She might be suffering today, but she hadn't had as much fun as she'd had yesterday and last night for a very long time.

Feeling the vibration from her mobile, she shuffled around and pulled it out of her back pocket.

Richie – Hey, are you still feeling rough? Happy to come & help get the shop ready after my shift? X

Balancing her mug on the arm of the chair, Molly grinned and typed a reply.

Molly – Will feel better after a coffee. It's fine, thank you though. Most of it is done now and have Lauren & Ellis coming back at 5 x
Richie – OK, glad most of it is done. I'll try & pop in to see you tomorrow if OK? X
Molly – That would be lovely x
Richie – Best go as got a call x
Molly – x

Swapping her phone with her mug, Molly wrapped her hands around the hot ceramic and smiled. Drinking the rest of her coffee, she balanced the mug on the arm of the chair and let her eyes close. Fifteen minutes wouldn't hurt and might actually get rid of her headache so she could get things done quicker.

* * *

Opening her eyes, she rubbed them and yawned. She could only have dropped off for a couple of minutes and would have slept longer if something hadn't woken her. Looking around, she shook her head. All was quiet. Maybe she'd had a weird dream which had cut short her nap.

No, there it was again, a banging noise. Shaking her head, she blinked, yes, it was the door. Richie. It must be Richie. Grinning, she pushed herself up from the chair and made her way to the door.

'One moment. Coming!' He was certainly eager to see her again if the incessant knocking was anything to go by. Pulling the door open, she stepped back. In front of her stood a woman whose bright red lips and high cheekbones dominated her features. 'Hi, I'm afraid we're not open today. We'll be open as usual tomorrow though.'

'I'm not here to buy anything. May I come in?'

Why would she want to come in if she didn't want to buy anything? 'What is it I can help you with? I'm happy to take an order.'

Flicking her long dark curls over her shoulder, the woman glanced behind her before looking pointedly up and down the road. 'I'd rather discuss this matter with yourself inside.'

'Umm, okay.' Shaking her head, Molly pulled the door further open. It wouldn't hurt to serve one customer, would it? Not if she'd travelled to the village especially. Although, Molly was sure she recognised her from somewhere, unless she'd just walked past her in the next town or something.

Stepping inside, the woman looked around the shop. 'Thank you, I didn't want to discuss things out on the street.'

Still holding the door open, Molly turned to her. 'What things? Has there been an issue with a purchase? I'm sure we can sort something out.'

Pulling her leather handbag higher up onto her shoulder, the woman's bottom lip wobbled. 'I'm Diane, Richie's ex-wife.'

Opening her mouth, Molly closed it again. Richie's ex-wife? Why on earth would she have come here? What could she possibly want from Molly? 'Right, okay. Nice to meet you. I understand you used to own the shop?'

'That's right.' Looking around her, she surveyed the shop floor.

Why hadn't she stocked up earlier? With the gaps on the shelves, Bramble Patch certainly didn't look its best. She shouldn't have had a rest. Shaking her head, Molly tried to push all thoughts of inadequacy away. 'Sorry, how can I help you?'

'I'm sorry to intrude but I really do feel I need to talk to you.'

Closing the door, Molly bit down on her lip before turning back to Diane. 'I don't understand?'

Taking a deep breath, Diane pulled a tissue from her oversized handbag and dabbed her eyes. 'I saw you with him last night.'

Shifting on her feet, Molly could feel the all too familiar rush of heat flush across her face. She hadn't spotted her at the dance. Not that she would have known who she was, but Richie would have mentioned if his ex-wife had been there. Surely? She shook her head. How did it have anything to do with her, anyway? She and Richie had split years ago from what he'd said, so surely she'd expect him to meet someone else. 'I didn't see you at the dance.'

'No, I didn't go. I saw you both together after.'

'Oh, right.' She had seen someone last night then, she'd been sure she had – a woman across the street. Had Diane been spying on them? 'I still don't understand how I can help you?'

'I... well I...' Wiping her eyes with the tissue again, Diane shook her head. 'I'm sorry, I promised myself I wouldn't get upset.'

'Are you okay?' Frowning, Molly reached out and rested her hand momentarily on Diane's forearm. 'Here, do you want to sit down?'

'Can I?'

Molly followed her across to the chairs and watched as she sank into the cushioned seat, before perching on the chair opposite her.

'I really shouldn't be making such a show of myself, it's just I've been so happy with Richie and now, after seeing him with you last night, I...'

Leaning forward, Molly perched her elbows on her knees. Did she seriously think that Richie would never have another relationship? 'I understand it's difficult when you see your ex with someone else. I remember when I saw my ex-husband with his new wife for the first time. It was a lot to get my head around even though I'd been expecting it and knew that he would move on at some point.'

'Yes, but I and Richie have just got back together and now after seeing you and him together I'm really worried that he's going to change his mind about us.'

Clasping her hands in her lap, Molly swallowed. He had said nothing about getting back together with Diane. He wouldn't, not after the way she had left him. He wouldn't. Diane must have misunderstood.

'He didn't say anything, did he?'

Shaking her head, Molly clasped her hands together.

'I'm so sorry for coming here and telling you like this but I just didn't know what to do. I didn't sleep at all last night. The image of you with him just kept going through my mind. You see, I have a teenage girl who's at such a vulnerable age and I worry about what it's going to do to her, if one minute she thinks her dad and I are getting back together and then the next, he's seeing you behind my back. Do you have any children?'

Molly cleared her throat and nodded.

'You must understand then. I'm sure it must have been tough for your children when you and their father broke up. Can you imagine what it would do to them if their parents had been given another chance at a happy relationship only to find out that another woman was trying to steal him away?'

Opening her mouth, Molly closed it again. She could imagine. She could picture what it would do to Lauren and Ellis. It had taken them years to get used to the fact that she and Trevor had split, and even now, something as simple as going to the same farm park they had visited as a family unit would trigger Ellis into asking why she and Trevor couldn't get back together. Molly shook her head. Even with Jessica and Ruby on the scene, Ellis seemed to still think it was a possibility.

Sniffing and patting her heavily mascaraed eyes, Diane looked over at Molly. 'You see, I'm now wondering what's going on and having visions of having to break my daughter's heart again. She's only just come to terms with me and her dad, Richie, splitting up and now...'

What was Molly supposed to say? She hadn't even thought that he was particularly friendly with Diane still. After what he'd told her, she had assumed that the only contact he had with her was when their daughter was picked up and dropped off. He hadn't mentioned anything else about her other than how they had split up. Lacing her fingers together in her lap, Molly looked down at the floor.

'I'm sorry. I'll go now. I just didn't know what to do, I didn't know whether to come and speak to you or not. I'm sorry.' Slipping her tissue back into her handbag, Diane stood and walked towards the door.

Staring at the floor, Molly heard the click of the front door as Diane left. Why would he get back with her after she had broken his heart?

And there it was. A slow low laugh rose up from her throat. There it was. When Richie had first told her about how Diane had run a clothes shop from Bramble Patch, he had been upset. Resting her head in her hands, she closed her eyes. How could she have been so stupid? So naïve? He'd been so funny with her when they'd first met and it had all been because she had bought Bramble Patch, and then when he'd stepped inside for the first time, he'd been talking about her. He obviously still had feelings for her.

But he had been telling her how Diane had hurt him so much, why would he risk another relationship with her? Molly shook her head. People in love, properly in love, don't see the obvious. They're blind to the doubts.

Pinching the bridge of her nose, she leant back against the cushions. She would not cry. She would not. It wasn't even as though they'd actually properly begun a relationship or anything. But she'd definitely felt a connection. She'd allowed herself to think what a possible future might look like. She should have known better.

15

Hold on, hold on. Placing the pile of clothes in her arms down on her bed, Molly ran down the stairs just as the doorbell rang again. It would be Lauren and Ellis. She checked her watch; they were actually fifty-five minutes early rather than the usual forty-five minutes late.

Turning the door handle, Molly jumped back as Ellis pushed the door open. Twisting, she watched him throw open the door to the flat and disappear up the stairs. 'Remember to take your shoes off, please, Ellis!'

'Hey, Mum.' Coming into the shop, Lauren dumped her rucksack down at her feet.

'Hi, Lauren.' Leaning forward, she kissed Lauren on the forehead before turning to Trevor. 'What's up with Ellis?'

Shrugging and rolling his eyes, Trevor glanced behind him at the car. 'He's in a strop because he got told off. I'd better get going, I need to get things ready for work tomorrow.'

'Right, okay. Thanks for bringing them back.'

'See you in a couple of weeks, Lauren. Bye, Molly.'

'Bye.' Shutting the door, Molly turned towards Lauren. 'Have you had a good weekend?'

'It's been okay.' Shrugging out of her coat, she picked up her rucksack. 'I'm going to go and watch TV.'

'Okay. Before you go though, do you know why Ellis is so upset?'

'He was told off, like Dad said.' Turning, Lauren followed Ellis up to the flat.

Frowning, Molly checked she'd locked the door and walked slowly around the shop. After Diane's surprise visit, she'd only just managed to get everything in place so Bramble Patch would be ready to open in the morning. She'd refilled all the shelves she could and anything that she hadn't had in stock out the back, she'd rearranged the other stock on the shelves so it didn't look obvious.

Closing the door joining the shop to the flat's hallway, she locked it and made her way up the stairs. She'd pop and check in on Ellis before jumping in the shower. After spending the afternoon shifting boxes and stock, she was sure she had a layer of dust covering her.

* * *

'Ellis? You okay, sweetheart?' Pushing his bedroom door open, Molly leant against the doorframe. Ellis was lying face down on top of his duvet. His coat and shoes still on. 'Can you take your shoes off, please? You know you're not allowed them on up in the flat. I don't want dirt trodden around.'

'Leave me alone.'

'Hey, what's the matter? Why are you so upset?' Leaning down, she moved the rucksack he'd taken to Trevor's out of her path and walked towards the bed. 'Come on, let's get those shoes off. I changed your bed this morning, you don't want your dirty shoes all over your clean duvet cover, do you?' Biting down on her bottom lip, Molly reached towards Ellis's feet. 'Hey, let me help you.'

'I said, leave me alone.' Squirming away from her, Ellis shouted out.

'Okay. Just take your shoes off and then I'll leave you alone.' She hadn't had time to put the washing machine on yet. If he got mud on his duvet, he'd have to sleep with it like that. Shaking her head, she tried to push away all thoughts of the germs his trainers would be carrying which were already all across his bed.

'All right, I'll take my stupid shoes off.' Sitting up, he pulled his trainers off and flung them across the floor before taking his coat off, scrunching it up and chucking it towards her.

Looking at his flushed red face, his eyes swollen from crying, Molly sat on the bed next to him, resting her hand on his back. 'What's happened, sweetheart? You can tell me.'

'I don't want to talk about it.' Taking a big gasp in between sobs, Ellis squirmed away from her touch. 'Leave me alone. Just... just leave me alone.'

'Oh, darling. Okay, I'll leave you be for a bit and come and check on you in a few minutes.' Pushing herself to standing, she looked back at him. She hated seeing him like this and not being able to help, but if she gave him a little space then hopefully he'd be more willing to talk and tell her what had happened. Trevor had told him off millions of times before and he'd never come home inconsolable before. Maybe Lauren would be able to shed some light on why he was so upset.

* * *

'Lauren, love. Can you tell me what happened to make Ellis so upset?' Perching on the arm of the sofa, Molly looked down at

Lauren who was sat curled up under the throw, remote control in hand, flicking through the channels.

'I don't know.'

'Stop for a moment, please?' Holding out her hand, she waited until Lauren had passed her the control. 'Thank you. You can have it back in a moment, I'm just worried about Ellis. I haven't seen him get so upset after getting back from Dad's before.'

'I've told you. He got told off.'

Slipping off the arm of the sofa, Molly sat down next to her. 'Okay. It just seems odd that he's so upset. I mean, your dad has told him off numerous times before and he's never usually like this. Are you sure there isn't something else?'

'I don't know. I don't know how his brain works, do I? Jessica told him off because he hurt Ruby or something. But she was being a brat to him anyway, so she got what she deserved, if you ask me. Now, can I have the remote back, please? I really need to watch this, everyone's going to be talking about it at school tomorrow.'

'Yes, sorry. Here you are.' Standing up, Molly passed Lauren the remote. 'Do you want a hot chocolate?'

'No, thanks.' Holding up a bottle of fizzy drink, Lauren took a gulp.

Shaking her head, Molly bit her tongue. However many times she asked Trevor not to keep giving them fizzy drinks, they still came home with them. Once in a while wouldn't be a problem, but from what Lauren had told her in the past, that's all they drank when they were with him.

She walked into the kitchen and switched the kettle on. It wasn't important. Not really. As long as they brushed their teeth, two days of drinking sugary drinks every fortnight wasn't going to hurt.

* * *

Balancing the plate of toast on top of the mug she was carrying, Molly gently tapped on Ellis' door before walking in. 'You okay? I've got some hot chocolate and some toast. With marmite and cheese, just the way you like it.'

Grumbling from beneath the duvet, Ellis rolled himself into a ball, the duvet mounding up on top of him.

Lowering herself down on the side of the bed, Molly rubbed his back with her free hand before taking the plate of toast back from its precarious position on top of the mug. 'Why don't you sit up and have a bit of toast and a drink? It might make you feel better?'

The lump under the duvet moved further up the bed.

'We don't have to talk about what happened, about why you're upset, if you don't want to. You can just eat your toast if you want.'

A mumbling noise filtered through the duvet.

'Sorry, sweetheart, what did you say?' Tilting her head, Molly strained to hear.

Peeking out from underneath the duvet, Ellis looked at her, his tear-stained face red from crying. 'I said, do you think I'm a horrible bully, too?' As quickly as he'd emerged, he flung the duvet back over his head.

'What?' Blinking, Molly reached across and set the plate and mug down on the bedside table. 'Who called you that?'

'It doesn't matter, forget I said anything.' His voice, each word interrupted by fresh sobs, sounded so quiet and young.

'It does matter, sweetheart. No one should call you that.' Shuffling closer to where he was curled up, Molly rubbed his back through the duvet again. 'You're a lovely, kind, thoughtful boy, you know that, don't you?'

'I'm not.'

Who had said that to him? Trevor, she'd be having words with him when she next saw him. How dare he call his own son a horrible bully? Yes, Ellis could get a little energetic sometimes, but when he did, that was just a sign that he needed a little direction. That he needed someone to suggest something for him to do. He didn't have a 'horrible' bone in his little body. And he certainly wasn't a bully. Taking a deep breath, she blew out through her nose. 'Daddy didn't mean to call you that. Sometimes, people say things when they get cross, but they don't mean them. Everyone gets cross sometimes. I do, don't I? Sometimes when you or Lauren aren't doing what I've asked you to do, I get cross, but I still love you and that's the same with Daddy.'

Not that she'd ever called him a bully and ever would. Taking her mobile out of the back pocket of her jeans, she scrolled through to Trevor's name. Whatever had happened, it was still upsetting Ellis so the sooner Ellis spoke to his dad again and realised all was forgotten and he hadn't meant it, the better.

'No, no. Don't call Dad.' Throwing the duvet back, Ellis plunged towards his mum, knocking the mobile to the floor.

'Ellis!' Jerking her head towards him, her face softened. His eyes were bloodshot as fresh tears streamed down his already damp cheeks. 'Okay, I won't ring him, but you need to tell me what happened and why he called you that.'

'It wasn't him.' Picking up his much-loved soft toy dog, floppy from the number of hugs it had received over the years, he rubbed the ears against his cheek.

'Who was it then?' If it hadn't been Trevor, who else had been there that could have called him that. Yes, Lauren teased him, and, yes, sometimes the way they teased each other did get out of hand, but if it had been Lauren, Ellis wouldn't have got this upset.

Covering his face with the dog, Ellis mumbled, 'It was Jessica.'

Opening and closing her mouth, Molly froze. She suddenly felt cold, very cold. Jessica had called her boy a bully, a horrible bully at that. Reaching out, Molly drew Ellis in for a hug and kissed the top of his head, his normally smooth blonde hair spiking up after being under the duvet for so long. 'What happened, sweetheart?'

Taking a deep shuddering breath, Ellis looked down at his toes. 'I was playing cars in my bedroom. I had them all set up on the car mat I've got there. You know, like the one I've got here but a bit smaller so I have to squash the cars up a bit. And I'd got them all where I wanted them, I'd laid the traffic jams out and the car park was full, so I was ready to play and Ruby came along and started kicking them about.'

'Oh okay. By accident or on purpose?'

'On purpose. She does that, she likes to mess up my games and when I tell Dad or Jessica, they just say she's too young to understand and she doesn't mean to mess them up. But she does, she does mean it. I know she does because she smiles and laughs when I get upset. And when they say she's too young to understand, I know she's not and that it's just their excuse for letting her get away with anything. She's four and she'll be starting school in September and I don't remember being allowed to kick toys and mess around with other people's games when I went to school. Mrs Packton would have counted down to me, wouldn't she?'

Molly could picture Ellis' Reception teacher, Mrs Packton having one of her silent meltdowns that she used to do when a pupil of hers didn't listen or was acting up. She used to close her eyes and count back from ten on her fingers before opening her eyes again. Molly used to laugh when Ellis used to tell her after some friend or other had been naughty at school until she'd witnessed it for herself when running late after a dentist's appointment and walking in to help Ellis find his peg. She remembered a child had begun playing with the Play-Doh when they should have been sat listening to the register. Molly shook her head, Mrs Packton had certainly had the magic. So, yes, Ruby was old enough to know what she was doing was wrong. 'Yes, Mrs Packton would have, but maybe Ruby doesn't know. She only has you and Lauren round twice a month, so maybe she just doesn't understand how to share yet.'

'Maybe, but Daddy and Jessica need to teach her before she goes to school then.'

'Yes, they do, and I'm sure if you had told them what Ruby had been doing they would have told her to stop.'

'They don't. They never do. It's always me in the wrong. They always say I should have played it up in my room or not where Ruby is playing. That's why I didn't play downstairs. That's why I played in my room so I was right away from her and she still came to find me and mess up my cars.'

'So, what happened after she'd kicked your cars? Did you tell your dad or Jessica?'

'Yes, I went downstairs and told them and they said the usual things, so I went back up and shut my bedroom door to play, but she still came in and this time she kicked them about again. So I gave her some cars of her own and set my other car mat up for her. It's a lot smaller and made of plastic, but I thought she'd still like to play with it.'

'And did she?'

'Only for a little while and then she got back up and kicked my cars again. She kicked them so hard at me that one of them hit my head. Look.'

Peering at Ellis' head as he held his hair apart, Molly smoothed her finger along his scalp. There was a cut, not a deep one, but one that must have hurt. 'Oh, sweetheart, are you okay? Did you have it cleaned up?'

'No, I didn't tell Daddy or Jessica.' Pulling away from her hand, he hugged his dog.

'Why not?'

Biting down on his bottom lip, Ellis then buried his face into the ears of his dog.

'Ellis. What happened? What's making you so upset?'

Keeping his face buried in the folds of the large floppy ears, Ellis mumbled through the fabric, 'I pushed her. I pushed Ruby, and she fell over. I only did it because I'd asked her to stop again and again and then she'd kicked that car at me and hurt me and I just stood up and pushed her and she fell on the floor.'

'Okay. Hey, don't cry. It's okay. Was she hurt?'

'No, she only fell on my rug but then she started screaming and crying and Daddy and Jessica ran upstairs. And she told them that I'd pushed her and Jessica called me a horrible bully and said I should be ashamed of myself. What does ashamed mean?' Fresh tears began streaking down his cheeks again before rolling down the ears of his dog.

Drawing his small body closer, Molly kissed his head. 'It doesn't matter. Did you tell them what she'd done? That she'd been kicking your cars and hurt your head.'

Ellis shook his head as his body began shuddering with sobs.

'Why didn't you tell them?'

'Because it wouldn't have mattered. I'd said before she'd been kicking them and they hadn't done anything. It's all about Ruby. Daddy loves Ruby more than me.'

Blinking back her own tears, Molly tried to suppress the hot angry muddle rising from her stomach. 'He doesn't, sweetheart. He loves you all the same.'

'No, he doesn't. He loves her more and Jessica doesn't even like me.'

Holding his shaking body, Molly stroked his hair and rocked him. 'He loves you, he loves you all the same. And Jessica loves you too. She's been with Daddy from before Ruby was born and loves you too.'

'No, they don't. They really don't. You don't understand. Ruby gets away with everything, but if me or Lauren says or does something wrong, we're always told off.' Lifting his head up, he took a rasping breath. 'They hate us and they think I'm a horrible bully.'

'Oh, sweetheart, they don't hate you. They love you. You should have spoken up and told them what had happened and then they would have understood.' Not that there was any excuse for calling him a bully. No excuse whatsoever.

Tearing away from her, he scooted backwards on the bed, his back against the wall. 'I knew you wouldn't understand. I knew I shouldn't have said anything.'

Biting down on her bottom lip, Molly turned around to face him and laid her hands on his knee. 'You should have told me. I'm glad you told me. You know if anything upsets or worries you, it's always better to talk about it, and I'm your mum, I want to know when you're upset or worried.'

'Then why don't you believe me when I say that it wouldn't have mattered if I'd told them or not. They're all about Ruby. They don't care about me and Lauren. Whatever she does, she gets away with.' Ellis took a long shuddering breath and wiped fresh tears from his cheeks with the body of the dog. 'They always say it's because she's younger and she doesn't understand or that me and Lauren are older and should know better.'

'Okay. What did Daddy say when Jessica said that to you?'

'He didn't say anything. He just told me to tidy up and went downstairs.'

'Oh, right. Okay. Look at me, Ellis.' Holding her hands out, she waited until Ellis had raised his head and he was looking. 'You are the most caring, kind and lovely little boy. Jessica should not have called you a bully and I can tell you, hand on heart, that she didn't mean it. She would have just said it accidentally without thinking. She does not think you are a bully. She knows you, remember, and she's known you longer than Ruby has even been alive so I can tell you she doesn't think that of you.'

'Why didn't she say sorry then? She just stayed in the living room when me and Lauren went. She normally says bye and gives us a cuddle.' Holding a dog ear with his thumb and forefinger, he rubbed it against his flushed cheek.

Looking across at the Lego strewn on the floor by Ellis' chest of drawers, Molly frowned. Had Jessica seriously ignored them? Was that why Trevor was early dropping them off? What kind of adult would act like that? Especially Jessica, who was supposed to be this all-maternal perfect being? How dare she? And how dare Trevor rush them out of their so-called second home? What kind of message was that sending to their children? Taking a deep breath, Molly smiled and turned back to Ellis. 'Why don't you have a bit of your toast now? I've got your hot choccie here too.'

Rubbing his eyes, Ellis crawled forward, sitting next to Molly as she passed him the plate of toast.

Wrapping her arm around him, Molly drew him closer as he bit into a slice of toast as his sobs began to fade.

16

Tucking the duvet around his small body, Molly stood up. Pausing by the door, she listened to him breathing. After eating the toast and taking a few sips of hot chocolate, Ellis had begun crying again before falling asleep exhausted. Pulling his bedroom door closed, Molly padded down the hallway.

'Mum? Is that you? You've been ages.'

Following Lauren's voice into the living room, Molly leant against the doorframe. 'Sorry, love. Ellis has only just stopped crying over what happened at your dad's.'

Shifting on the sofa, Lauren looked across at her mum. 'Can we have dinner now? I'm starving?'

Frowning, Molly shook her head. 'I thought you had dinner at your dad's? You normally do.'

'We didn't today, even though Jessica had spent the entire after-noon cooking a roast dinner. I assumed you'd asked Dad to bring us back early? Unless it was because of what happened with Ellis. It was straight after him being told off that we left.'

Molly frowned. It wasn't fair on Ellis, or Lauren for that matter, to think that Trevor had wanted to get rid of them. She cleared her throat. 'I think it must have been a miscommunication. He must have thought I was doing dinner. Sorry. What did you want?'

'I don't mind. Can we have something quick, though?'

'Yes. How about I shove some oven chips in and we have chip butties?' Ellis had only had toast. If she'd known he hadn't had dinner... Never mind, he probably wouldn't have been up to eating a big meal anyway, not the way he was feeling. If he woke up later, she could always make him something quick then.

'Ooh yes please! Have we got tomato sauce?'

'Yep. I'll go and pop the oven on.'

* * *

Checking the time, Molly closed the door leading up to the flat and walked towards the counter. She had ten minutes until the oven heated up. Ten minutes to ring Trevor and find out exactly what had happened. Shuffling the stack of leaflets next to the till, Molly took a deep breath and scrolled to Trevor's name in her mobile. She had a feeling this would be a conversation she didn't want Ellis or Lauren overhearing.

'Hello?'

'Hi, Trevor. It's me, Molly.' Why did she always do that? Introduce herself? She knew full well that Trevor had her number saved and he would have known it was her before he'd picked up.

'What's up?'

'I think you probably know why I'm calling.' Molly listened as the phone was muffled. She heard him speaking to Jessica presumably, and then the dull bang of a door closing.

'Is this about what Ellis did?'

'Not so much about what Ellis did, but the way he was told off. Yes.'

'Before you jump down my throat about how to parent, he had pushed Ruby. I'm assuming he didn't tell you that part.'

'Yes, he did. He told me that Ruby had been kicking cars at him and he had asked her to stop but she'd continued so he'd closed his door only for her to come in and kick cars again. He'd even set up his other car mat for her and she'd carried on.'

Trevor scoffed. 'Remember he is a child and his perspective on things might be slightly biased to save himself from getting into trouble.'

'Are you telling me you think he's lying?'

'Kids do lie. It's nothing to be ashamed of. It's not the way you're parenting them or anything. It's just a stage they go through.'

Holding the phone away from her ear, Molly stared at it. Was he actually being serious? Closing her eyes she brought her mobile to her ear again. 'Trevor, he's telling the truth. He's not lying. This is Ellis we're talking about here. Your son. Not some stranger.'

'I know that, but I also know that children go through phases of lying. And if he's feeling threatened by Ruby, then this phase may be more magnified than it may have otherwise been.'

Molly shook her head. That was Jessica talking. She knew Trevor, and Trevor would never in a million years say something like that. 'He's telling the truth. He's been inconsolable since you dropped him off. He's been sobbing in my arms thinking that you and Jessica hate him.'

'That's a bit of an overreaction.'

'Is it? Jessica called him a horrible bully and then basically chucked him out of the house without giving him any dinner! How do you think that made him feel?'

'Look, I'm sorry if he's been upset but he really shouldn't have pushed Ruby.'

'No, he shouldn't have and he knows that, but he'd had her kicking his cars around for goodness knows how long before. He's even got a gash on his head from where she kicked a car at his head. But, I guess you didn't know that, being as it hadn't been cleaned up. I guess you just took what had happened at face value, and because Ruby was, no doubt, upset, you automatically assumed Ellis had pushed her for no reason.'

'I... I didn't know he'd got hurt, no. Is he okay?'

'His head is fine. His mental health not so good.'

'Look, I didn't know that she'd kicked a car at him. He didn't say anything. Are you sure he did it here?'

Molly shook her head. 'Are you asking me if, in the few minutes it took me to go after him when you'd left and seen him running upstairs crying, that he did it then? In those few minutes? No, he didn't. And if you need any proof, I'm happy to send you a photo. You can tell it's not fresh.' Why couldn't he just see that Ruby wasn't the perfect little princess he thought she was? All kids had their naughty moments, and that was normal, what wasn't normal was the parents not believing their little darling could put a foot wrong. Their expectations of Ruby's behaviour were so screwed up, they were risking not teaching her any boundaries at all.

'Okay, okay. So, maybe she kicked a car at him. You don't know if it was on purpose though.'

'For goodness' sake, Trevor. Ellis is your son too. It's not all about Ruby and your so-called perfect little family you have now. You have other children and you're risking alienating them if you carry on with this favouritism lark. Do you remember before we split up? Think back to when Ellis was Ruby's age, you used to tell him off when he teased Lauren. I know you weren't about much then, but you must still have some memories of them at that age. I'm not telling you that Ruby isn't lovely, she is. But you also need to realise that she's a kid. She's a child, and she needs you and Jessica to step up and take control. She's got you both wrapped around her little finger. You both think she's this perfect little thing that can do no wrong. But she's a child. Children learn by making the wrong choices sometimes, or she would do if you set her boundaries.'

'She has boundaries. She's so good with her bedtime routine. You can't say the same for Ellis and Lauren.'

'And what about Jessica calling Ellis a horrible bully, I suppose you think he deserved that?'

'I'm quite sure she didn't say anything of the sort.'

'So again, you're calling him a liar?'

'What? No, all I'm saying is that he's probably got things a bit confused.'

Gripping the side of the counter, Molly could feel her nails sink into the wood. 'I give up. Do what you want, but I doubt Ellis will want to go to yours next time.'

'You can't cut contact. I'm their father. I have rights.'

'I'm not cutting contact. I'd never do that, but if you carry on treating Lauren and Ellis like second-class members of your family, then they won't want to come.' Ending the call, Molly turned and leant her back against the counter. Chucking the mobile behind her, she listened as the dull thud of glass hit the wooden counter.

Great, now she'd have to get her screen repaired. Covering her eyes with the palms of her hands, she sank to the floor and pushed until all she could see was a black expanse and dancing white spots. She couldn't do this. How was she supposed to protect Ellis when he was at Trevor's? She couldn't be there for him, and she couldn't control what was said to him or how he was treated by the two other adults who were supposed to love him like she did. When were things supposed to get easier?

The shrill ringtone of her phone filled the shop. Standing up, she looked at her mobile as it danced across the counter, vibrating on each beat of the tone. Bracing herself for another argument, she picked it up.

Pausing her finger over the answer button, she read the name flashing on the screen. It wasn't Trevor looking to have the last word after all. It was Richie. Slamming it back down on the counter, Molly stared at it until the voicemail kicked in. She really couldn't deal with him. Not now. Not today.

Gingerly picking up her mobile, she went into the back kitchen and put it on the table. She needed a strong coffee and five minutes to collect her thoughts before going back up to Lauren. She just needed a bit of time to work out what she should do next.

Flicking the kettle on, she spooned a heaped teaspoon of coffee powder into a mug, mixing in a heaped teaspoon of sugar for good measure.

It had only been yesterday when everything had felt right. More than right. For once she'd felt as though her life was actually turning out okay. That she was finally getting things on track. Yesterday, she'd thought she'd finally met someone she could actually see a future with. Things had been so perfect with Richie. He'd seemed so perfect.

Molly poured the boiling water in, stirring vigorously as the brown and white granules mixed and dissolved. Why had she been so stupid? Why had she dared to think that her car crash of a love life had turned a corner? She'd always attracted the cheats and the liars. Why had she dared to think that Richie was any different?

And then there was Ellis. How was she supposed to try to fix the relationship between him and his dad when Trevor couldn't even see there was anything wrong in the way he and Jessica had treated him?

Taking her mug to the table, Molly slumped into a chair and wrapped her hands around the boiling ceramic. She hadn't put enough milk in. Shrugging, she took a sip, instantly regretting it as the boiling coffee burnt her tongue.

What was the point? She couldn't even make a cup of coffee properly. Standing up, she tipped the coffee down the sink, watching it swirl and discolour the plughole, before putting the mug on the side, grabbing her phone and heading up the stairs to the flat.

* * *

Sliding the oven tray full of frozen chips into the oven, Molly straightened her back.

'Mum, are the chips done yet?'

'Shh, you'll wake up Ellis!' Rushing to the living room, Molly put her finger to her lips.

'Sorry! Are they done yet though? I'm starving.' Turning around, Lauren peered over the back of the sofa.

'I've just put them in. They'll be done in twenty minutes or so.'

'Seriously? I thought you'd put them in ages ago?'

'Well, I had to make a quick phone call. It's not long. You'll survive.' Sitting down next to Lauren, Molly put her feet up on the coffee table in front of her. She hadn't felt this tired in a long time. And she still hadn't had her shower.

'Is that your phone? And you moaned at me for calling you quietly. That's more likely to wake him up.' Raising her eyebrows, Lauren shook her head.

Glancing at Lauren, Molly pushed herself to standing and made her way back to the kitchen.

'Is there anything I can have to eat now?'

Molly looked down at her mobile. It was Trevor. She'd have to get it. 'Yes, just have a look. I need to get this. I won't be long.'

'Okay.'

'Trevor?' Speaking quietly, she made her way back downstairs again.

'Molly. Do you think we can have a civilised conversation about this now? Without you hanging up on me?'

Breathing hard out of her nose, Molly shut the door leading back up to the flat firmly behind her. 'I hung up because you weren't listening to me.'

'Just because I didn't agree with you, it doesn't mean I wasn't listening.'

'Right, okay.' Molly rolled her eyes and sunk back into the kitchen chair. This was going to be a long conversation.

'I don't like the way you imply I don't treat Ellis and Lauren the same as I treat Ruby. You've got to understand that it's very difficult. Ruby lives with me and so naturally I do spend more time with her, but when Ellis and Lauren visit, I treat them the same way. If you'd gone on to have another child, you'd understand how tough it can be.'

Opening and closing her mouth, Molly fixed her eyes on a mark on the paint in the far corner of the room. If she'd had another child? He damn well knew that she'd have loved to have another child. Fat chance of that ever happening now though. Talk about rubbing salt into the wound. 'I sympathise that it must be tough, but it has nothing to do with how much time you spend with them all, it's to do with how you treat them when you do have them. You've got to admit that by the sounds of it you're a lot more lenient towards Ruby than you are with Ellis.'

'She is a lot younger than him.'

'Yes, she's younger, but this isn't the first time that Ellis has come home really upset over the way Jessica has spoken to him after a clash between him and Ruby.'

'Yes, well?'

'Just that. She needs to watch what she says to him, she's really upset him.'

'Look, I didn't hear what she said. I was downstairs when Ellis got pushed, I only saw the aftermath and told him off.'

Molly sighed. 'Why didn't you say that before?'

'I didn't think it was important.'

'Well, it is. If you were downstairs, how do you know what Jessica said to him? Do you agree with the way she handled it?'

'She told him off. That's what I would have done too. Look, it's not her fault if Ellis didn't say that Ruby had kicked a car at him. She's not a mind reader and neither am I.'

Laying her hand palm down on the surface of the table, Molly scrunched her fingers into a tight fist before releasing them. 'I've already told you that he doesn't feel the point in telling on Ruby any more. Surely we don't have to go through all of this again? What I want to know is are you happy that Jessica called our son a horrible bully?'

'No.'

'So, you believe Ellis now? You believe he didn't make that up.' He wasn't denying it now, not like he did earlier.

'Yes, I do.'

Frowning, Molly ran her index finger over the tabletop, drawing star after star. Well, that was certainly a turnaround. What? No sticking up for Jessica any more? Lowering her voice, she spoke quietly. 'You've changed your tune. Has she admitted it?'

'I asked her if she'd said that, yes, and she said she may have done.'

'She may have done? What's that supposed to mean?'

'It means she doesn't remember. She knows she told him off, but she doesn't remember what she said.'

'Seriously? I think I'd definitely remember if I'd said that, especially to my stepchild!' Molly scoffed, Jessica knew what she'd said. It was ridiculous of her to lie.

'She's very sorry if she's caused him any upset. She's crying herself now. Can we just leave it at that?'

Pursing her lips, Molly could feel the telltale bubble of anger stirring again. 'Trevor, for goodness' sake, she's an adult! Don't you dare tell me she's crying and expect me to feel sorry for her when I've had to sit with our son – a nine-year-old – and have him sobbing into my arms until he finally fell asleep!'

'I understand you're annoyed...'

'Annoyed? That's the least of it! You really don't seem to comprehend how much this has affected him! And it's not just her calling him a bully, it's the fact that you rushed both him and Lauren out of your home – their home – without their dinner. That just reinforced the fact that you put Ruby first and don't feel they are a true part of your family.' Laying her free hand down flat on the table, she tried to stop it shaking.

'I just wanted to get them out of the situation.'

'What do you mean, out of the situation? Kids argue, that's kids, but reacting the way you both did is not normal. It's not right.'

Silence.

'Trevor?'

'You're right. I, we, could have handled it better.'

'That's an understatement.'

'I've said we were in the wrong.'

'I know, but it's easy to say. Now you've got to try to make it up to him.' Molly shook her head. 'I just can't believe how something as normal as kids arguing could have been so blown out of proportion.'

'All right. I get it. How many times do I have to say we were in the wrong? I suppose you're the perfect parent?'

Taking a deep breath in, Molly bit down on her bottom lip. It was done. There was nothing any of them could do to change the past. 'Sorry. It was just so heartbreaking to see how upset he was. But now you just need to figure out how to fix it.'

'Can I talk to him?'

'He's asleep.' She'd already told him that. 'Look, why don't you give him a call tomorrow and sort it all out then?'

'Okay.'

Lowering the mobile to the table, Molly leant her elbows on the hard surface and rested her chin on her hands. It was good that he could see what he'd done wrong, that he could have, should have handled the situation better. How could Jessica not have told him what she'd said straight away? Unless he'd been covering for her and was trying to blame Ellis' overactive imagination?

She shook her head. No. She needed to take this at face value. She had to. There was no point in always thinking the worst of Trevor.

'Mum! Here you are! I've been calling you, the timer's going off on the oven.' Bursting through the door, Lauren folded her arms and glared at Molly.

'Oh right. Sorry, sweetheart, I just had to take a phone call. Did you get them out?'

'No, I didn't know if they were ready or not.'

'The timer going off would suggest that they are.' Forcing a laugh, Molly pushed herself to standing.

17

'And then if you just pull the wool a little bit taut, it's got less chance of falling off your needle.' Patting Bill on the arm, Molly stood up and glanced around the group. They had two new people join them today. Tara and Catherine. She recognised them both from the Village Fete.

'I'll just get you another ball of wool, Pat. It looks like you're about to run out any minute now!'

'Thanks, love.' Glancing up from her knitting, Pat smiled.

Walking across to the basket, Molly dipped her hand into the soft balls of wool, rummaging around until she found the correct shade of pink Pat was using.

'Morning, everyone. Hi, Molly.'

Keeping her eyes on the basket of wool, Molly momentarily closed her eyes. She knew that voice. It was Richie. What with everything that had happened with Ellis yesterday, she hadn't been able to give much thought to what he'd done, but now... Now, she could feel her cheeks redden.

Straightening her back and focusing her eyes on Pat, she walked over and passed her the soft pink ball. 'Anyone for another drink?'

'I think I've still got...'

Placing the mugs hurriedly onto the tray, she ignored the coffee spilling onto the surface of the coffee table before she turned her back and walked towards the kitchen. Plastering a smile on her face, she focused on putting one foot in front of the other, trying to appear as natural as possible.

Kicking the kitchen door shut, she placed the tray on the work surface before resting her hands, palms down, either side of the tray and dipped her head.

'Molly? You okay?'

Jerking her head up. Molly spun around. 'What are you doing in here, Richie?'

Blinking, Richie ran his fingers through his hair. 'Sorry, I just... I came to see if you were okay. You just seemed to blank me out there.'

'Yes, well, some of us have things to do. We can't just gallivant around chatting to people when we're supposed to be working.'

Fiddling with his radio attached to the front of his uniform, he frowned. 'Have I done something to upset you?'

Say nothing, say nothing. He wasn't worth getting upset for. Turning around slowly, Molly bit her bottom lip. He looked so casual, though. So together. How could it not be affecting him in the slightest? How could he not feel a smidgen of guilt? Feeling the flush of anger return to her cheeks, she looked him in the eye. 'I know, okay? I know.'

'You know what? What's happened?'

Why could he not just admit it? 'Just go.'

Stepping forward, Richie laid his hand on her forearm. 'I don't understand. What's happened?'

Pulling her arm away from him, she took a step back. 'Please leave.'

'Molly, please? I have a right to know what's happened. Every-thing was so good Saturday night. I really enjoyed spending time with you and I thought you did too?'

'I did.' She would not cry. She would not cry. Scrunching her eyes up, she looked away, blinking back the tears.

'Molly?'

Turning back to him, she looked him up and down, trying to find a chink in his armour, trying to find a telltale sign that told her who he really was. What he was really capable of doing.

'Hey, sorry to bother you, but I've got myself into a bit of a pick-le.' Tara pushed the door to the kitchen ajar and held up a muddle of knitting needles and wool, a sheepish grin spreading across her face.

'That's all right. I'll bring these out and come and help you.' Pouring the boiling water into the mugs, Molly stirred as the door gently swung shut again. 'Richie, I'm sorry, do you mind if we do this another time? I'm just in the middle of something.'

'Right, of course.' Looking down at his shoes, he looked back up at her, shook his head and left.

Gripping the side of the work surface, Molly took a deep breath. She would speak to him. She would tell him that she knew about Diane, just not at the moment. Not with the knitting group in the next room, and not until she'd got her own head around everything.

* * *

The ceiling above Molly's bed had a blue mark on it. She'd never noticed it before, but every time the lightning struck and illumi-nated the room, she caught a glimpse of it. Maybe it was a stray lick of paint. Maybe before Diane or Richie or whoever had painted the walls magnolia, they had been blue. Maybe Richie had painted it to help it to sell. That was the advice, wasn't it? Strip the property of all colour in order to help prospective buyers to visualise their belongings in place.

She wouldn't have minded the blue, it was a bright colour. The colour of peacock feathers. She liked peacocks. They reminded her of the country estate she used to take Lauren and Ellis for picnics with Florence and her daughter when they were young. She missed her friend, Florence, but she and her family had moved to the coast. Maybe she'd call her sometime, invite them to come and visit.

'Mum?'

Pulling the duvet down, Molly peered into the dark. 'Ellis? Do you want to come and snuggle?'

'Can I?' The sleep in his voice carried across the room.

'Of course, you can, sweetheart.' Holding the duvet open for him, Molly held her other hand out to guide him.

Just as Ellis began padding towards the bed, a bolt of lightning lit the room, as bright as a floodlight, before an almighty clap of thunder vibrated the flat. Running the short distance towards her, Ellis dived into Molly's arms.

'It's okay. It's outside. You're safe.' Pulling his shaking body towards her, Molly hugged him tightly and kissed the top of his head. 'Try to go back to sleep now.'

Nodding, Ellis pulled the duvet further up, covering his face as another bolt of lightning lit the room.

He had never liked thunderstorms, not like Lauren, whose favourite thing to do was to sneak out into the garden mid-storm and hold her arms out wide, catching the pelting rain and vibrations from the thunder. It wouldn't surprise Molly if she had opened her bedroom window and was leaning out, revelling in the storm's electricity.

As another bolt of lightning shot across the sky, flashing behind the curtains, Ellis squeezed his arms tight around Molly's forearm.

The clash of thunder which ensued filled the room just as an enormous thud shook the flat.

'Mum? What was that? What was that bang? Has it hit us? Has the lightning hit us?'

'No, no, sweetheart, it hasn't hit us.' Staring into the darkness enveloping them, Molly bit down on her bottom lip, the metallic taste of blood quickly filling her mouth. Something had been hit, she was sure of that. Not the flat, not Bramble Patch, but something close. Very close.

'Are you sure? It sounded like it did. It sounded on top of us.'

'Don't worry, it hasn't hit the flat. Let me just go and have a look out of the window.' As she tried to slip her arm from underneath Ellis' head, he gripped tightly.

'No, don't, Mum. Don't leave me. Please?' The fear in his voice echoed in the momentarily silent room.

'Okay, okay.' Positioning her arm back beneath Ellis' sweaty head, Molly twisted her head to look towards the window. She couldn't see the glow of fire or anything, so maybe nothing had been hit, maybe it had just been the noise of the thunder. She looked back down at Ellis, his eyes still wide open with fear. She'd slip out and take a look to be on the safe side when he'd fallen back to sleep.

As another flash flooded the room, Ellis' body stiffened.

'One, two, three.' The rumble of thunder interrupted Molly's counting. 'There, see, it's getting further away now. It's not right above us any more.'

'It's still close though.' The shudder in Ellis' whisper penetrated the night.

'Not for long. It's on its way. Close your eyes and we'll count together.' On cue, the bedroom illuminated once again. 'One, two, three, four, five.'

* * *

Yawning, Molly peeked down at Ellis, his eyes were closed and his breathing had slowed. He was almost asleep. She just had to stay awake that little bit longer so she could go and check out of the window. 'One, two, three, four, five, six, seven, eight.'

18

'Ellis, stop being a slow coach! You're going to make us late!' Chucking Ellis' rucksack at him, Lauren checked her reflection in the mirror for the third time in as many minutes. 'Tell him, Mum.'

'Calm down. Let him put his shoes on. Throwing his bag at him isn't going to help. It will only slow him down.' Shrugging her arms into her thin jacket, Molly glanced in the mirror too. Not that it mattered that she hadn't had time to put any make-up on or even to brush her hair. She wouldn't be getting out of the car, anyway. She could sort herself out when she got back from dropping them off.

'Come on!'

'That's it, Ellis. Now grab your coat. I'll get your bag.' Stooping down, Molly retrieved Ellis' rucksack from the floor.

* * *

Pulling the front door open, Molly stepped out into the light, the fresh clean air only a thunderstorm could bring filled her lungs as she shielded her eyes from the low morning sun. 'Oh.'

'You've got to be kidding me?'

Standing still, her keys in her hand, Molly stared in front of her.

'Was that what the bang was last night? I told you something got hit, didn't I, Mum?' Taking his rucksack from Molly's hand, Ellis shifted it onto his shoulder.

'You sure did.' Looking at the tree lying sideways across the entrance to the parking bays in front of Bramble Patch, Molly tucked her hair behind her ears. Tilting her head, she followed the thick tree trunk with her eyes. Before last night it had stood on the small green outside Richie's mum's house next door. Now, though, over half the length of the tree, complete with branches, leaves and a smattering of blossom, lay awkwardly across the pathway and parking bays, while a stub of trunk remained stubbornly in the ground where it belonged.

'How come it didn't catch fire?' Lauren dropped her school bag by her feet.

'It probably had too much moisture in or something.' Walking around the back of their car, Molly blinked. Apart from a small twig full of blossom having got caught on the back wiper, the car had got away unscathed. 'The car's okay.'

'That's not much use when we can't actually get out though, is it, Mum?'

'It's a lot better than having a squashed car, Lauren.'

'Yes, but... what do we do now? How am I going to get to school without the car? I'm going to be mega late now and I wanted to be early.'

'All right. There's nothing we can do about you being late now, anyway. We'll just have to get the bus.' Rummaging in the pockets of her jacket, Molly pulled some coins out. 'Come on. I should have enough change here.'

'What time does the bus come?'

'I don't know, we can look at the timetable when we get to the bus stop.'

'Oh great, so I will definitely be late then. Won't I?'

'Yes, you'll be late but don't worry, it's not like there's anything we can do about it. I'll ring the office and let them know.'

Lauren kicked at a twig. 'It's going to be so embarrassing.'

'No, it won't. I bet people are late all the time. You won't be the only one who's ever been late.' Bending down, Molly picked up Lauren's bag and handed it back to her. 'Come on.'

* * *

'Thank you.' Smiling to the bus driver, Molly stepped down onto the pavement before checking her watch. Momentarily closing her eyes, she shook her head. Although the journey to and from Lauren and Ellis' schools had been pleasant, the bus had taken them around all of the narrow windy roads and through at least five other villages, none of which Molly had realised had existed, meaning the journey had taken at least four times the time it would have taken to do the school run in the car. She had fifteen minutes until Bramble Patch was due to open. Not that any would-be customers would have anywhere to park, anyway.

Glancing each way before she crossed the road, she reminded herself what she'd told Lauren; they were lucky the tree hadn't hit the car. Or Bramble Patch, for that matter. If the lightning had struck further down the trunk and in a different position then it could easily have fallen towards them. Yes, they'd been lucky. She'd have to get on the phone to the council or whoever dealt with fallen trees. Hopefully, they'd be able to sort it sooner rather than later.

Turning the corner, Molly frowned and slowed down. Richie was hanging over the garden gate to his mum's bungalow, chatting to her. Glancing behind her, Molly cursed under her breath. In a small village, what were the chances that someone would be walking behind her, along this particular road, at this particular time?

Yep, and now he'd noticed her. Zero chance of her avoiding him now. Slowly raising her hand, she gave a slight wave, telling herself she was waving to his mum rather than him. Looking down at the ground, she counted the steps until she crossed over to Bramble Patch.

'Hi, Molly. You okay? Looks like you had a lucky escape last night!' Waving to his mum, Richie walked over towards the front of Bramble Patch.

'Yes, I know.' Digging in her pocket for the keys, she eventually pulled them out and unlocked the front door.

'I'll put a call in to the council, see if we can get someone out to shift it.'

'It's fine, I can do it.' Slipping inside, Molly went to shut the door, stopping as Richie followed her in.

'I'm happy to call.' Grinning, Richie pulled his mobile from the pocket of his uniform.

Taking a step back just inside the doorway, Molly looked him up and down. He really didn't have a clue that Diane had paid her a visit, did he?

'I was going to ask if you'd like to pop out for a coffee sometime if you get the chance.'

'I don't think that's a good idea.' Even if Diane hadn't warned her off him, she normally worked through lunch, anyway.

'Oh, right.' Running his fingers through his hair, Richie looked down before looking her in the eye. 'Have I done something wrong? I feel that yesterday and today you've been a little off with me.'

'No, I just...' This was silly. They were both adults. She had nothing to feel ashamed of. It was Richie in the wrong, not her. 'I had a visit from Diane.'

'Diane?'

'Yes. She told me everything.'

'Oh right. She told you how we broke up?'

'No, not about that.'

'About what then? About the shop?'

Was it that hard? That difficult to realise what she meant? Surely he should have twigged by now? Breathing out hard, Molly shook her head. 'She told me about you two starting to see each other again.'

Opening and closing his mouth, Richie stood there watching her.

'Well?'

Shaking his head, he glanced towards the front door and back to Molly. 'I don't know what to say.'

'Have you been seeing her?' Molly cleared her throat.

'What? No. No, of course I haven't been seeing her. I wouldn't have gone to the dance with you if I was with her again, would I? Not that there will ever be anything between me and Diane again.' Richie rubbed his hand over his face and tilted his head. 'I did tell you how we split up, didn't I?'

'Yes, you did.'

'Then you'll understand why I'd never get back with her even if I liked her that way. Which I don't before you ask.'

'Right, okay.' Molly crossed her arms.

'I am so sorry that she came to you like that but I can honestly say nothing is going on at all between us. She barely even talks to me when I drop off or pick up our daughter.'

Molly crossed her arms. He looked as though he was telling the truth, and she knew how Diane had cheated on him. Had she got this completely wrong? She was normally such a good judge of character. Had she really let Diane lie to her?

'Honestly, I'm telling you the truth.' Looking down, he adjusted his shirt collar. 'I don't lie.'

She had, she'd got it all wrong. Holding her hand against her cheek, she could feel the heat radiating from her skin.

'Please? Please believe me.' Touching her on the forearm, Richie glanced at her, deep creases appearing above his eyes.

Putting her hand over his, she looked up at him. 'I'm so sorry. She was crying and upset because she'd seen us together and I just... I guess I just jumped to the wrong conclusion.'

Richie nodded.

'I really am.' Looking down at her feet, Molly kicked at an invisible mark on the floor. 'I guess I've just been hurt in the past and it was easy to believe her.'

'Don't worry, I understand.'

'Really?'

'Yes, really. Remember, I know how convincing she is.' Chuckling, Richie stepped closer.

'I guess you do.' Grinning, Molly lifted her head up, his lips millimetres away.

'Are we okay now then?'

'We are.' Closing her eyes, Molly felt the tender warmth of his lips against hers. How could she have believed Diane after what Richie had told her about their break-up? She should have known he wouldn't lie.

'Was that okay?'

Looking down at her feet and back up at him again, Molly nodded.

'Good. Right, I'll pop a call in and see if we can get that tree moved sooner rather than later then. If that's all right with you, of course?'

'Yes, that'd be great thanks.'

* * *

'Thanks for letting Marissa stay for dinner. Are you sure it's okay at such short notice?'

Stirring in the pasta sauce, Molly looked up at Lauren and smiled. 'Yes, it's fine. I'm just glad you're making friends.'

'Great, thanks. Her dad is on a late shift so won't finish until about eight, can she stay until then?'

'Yes, that's fine. Does she need a lift home?' Richie had been true to his word, and the tree had been removed just before she'd had to go out and do the school run.

'Nah, she only lives a couple of streets away.'

'Oh, she lives in the village too?' Molly grinned. It would be great for Lauren to have someone so close, someone she could meet up with on the weekends.

'Yep. Her dad's going to come to pick her up on his way back from work before you panic about her walking home in the dark. I know what you're like.'

Molly laughed. 'It's always better to be overprotective and...'

'Keep safe. Yes, I know.'

'Right, time for dinner.'

* * *

'Mum, that'll be Marissa's dad. Can you tell him she'll be down in a couple of minutes? We're just finishing off our nails.' Lauren's voice floated down the hallway from her bedroom.

Pushing herself to standing, Molly passed the popcorn to Ellis. 'I won't be long.'

'Do you want me to pause it until you get back?' Holding up the remote to the TV, Ellis popped some popcorn in his mouth.

'No, you watch it, sweetheart. You can tell me what happened when I come back up.'

Shrugging, Ellis dipped his hand back into the paper bag and looked back at the film.

* * *

Pulling the door to Bramble Patch open, Molly smiled. 'Hi, Richie. This is a surprise, I wasn't expecting you to pop round.'

'Hi. I'm actually here to pick Marissa up. Not that I'm not happy to see you, I am.' Grinning, Richie shrugged out of his jacket and stepped inside.

Shutting the door behind him, Molly felt the hot heat of embarrassment flush across her face. 'I didn't realise you were Marissa's dad. I knew you had a daughter, but you never mentioned her name.'

'Yep, that's me.' Richie glanced at the door up to the flat. 'Are they upstairs?'

'Yes, they're just finishing off painting their nails, but they shouldn't be too long now.'

Stepping forward, Richie flung his jacket onto one of the comfy chairs and pulled her towards him. 'Do you think we have enough time for this?' Cupping his hands around her chin, he tipped her face to meet his.

'I should think so.' Moving her lips towards his, she closed her eyes as she felt his lips against hers, soft and warm and gentle. Feeling his hands move from her face to her back, she let herself be pulled in closer to him, the kiss stronger now, more urgent.

Stepping back, Richie grinned. 'I've missed you these last couple of days.'

'I've missed you too.' Tucking her hair behind her ears, Molly smiled. She really had. She'd missed their chats, the jokey chats and the more serious conversations too. She'd missed the general feeling that he was there for her. She knew they'd only really become close at the dance, but before that, when they'd been getting to know each other, he'd always made her feel special. Always made her feel as though he really cared about her opinion, listened to her. She'd missed that these past couple of days. She'd missed looking forward to him coming into the shop, seeking her out, wanting to spend time with her. Threading her fingers through his, she smiled up at him. 'Have you got time for a coffee?'

'I should think so, we all know how long girls take painting their nails.' Chuckling, he followed her through past the counter and into the back kitchen.

'Oi!' Letting go of his hand, Molly switched the kettle on. 'You're right though, Lauren normally takes forever painting her nails and redoing them until they're perfect.' Turning around and leaning against the work surface, she tucked her hands in her pockets, hiding her own naked and bitten fingernails. She'd never been one for pampering herself or painting her nails and she'd definitely not had the time or inclination since moving into Bramble Patch.

Slipping into a chair, Richie laid his hands on the tabletop. 'I've been thinking, I will speak to Diane about what she said to you. It was unfair of her to make you feel the way she did.'

Turning around, Molly spooned coffee granules into two mugs. 'Please don't. It's fine. I should have been more trusting of you.'

'No, you shouldn't. We've not known each other long, you had no reason to doubt her.' Standing up, he walked over towards Molly and wrapped his arms around her waist. 'I'm so glad it's all sorted now though.'

'Me too.' Twisting around in his embrace, Molly looked him in the eye and smiled.

'Mum, we've finished our nails.'

Jumping away from each other, Molly and Richie looked towards the door just as Lauren and Marissa barged in.

'Hey, Dad. Look, what do you think?' Grinning, Marissa held

her hands out for her dad to see her bright pink nails emblazoned with nail stickers featuring the black silhouette of flamingos.

'Oh, yes. Very nice. I like the flamingos.'

Molly nodded. With them both stood together she could see the family resemblance. In fact, she was surprised she hadn't spotted it before. Marissa had Richie's same large eyes and sandy hair.

'What do you think, Mum? We used that new colour you got me the other day.' Holding her hands out, Lauren looked across at her mum.

'It's a lovely colour, isn't it? It's come out really nice. You've done a really good job. Very professional.'

'Thanks.' Lauren grinned and turned to Marissa. 'We forgot to put the topcoat on to protect them.'

'Have we got time to quickly do that? Please, Dad?'

Richie looked at his daughter and nodded. 'Off you go then.'

Smiling, Molly went back to finishing the coffees. That had been a close call. Feeling Richie's strong arms around her waist again, she leant back, holding her face up towards him. His kiss, although quick, was so full of passion, she closed her eyes and could almost picture themselves anywhere – the beach, the Eiffel Tower. Pulling away, she laughed. 'Here's your coffee.'

'Thanks.' Taking his mug, he immediately placed it back on the work surface. 'How long do you think we've got?'

'Oh, I don't know. Five, ten minutes.'

'Then let's make the most of them.' Taking Molly's coffee, he placed it next to his and brought her in towards him.

She really hadn't felt like this about someone since Trevor. No, that was a lie. Even at the beginning of her relationship with her ex-husband, he hadn't made her feel this comfortable, this special. As she kissed him back, she looked into his eyes. How could she have doubted him? How could she have believed a total stranger over him? She knew she hadn't known him long at all, and they'd only been together a mere few days really, but she knew, just knew that they could actually have a future together. And she'd been on enough dates with men she'd met online to know that this feeling was different. To know that there was a real connection between them.

Pulling away, Richie held her at arm's length, tilting his head as he looked at her. 'I feel as though I'm really falling for you.'

'Me too.' Looking down, she hoped the blush she could feel speeding across her skin wouldn't be too obvious.

'Do you think you'd be able to take a lunch break tomorrow? There's this really nice pub in a hamlet a few miles down the road. I think you'd really like it there.'

'Umm.' She didn't usually take lunch breaks, it would mean closing up the shop and potentially missing out on customers and profit. But then, she couldn't carry on forever not taking any breaks, could she? 'Yes, okay. Why not?'

'Great, I'll pick you up at half twelve then, shall I?'

'Looking forward to it already.' Molly grinned and picked up her coffee. Maybe moving here had been the right decision in more than a few ways.

19

Switching the door sign to Closed, Molly stepped out into the warm spring air. The sun was beaming down and if she hadn't just written an order form out for a delivery for the end of May, she could have been forgiven for thinking it was July or August. Slipping out of her grey cardigan, she threw it over the crease of her elbow and waved at Richie who was sat waiting for her on the small wall next to the planter in front of the shop.

Holding up two motorbike helmets, he pointed to a big black and silver beast in the parking bay. 'Are you up for it?'

Looking at the motorbike and then back at Richie, Molly let her mouth drop open. 'I've never ridden one before.'

'Don't worry, I'll drive, all you'll need to do is hold on tight. What do you reckon?'

Biting down on her bottom lip, Molly grimaced. Throughout her childhood, her mum had always told her how dangerous they were and always chided Molly's dad when he went out for a ride. She tilted her head and stared at Richie. She trusted him, he'd keep her safe. After all, he was a police officer. If he'd deemed it too dangerous, he wouldn't even be suggesting it. 'Okay, why not?'

'Great.' Coming towards her, he placed his helmet on the floor and gently fitted the spare one onto her head, pulling the strap tight under her chin. 'How does that feel?'

'Heavy.' Molly nodded her head and grinned. Maybe it was time she started trying out new things.

'You'll get used to it. I'd pop your cardigan back on though if I was you. It might get a little drafty on the bike.' Taking Molly's cardigan, he held it out for her as she shrugged into it. 'Ready?'

'Yep. Yes, I guess so.'

Taking her hand, Richie led her to the bike and helped her on before throwing his leg over and taking the handlebars. Looking back at her, he grinned before reaching back, taking her hands and positioning them around his waist. 'Hold real tight, right?'

'Right, will do.' Moving her chin from side to side, she wished he'd look away from her, she was sure her cheeks must be squashed at a weird angle, she could feel the fat in her face pushed upwards by the helmet.

'Okay, great. Here we go then!'

As Richie revved the bike into action, Molly could feel the power from the engine vibrate through her. Lifting her feet off the ground, she tightened her grip around Richie's middle. Could she really hold on for any length of time? What if she let go accidentally? Did people even do that? You never heard on the news that someone had lost their life due to letting go and falling off though, did you? Maybe it would be an automatic reaction to grip on for dear life when going at speed on one of these things. Closing her eyes, Molly hoped it would be. She hoped she wouldn't do anything silly like push a loose hair out of her eye or something.

Pulling out of the parking bays, Richie turned right and drove the motorbike slowly out of the village. Maybe it wouldn't be too bad. She could cope with this speed, and if she did let go, as long as she made sure she didn't fall beneath the wheels, the worst she'd sustain would be a bruise or two.

Plastering a grin on her face as Richie quickly glanced back at her, Molly hoped he thought she was having a good time. And it was quite nice, really. She noticed flowers in the hedgerows she hadn't seen when driving past; she noticed the horses which were kept in the fields just outside the village.

She could do this. Maybe she'd even have a go at driving one of them some day. Grinning, she nodded. Yes, maybe. Feeling Richie's hand fleetingly on hers, warm and strong, she let him move her hand tighter around his middle. As she turned back to look at the flowers, the hedgerows quickly turned to woodland. The bike was speeding up. Molly could feel the vibrations beneath her quicken and the trees began to blur, the flash of bluebells smattering the ground beneath the trees.

Gripping even tighter, Molly wondered whether the blood would be able to get through to her fingers. Was she hurting Richie? No, he'd slow down if she was and he was doing just the opposite, he was speeding up. Looking down, she could see the tarmac beneath them, the white lines in the middle of the road becoming a long white ribbon of continuous colour.

Trying to lean back to keep her head up, her neck strained as they sped along. Lowering her face against Richie's back, the warmth emanating from his leather jacket warmed the skin of her cheek.

Faster and faster they went. Molly felt as though the world was spinning beneath them. She could feel the air through the thin material of her cardigan, colder than she would have imagined on a day like this.

* * *

As she lifted her leg over the back of the bike and planted herself on the safety of the earth again, Molly could feel the rush of adrenaline pulsing through her body still. Now she was safe, now she knew she had arrived in one piece, she felt more awake and alive than she had done in a very long time.

'So?' Taking his helmet off, Richie hooked it onto the handlebars and ran his fingers through his hair. Stepping forward, he unclipped Molly's helmet and pulled it off. 'What did you think?'

Smoothing her hair down with the palms of her hands, Molly grinned and nodded. 'It was great! Really good fun.'

'You really think so?'

'Yes. I mean it was completely petrifying and at numerous points along the way, I seriously thought I might die, but, yes, it was great. I haven't felt this alive in a long time.'

Richie laughed. 'I hope I didn't scare you too much! I kept to the speed limit. Obviously. And I thought I'd taken it pretty slow and steady.'

'If that's what you call slow, I definitely do not want to go on it when you're not taking it slow and steady.' Laughing, Molly reached out and brushed a leaf off his arm. 'You must be boiling in that jacket.'

'I am.' Grinning, Richie slipped off his leather jacket to reveal a pale blue short-sleeved shirt and held out his elbow.

Slipping her arm through his, they walked towards the pub. It was a beautiful old stone-built building, low and squat with ivy growing up the front wall. With her free hand, Molly smoothed down the hair on the top of her head again. She must look an absolute mess after wearing that helmet. And that was just her hair, she dreaded to think what her make-up looked like. She never wore much, but she had put some foundation and a little eye shadow on for their lunch date. She'd have to pop to the toilets and try to sort herself out.

Puling the heavy wooden door open, Richie held it open and let Molly walk through first before they both headed towards the bar. 'Shall we eat outside?'

'Yes, it would be a shame to be cooped up in here on a day like today.' Not that the inside didn't look lovely. It did. With its green and white checked covered seats and benches and dark wooden tables, it looked cosy and a roaring coal fire and old oil paintings added to the ambience, but it was so nice outside and especially after the ride getting here, it would be good to be outside. More refreshing.

'Great, what did you want to drink?'

'Umm, could I have an orange juice, please?' Looking towards the bartender who was serving an elderly gentleman at the other end of the bar, Molly turned around and scoured the walls for a sign indicating the whereabouts of the toilets. There. 'Are you okay if I pop to the toilets? I feel bad making you wait.'

'Don't worry. It's fine. I'll grab some menus too.' Leaning across, Richie pecked Molly on the cheek before turning back to the bar.

* * *

Staring at her reflection in the mirror, Molly laughed. There had literally been no point straightening her hair before their date. Patches were fine, but the vast majority of it looked something like a spider web. In place of a brush, she held her fingers apart and raked them through her hair.

Standing back, she looked at herself. That would have to do. Yes, she hadn't managed to get her hair as smooth as it was earlier, and where the helmet strap had done up the foundation on her chin and cheeks was a little smudged, but, hey, Richie had seen her with no make-up. Heck, he'd seen her with tears streaking down her face. This was still an improvement. She shrugged, Richie liked her for her, not for the amount of make-up she wore or how frizz-free she could style her hair.

* * *

As she walked back out into the pub lounge, Molly made her way towards the open doors leading to the garden. Stepping outside, she blinked. The sun was bright after the dim lights inside. Taking a deep breath, she could smell the unmistakable sweet aroma of freesias and lavender mixed together into some beautiful perfume. The garden was laid to lawn, sporadic flower beds springing from the green of the grass between old-style wooden pub tables. A river ran past the side of the garden where ducks emerged from the reeds, quacking around the tables looking for scraps before heading back to immerse themselves into the cool water.

Holding her hand up, Molly spotted Richie sat at a table by the river and waved before making her way over. 'It's beautiful here.'

'It is, isn't it? I thought you'd like it. I sometimes come here if I manage to get a lunch break or after a particularly difficult shift, just being this close to nature helps me to put things into perspective.'

'I can imagine it would.' Slipping onto the bench opposite him, Molly picked up her orange juice and took a sip. 'Thank you.'

'You're welcome.' Shuffling in his seat, Richie laid his hands on the table in front of him. 'So, I need to tell you something.'

'Okay, that sounds ominous.'

'No, not really. Well, I hope not anyway.' He cleared his throat. 'You know I said that I was falling for you?'

Trying to keep her eyes focused on his, Molly dismissed the heat quickly rising to her face and nodded. He'd made a mistake. He wasn't falling for her at all. This was some elaborate break-up date. She'd had it once before, instead of the usual text or phone call to end a relationship, which, yes, wasn't the 'right' thing to do but was definitely a fairly kind route leaving the dumped to break down in the safety of their own home, a guy she had been dating, had taken her for dinner when he'd got back off of a holiday and dumped her then. She shivered, she still remembered it, the awkward conversation over dinner. Her, happy to see him but aware of some underlying tension. Him, obviously trying to be a gentleman by paying for the meal and drinks. Afterwards, he'd suggested a walk around the village and by then she'd been quite certain what had been coming and, just as she had begun to suspect, he'd 'let her down gently'. She understood why he, and now Richie, thought they were being kind but she'd much much rather a text or at worst a difficult conversation over the phone.

'You okay?'

Molly nodded. She could already feel the tears welling up in her eyes and he hadn't said anything yet. It was just that, unlike when she'd been dumped this way before, she actually had real feelings for Richie. If she was honest, she'd already had visions bouncing around in her head about how they'd tell the children about their relationship, their first holiday together as a proper family, even him proposing. She shook her head; it was daft; she knew it was. She was daft. She'd let herself get way too involved emotionally way too quickly. She'd just felt such a powerful connection with him. Placing her hands in her lap, she laced her fingers together tightly.

Running his fingers through his hair again, he tilted his head. 'I'm just going to come out with it.'

Closing her eyes, Molly nodded. Here we go.

'I think we could have a real future together.'

Nodding, Molly bit her bottom lip. 'I understand... what? Sorry, what did you say?'

A nervous throaty laugh escaped Richie's mouth. 'I said I can see a future with you. Ever since we met, I've felt different, I've felt as though I could picture a future with you.' Sitting back, he looked out to the river and then back at Molly. 'I'm sorry. It's too soon. I know it is. I shouldn't have said anything.'

'No. No, it's fine.' Placing her hands on the table in front of her, she waited until Richie had slipped his into hers. They laced their fingers together, Richie's a little sweaty from nerves. 'I feel the same. I feel as though I can picture a future with you too. I really can.'

Laughing, Richie leant forward, their lips meeting. 'Thank goodness for that! I really thought you were going to think I was completely crazy to feel that way in such a short space of time.'

'Maybe. But we can be crazy together.' Laughing, Molly kissed him again, a little stronger, a little more passionate this time.

———————

20

'Molly, there's someone here for you, love.' Walking into the back kitchen, Gladys shut the door behind her. 'It's Diane, Richie's ex. She seems quite upset. Shall I tell her you're busy?'

'Diane?' Placing the bottle of milk back down on the work surface, Molly frowned. What did she want now? Was she going to spread more lies? Well, it wouldn't work. She knew Richie was telling her the truth. Plus, he had good reasons not to want to get back with her. It made no sense. 'No, it's okay. I'll see her. I'll just take these out.'

'Here, I'll do that. I'll send her through then, shall I?' Taking the tray, Gladys turned and went back to the Knit and Natter group.

Great, she'd just been trying to help one of the new people get to grips with knit one, purl one and now Diane was demanding to see her. She shook her head, she knew she didn't have to worry about the knitters, Gladys, Susan and Lucy were more than capable of looking after the newbies, but, still, Diane knew the shop was open and when she'd come in she would have seen the group going on. Instead of walking away, she'd made the choice to barge in, probably just to spin more of her lies.

Seeing the door open, Molly took a deep breath. She could handle Diane. 'Hi, Diane.'

'Hello, Molly. I'm so sorry to bother you, especially when you're working, but I just didn't know what else to do. I needed to speak to you and I really don't think it can wait.'

Nodding slowly, Molly took in the dishevelled hair and the wonky sunglasses. It really did look as though she was upset. Properly, this time, not like she was last time. Molly knew she'd been playing a game, lying, last time, but this time she looked genuinely upset. She shook her head, she'd thought Diane had been genuine the last time too. Crossing her arms, Molly stared at her. 'I don't have anything to say to you.'

'Molly, please listen.' Stepping forward, Diane placed her hand on Molly's arm.

Backing away from her touch, Molly shook her head. 'No, I'm sorry. I don't have the time today.'

Diane looked down at the floor before sliding her sunglasses to the top of her head, revealing her eyes, eyeshadow smudged and mascara running. 'You know I'm not in a relationship with Richie, don't you?'

Molly nodded.

'I'm sorry for misleading you, I was desperate and didn't know what to say to get you to listen.'

'Well, I listened, but your plan didn't work. Me and Richie are still together.' Why on earth had she lied to her?

'I know.'

How did she know? Had she been spying on them again? 'Look, I don't understand what you want from me? And to be honest, I don't want any part of it. If your plan is to try to break us up by pretending to be having a relationship with him again, it's not going to work. He's told me how you both split up, he's told me how you cheated on him. So whatever you've got to say won't work.'

Looking towards the table and back to Molly, Diane pointed to a chair. 'Do you mind if I sit down?'

Shrugging, Molly stayed standing.

Slipping into a chair and placing her sunglasses on the table, Diane clasped her hands in front of her. 'I realise I'm probably not very welcome here. In the village, I mean. I know how much everyone likes Richie and cares about him, and I know what I did to him in the past was inexcusable. I regret it every day. I really do.'

'That's something then.'

Unclasping her hands, Diane began fiddling with her sunglasses.

'I don't mean to be rude, but why are you here?' That was a lie, she did mean to be rude. Diane had almost destroyed her relationship with Richie. Molly really wasn't in the mood to be friendly to her.

Shuffling in her seat, Diane looked at her. 'I understand why you're so hostile towards me, I would be too if it was the other way around. I really would. I'm here because I need to speak to you mother to mother. I'm worried about my daughter, Marissa. She's fourteen, right at that difficult age when life seems impossibly hard.'

Molly nodded. Yes, life could be difficult for teenagers, but what did that have to do with her? Marissa had seemed perfectly happy yesterday, not that she was about to tell Diane that their daughters were friends. She didn't want her spying on Lauren as well.

'There's no easy way to say this, to ask this, but Marissa's been struggling a lot recently with the split between me and her father.'

'It can be difficult.'

'I know it sounds silly, because, as you probably know, Richie and I split up years ago but I think it's her age or something. She's been questioning me and getting upset over the fact that her dad and I aren't together any more.'

It didn't sound silly. It was completely plausible. Ellis, in particular, kept going through phases asking why she and Trevor couldn't get back together again, and he was remarried. So she did understand. 'I do understand, but I still don't know how that affects me?'

Laying her sunglasses back on the table, Diane looked straight at Molly. 'Richie and I have been spending some time together discussing Marissa, and there's a connection between us still. Marissa has moved in with him now and we've been spending even more time together as a family again.'

'Sorry?' A connection? Was she being serious?

'A connection. Between myself and Richie. I really think we could make another go of it. Be a family again. Provide that family life and stability for Marissa at this difficult time.'

Molly frowned. She knew Richie had been talking to Diane about Marissa's living arrangements but from what he'd said she was certain there wasn't any connection felt on his part.

'He's probably not told you we've been spending some time together.'

'He's told me.'

Diane nodded slowly. 'Of course. Well, I'm sure he's not mentioned about wanting to get back with me to you, but I definitely feel a connection and if you weren't on the scene...'

Biting down on her bottom lip, Molly tried to suppress the red fiery feeling of anger rising from the pit of her stomach. Diane really thought she could spin another web of lies and Molly would drop Richie? Richie didn't want to get back with Diane. Molly was sure of that. She was positive. 'I think you should go.'

'Okay, but please do have a think about what I've said. Please, if you can, step back and let us put our family back together. For Marissa's sake. She really does need us both there for her. I'm sure you look at your children and feel the same?'

Closing her eyes, she chuckled to herself. No, she really didn't feel that way. Yes, the 'happy, perfect family' with both parents did seem ideal, but she and Trevor could never have provided that for Lauren and Ellis. They would have grown up in a household of arguments. That wouldn't have been better for them than this. Two happy homes were always going to better than one unhappy home. She really did believe that. And she also believed that Richie and Diane would never be able to provide that ideal for Marissa together. Not from what Richie had told her. Opening her eyes again, Molly walked towards the kitchen door and held it open. 'Please leave.'

Nodding, Diane pushed her chair back and stood up. 'I will, but please, think about what I've said.'

Letting go of the door, Molly watched as it swung shut before running her fingers through her hair. She would not let Diane ruin this. Not for her, and not for Richie. Richie didn't want to get back with Diane and he wouldn't. Not after how she had treated him. Richie wanted the best for Marissa. She knew that. And him and Diane getting back together wouldn't be the best for any of them. Least of all for Marissa.

21

'Mum, Ellis is asking for you upstairs.' Letting the door to the flat bang shut behind her, Lauren walked behind the counter towards her mum, oblivious to the resounding slam of the door.

'Thank you. Hope to see you again soon.' Smiling at the customer in front of her, Molly handed the bag of ribbons the silver-haired lady had just purchased over the counter to her before turning to Lauren. 'The shop's still open. You know I have to stay down here. Can you ask him to come to me, please?'

'I really think you should go up. He's on the phone to Dad and he's getting pretty upset.'

Molly bit down on her bottom lip, Trevor normally rang the kids in the evenings when he got back from work. She looked across at the lone customer in the shop, a yummy mummy pushing a toddler in a buggy whilst having a baby strapped to her front.

'It's cool. I'll serve.' Sidling up to her, Lauren placed her hands over the till, gently laying her fingers across the keys.

'You've never used a till before.'

'I have. Gladys showed me once when you were getting a delivery in and she'd stepped in to help.'

'Oh, right.' Of course, Bramble Patch had been uncharacteristically busy the weekend after the Village Fete and Gladys had popped in just as a delivery truck had pulled up. She glanced at Lauren and nodded slowly. 'Okay. Any problems though, shout me. Any problems.'

'Uh-huh.' Nodding, Lauren blew a bubble with the gum in her mouth.

Looking back at Lauren as she pushed the door to the flat open, Molly nodded. Lauren could handle the till. Molly had only been less than a year older when she'd got her first job at the local corner shop.

* * *

Walking quietly up the stairs, Molly tilted her head and listened. She couldn't hear anything. Maybe the call had finished.

Walking across the hallway, she pushed Ellis' bedroom door open. He wasn't in there. Making her way to the living room. Molly peered in. Curled up on the sofa, Ellis had used cushions to barricade himself in the corner. 'Ellis, sweetheart, are you okay?'

Shuffling himself further back into the sofa cushions behind him, Ellis dipped his head into his lap.

Lowering herself onto the sofa next to him, Molly held her arm open. 'Come here, sweetie.' Waiting for him to sidle up to her, she wrapped her arm around him. Pulling him closer and kissing him on the top of the head. 'Do you want to tell me why you're upset?'

Keeping his eyes down, Ellis shook his head.

'Okay.' Staring ahead, Molly looked at the TV screen as a bright green mouse chased a yellow cat. 'Did Daddy call you?'

Ellis shook his head. 'I rang him.'

'Okay.'

'He said he's sorry that Jessica called me what she did.'

Molly nodded. Maybe she should have given Trevor more credit. Not in a million years had she thought he'd apologise. Yes, it should be Jessica saying sorry to Ellis, but, still. 'That's good then. Why has it made you upset?'

'He said he will pick us up early on Friday because he's got a half-day at work.'

Molly nodded. As the children had become older, Trevor tended to change arrangements through them rather than speaking to her and actually checking to see if it was okay with her. She shook her head. After all these years she should have got used to the way he was. It would never cross his mind that she might have something arranged. 'That will be nice then.'

Pushing himself up, Ellis looked at his mum. 'I don't want to go. I don't want to go to Daddy and Jessica's.'

'Why not, sweetheart? Why don't you want to go?'

'Because I don't. I don't want to see Jessica again and I don't want to see Ruby again. She'll just get me into trouble again and then Daddy and Jessica will hate me even more. I don't want to. I don't have to, do I?'

Twisting around to face him, Molly held his hands in hers. 'Daddy and Jessica love you. Jessica only said what she did because she didn't know what had happened and it was in the heat of the moment. Like I explained before, we all say things we don't mean sometimes, don't we? It's like when you and Lauren have an argument, you sometimes tell her you wished she wasn't born, don't you? And you don't mean it, you just say it because you're cross. You love her really, and she loves you, and you both know that, don't you?'

'That's different.'

'How is it different?'

'Because Lauren is my sister and we're supposed to fight.'

Molly nodded her head. 'Yes, but it's the same kind of thing.'

'No, it's not. Jessica has never liked me, she's always treated me and Lauren differently to how she treats Ruby. I don't want to go.'

'Let's see how you feel nearer the time, shall we?' As much as she didn't want to make Ellis go, as much as she'd love to have them both at home with her all of the time, she knew it would be best for Ellis to go as normal. If he didn't go this time, he'd only build it up more in his head and it would be even harder to go the next time.

'I mean it, Mum. I don't want to go ever again. She hates me, and I hate her too. Why couldn't you and Daddy have stayed together? Why can't you get back with him now? I hate you not being together. I hate having a stepmum.'

Turning to face him, Molly wiped the tears streaming down his cheeks. What was she supposed to say to him? How was she supposed to make it right? 'It will all be okay. When you see Jessica again on Friday, you'll see everything is back to normal.'

'No. No, I'm not going.' Flinging his cushion barrier from the sofa, Ellis jumped up, his voice hiccupping with tears. 'I hate it. I hate my life. You don't understand. You always say you understand, but you don't. When you were my age, Nanna and Grandpa were together. You didn't have to go from home to home and have to get to know a complete stranger who tried to be your mum.'

'Ellis, wait.' Standing up as he stormed out of the room, Molly listened as his bedroom door slammed. Sinking back down onto the sofa, Molly clasped her hands in her lap. The bright green cartoon mouse had just climbed to the top of a mountain with a grand piano on his back. Standing still for a second, he laughed before throwing it on top of the yellow cat standing at the bottom of the mountain.

What was she supposed to say to Ellis? How was she supposed to make it all better for him?

'Mum! Are you coming back down? Marissa's calling me!' Lauren called up the stairs.

Pushing herself to standing, Molly tucked her hair behind her ears and made her way past Ellis' closed bedroom door and back down the stairs to Bramble Patch.

* * *

'Thanks for that, Lauren.'

'It's okay. It was pretty fun, to be honest. Ellis, okay?'

Joining Lauren behind the counter, Molly looked across at her. It wasn't like Lauren to ask about her brother, she must be really worried about him. 'Not really. He's getting upset about going to your dad's on Friday. He's rung to say he's got the afternoon off work so is going to pick you both up early. I think Ellis is worried about seeing Jessica again after what happened.'

'Umm, I don't blame him. She shouldn't have called him a bully. And Ruby's annoying. I know she's my kid sister and I'm supposed to love her, and I do, but she really is annoying. More annoying than Ellis. Jessica and Dad let her get away with too much.'

'Hopefully, after what's happened they'll start to see she's a real kid rather than one who can do no wrong.'

'Maybe.' Lauren shrugged. 'Anyway, can Marissa come over?'

Looking towards the front door of Bramble Patch, Molly bit down on her bottom lip. 'Do you mind if we just have a quiet one this evening? I think I'm going to shut the shop early and maybe we can get takeaway or something.'

'Okay. Can we get pizza though?'

'Yes, pizza sounds good. Why don't you go on upstairs and make sure you've done all your homework while I cash up?'

'It's all done. Me and Marissa went to the library at lunchtime and we didn't get any this afternoon.'

'Wow, okay. Well done.'

'I'd better ring Marissa back though.' Picking her mobile up from the counter, Lauren headed towards the flat.

'See you in a bit then.' Too late, Lauren was already chatting on the phone. Turning around, Molly slumped against the counter. Ellis had mentioned on and off that he'd wished her and his dad could get back together over the years, but she hadn't realised he wasn't happy going there. Until a week and a half ago, she hadn't realised that Ruby had her parents wrapped around her little finger, and she hadn't realised how differently Trevor and Jessica treated them all.

What was she supposed to do now? She could ring Trevor and explain, and she probably would, but what good that would do she wasn't sure. What she was sure about now though was that she couldn't come between any chance, however slight, of Richie getting back with Diane. She needed to step back; she needed to give Richie space to see if he wanted to get back with Diane. She couldn't ruin any hope Marissa might still have of them being a happy family unit again. No, she couldn't be the reason Richie didn't get back with his daughter's mum.

Placing her thumb and forefinger over her temples, Molly pushed down, hoping for even a slight relief to the pain piercing through her skull. A few hours ago all had been fine between her and Richie. She'd vowed not to let Diane come between them. She'd promised herself she wouldn't listen or react to Diane's emotional blackmail, but after trying to comfort Ellis she just couldn't inflict that pain on another child. She had to give Marissa that chance. She had to give them all the chance of having their family unit back.

22

Looking behind her at Richie's motorbike on his drive and the police car parked on the street, Molly knocked again. She knew he was there. Why else would the police car be out the front? He'd often told her he popped home on his lunch breaks.

Standing back, she ran her fingers through her hair again and looked towards the open back gate. No, she couldn't just walk around the back. But then again, the back gate was open, wasn't it?

Glancing at her watch, Molly turned and began walking back down the driveway. Pausing at the top of the drive, she looked back at Richie's house and shook her head before turning around and retracing her steps. She probably wouldn't be able to pop out later, and even if she could, Richie wouldn't still be on his lunch break. She'd go round the back. He wouldn't mind, and she really needed to talk to him today. Before she changed her mind again.

Glancing behind her, she slipped through the gate into his back garden. That's why he hadn't answered the front door then. Standing still, she watched as he hung another bright white shirt on the washing line.

'Hey, Richie.'

Turning around, a slow grin spread across his face. 'Molly! What a nice surprise.'

'I hope you don't mind me coming round the back, the gate was open so...'

'Of course, I don't. It's just nice to see you.'

'Are you on your break?'

'Yes, on a forced break I guess. I got thrown up over so I popped back to shower and change and thought I'd take advantage of the nice weather.' He indicated the washing line. 'I've never known someone to get through as many clothes as Marissa.'

'I think it must be the age, Lauren is the same.'

'What can I get you? Coffee? A cold glass of orange juice?'

'Umm, I'll just have an orange juice, please?' Wringing her hands together, Molly looked around the garden as Richie disappeared into the house. She hadn't planned on staying for a drink.

'Here you go.' Leading the way to the end of his long narrow garden, Richie ducked beneath the sprawling branches of an old apple tree before climbing two shallow steps up to a decking area.

'This is lovely here.'

'Thanks. Marissa says it reminds her of a secret garden because you can't see it from the house.'

'It's beautiful.'

'Maybe we could enjoy something a bit stronger down here at the weekend? Your two are at their dad's, aren't they? And Marissa is spending the weekend with her mum. Well, at the moment she is anyway, Diane has a tendency to change her plans at the last minute. Although now that Marissa has officially moved in with me, hopefully she'll start to spend some decent quality time with her. I know it's not been long but we can live in hope that she steps up.' Richie rolled his eyes.

'I, uh, that's why I came over to see you.'

'To make plans for the weekend?' Sitting down on a metal

garden chair, Richie placed his glass on the table, indicating the chair next to him.

'Not really.'

'Oh, okay.' Leaning forward, he cupped her chin with his hand and inched towards her.

Closing her eyes as his lips met hers, Molly could feel the all familiar warmth rising from the pit of her stomach. This was going to be so hard. As she began kissing him back, she frowned. However hard it was going to be to put a stop to this, she had to. She knew she had to, for Marissa's sake. She wasn't ending things. Not completely. Well, yes, she was, but it was only to give him the space he needed to decide what was best for his daughter. She just needed to put things on pause. She needed to let Diane have a chance at getting back with him. Pulling away, she pushed her chair back.

'You okay?'

'Yes. No.' Setting her jaw, she took a deep breath. 'I'm going to have to step back from this.'

'You need to get back to the shop? Don't worry, we can do this another time. I should be getting back soon, anyway.' Richie checked his watch.

'No, I don't mean that. I mean us. I need to step back. That's what I'd come round to tell you.' There, she'd said it.

Frowning, Richie picked up his glass, holding it in one hand and running the pad of his forefinger around the rim. 'I thought we'd just got back together? Has Diane been to see you again?'

Holding her glass on her lap, Molly looked across at him and nodded.

Looking down at his shoes, Richie shook his head slowly. 'I really am not back with her.'

'I know.' Shifting in her seat, Molly placed her hand over his. 'The last time Lauren and Ellis went to their dad's Ellis had a bit of a disagreement with their daughter and his so-called stepmum told him off. She said some things she really shouldn't have. Since then he's been really upset about me and his dad not being together any more.'

'I thought you'd split up years ago?'

'Yes, we did.' Taking her hand from his, she wrapped it back around her glass. 'Sorry, I'm not making any sense. What I mean is, I can see what our split has done to my kids and how it's still affecting them all these years later. And although with me and Trevor we did absolutely the right thing splitting up, if you and Diane have any chance of getting back together, I don't want to be the one in the way.'

Sitting back in his chair, Richie rubbed his hand over his face. 'What did she say to you this time?'

'Just that she thinks you both have a chance of getting back together and that Marissa's been struggling with your split recently.'

A low chuckle escaped Richie's throat as he leant forward in his chair, his elbows resting on his knees as he cupped Molly's hands. 'If that's the only reason you're calling it a day then you have absolutely nothing to worry about. There's no chance of me getting back with Diane. Zero chance. I can promise you that.'

Closing her eyes, Molly turned her hands over in his until their fingers interlocked. She could stay like this forever, the warmth from his skin warming hers, the electricity buzzing between them. Opening her eyes, she pulled her hands away and picked up her orange juice. Taking a long sip, she tried not to look in Richie's direction. She knew what she had to do; she didn't need to make it more difficult for herself. 'I'm sorry, I've made my decision. I need to give you and Diane a chance, time.'

'What? But you know how me and Diane ended and, to be honest, our relationship before she began cheating wasn't great either. Not even good. We were a bad mix. She didn't want me, never had, but for years after Marissa was born I tried to do the right thing. I stayed with her, tried to keep the family together. I turned many a blind eye to what I knew deep down she was doing. The affair that ended us, it wasn't the first one. Had she told you that?'

Shaking her head, Molly put her empty glass on the table and stood up. 'I can't do this. Not now. I have to give you space, time to think about what you really want. If not for your sake, then for Marissa's.' Stepping down from the decking, Molly strode back down the garden.

'Molly, wait. I don't understand.'

Quickening her step, she ducked her head beneath the low branches of the old apple tree before making her way through the gate. If he got back with Diane, he'd thank her one day. If he didn't, then that was his choice. She would have nothing to feel guilty about.

Closing the gate behind her, Molly wiped her eyes as she walked past his motorbike. Diane had better treat him better this time around.

Looking down at Ellis as he gripped her arm in an attempt to pull her back, she paused and stooped to his level. 'It's going to be all right, sweetheart. Just let me answer the door and you'll see.'

'No. I don't want to go. I really, really don't want to go to Daddy's house. Please don't make me. I don't have to, do I? Lauren can go and I can stay with you, can't I? Please?' Glancing at the silhouette of his dad on the other side of the door to Bramble Patch, Ellis tightened his grip around his mum.

Gently loosening his grip finger by finger, Molly held his hands in hers. 'This is your home and you are always welcome to stay here, you know that, but I think today it will be best for you if you go to Daddy's.'

'No, no. I don't want to.'

'Hey, I know you're worried, but if you don't go today, you'll only worry until it's time to go again and then you won't want to go that time either. Sometimes it's best to do things we're worried about and get them over and done with. Things will be absolutely fine, I promise you that. It will be better for you if you go today so you can see that things are all okay and then you won't be worried any more.'

'Please, Mum? Please, I want to stay.'

Gently wiping a lock of hair from his forehead, Molly hugged him tightly. All she wanted to do was to carry him upstairs and tell him he could stay with her forever, but she knew the best thing for him would be to face the music. From what Trevor had said on the phone, Jessica really was sorry for what she'd said and wanted to make up for it. Molly might not be able to forgive her, but she knew that Ellis needed to put it behind him for his own sake. 'How about you go to Daddy's now and I'll come and get you later? That way you can see that it's all okay?'

'You'll really come and pick me up?' Looking up at his mum, the tears in Ellis' eyes shone in the stark light of the shop.

'Of course, I will. You're my little lad, aren't you? I'd do anything for you.' Wrapping her arms around him, she pulled him close. 'So, what do you think?'

'Okay. Okay, I'll go. As long as you promise you'll come and get me?'

'It's a deal.' Smiling, she used the pads of her thumbs to wipe the tears from his cheeks.

'Mum, Dad's at the door! Can't you hear him?' Bustling through the shop from the flat, Lauren shifted the rucksack higher up on her shoulder before walking past them to the door. 'Hi, Dad.'

'Hi. All ready?' Stepping into Bramble Patch, Trevor let the door swing shut behind him.

'Yep, all ready.' Lauren patted the strap to her rucksack.

'How about you, Ellis? Are you ready to come for a fun weekend?' Looking across at Ellis, Trevor gave him the thumbs up.

Straightening her back, Molly narrowed her eyes. Why did he always do that? After all these years, why did she still let him annoy her? He always had a knack of implying that the weekends Lauren and Ellis went to his were super fun, as if she did nothing nice with them at all. She shook the thought away; he didn't mean anything by it. She was sure he didn't. Almost sure.

'Mum?'

Looking down at Ellis, Molly nodded. 'Ellis and Lauren, why don't you both go and get your books from upstairs to take with you while I have a quick word with Daddy?'

Rolling her eyes, Lauren followed Ellis up to the flat.

'Everything okay?' Picking up Lauren's discarded rucksack, Trevor flung it over his shoulder.

'Ellis is a bit worried about coming over.'

'Not this again. I thought we'd sorted all this over the phone?' Flaring his nostrils, Trevor crossed his arms.

Taking a deep breath, Molly crossed her arms too. He really didn't get it, did he? Did he really think that one conversation, now almost a whole week ago, had fixed things between him, his son and his new wife? 'I've said that I'll come and pick him up later. That way he can go over, see that everything's okay with Jessica but not have to worry about staying the whole weekend if he feels uncomfortable.'

'Tonight? You're seriously going to travel over this evening? That's a bit excessive, don't you think? I'm his dad.'

'I know that, but the way he was treated last time he went to yours has really upset him.'

Shaking his head, Trevor looked behind him towards the door and back at Molly. 'Seriously? I've spoken to him about what Jessica said. Can we just put it behind us?'

'It wasn't just what Jessica said though, was it? It was the way you both treated him, and Lauren, bundling them out of the house without any dinner like that.'

'I've apologised for that, what else do you want me to do?'

'I want you to understand that just because you've said sorry, it doesn't erase the memory. All I'm asking is for you to let him go to yours for a bit and see that it's all okay. I'll come and get him before bedtime.'

'It's my weekend with them. You can't cut access.'

Really? He was really going to pull that one? If he'd managed to treat all of his children the same in the first place then none of this would have happened, but now it had, because of what he and Jessica had done, she was the one being made to feel as though she was in the wrong. Uncrossing her arms, she circled her shoulders back. 'I just want him to feel safe and secure. If this is a way of getting him out of the door to go to yours then that's got to be better than you dragging him out crying, hasn't it?'

'And what if when he comes over he enjoys it? You're still going to come and collect him?'

'What? No, of course not. I'm half expecting him to change his mind when he gets there, anyway. And if he does, he can ring me and tell me.' Why was he making her feel so bad? If she hadn't suggested picking him up in a few hours, Ellis would now be hiding in his room.

'I suppose I haven't really got a choice, have I?'

Turning towards the door to the flat as Lauren and Ellis came back, Molly rolled her eyes. 'Did you get them? Great. Pop them in your bags then.'

'Yes, come on. We need to get back.' Shrugging the rucksack from his shoulder, Trevor passed it to Lauren. As soon as the books had been packed, he turned on his heels and headed outside. 'Come on, you two.'

Picking his rucksack from the floor, Ellis crept over to Molly. 'You will come and get me, won't you? You won't forget, will you?'

'No, of course I won't. Try to enjoy yourself and if you change your mind and you want to stay then give me a call, okay?'

Nodding, Ellis accepted Molly's hug before following Lauren out to the car.

Swallowing hard, Molly stood in the doorway and watched as Trevor bundled the rucksacks into the boot. This was always the most difficult time, waving them off. It didn't get any easier, it was still the same bitter pill it was when Trevor had first started having them overnight.

* * *

Laying the sewing patterns back in the box, Molly reached for her mobile on the first ring. It was probably Ellis. 'Hi.'

'Molly.'

Trevor. It was Trevor. Slumping her shoulders, she leant against the shelf behind her, the box she was unpacking by her left knee. 'Are the kids okay?'

'They're fine, actually. More than fine. Jessica's niece and nephew, Max and Freya, have come over for a sleepover and they're having a really fun time.'

'Great, that's good then.' Shifting on the hard floor, Molly brought her knees towards her chest.

'So Ellis doesn't need you coming to rescue him.'

Closing her eyes momentarily, Molly took a deep breath in. He didn't have to speak to her like this, not with that tone. He had no right. They weren't even together any more. Not that he should have spoken to her like that when they were married anyway. 'I wasn't "rescuing" him as you put it. We spoke about this.'

'Yes, well, whatever. He's fine. You don't need to come and get him, he wants to stay.'

'That's good then. That's what I wanted, and half expected would happen, but the way he was feeling before he went with you, he needed to know that he had that option.'

'They might live with you the majority of the time, but that doesn't mean I don't have as much right over them. They're still my children.'

Narrowing her eyes, Molly stared at the shelf opposite. When had she ever suggested otherwise? 'I never said anything against that, I simply told you that Ellis was a bit nervous about going over after what Jessica had said to him and how you had both treated them. That's why I gave him the option of coming back. I wasn't undermining you. I was acting in the best interests of our children. You'd have done the same.'

'Well, he's fine. I've got to go now. Bye.'

Placing her mobile on the floor next to her, Molly pinched the bridge of her nose. And that was one of the reasons she didn't miss him. Yes, it had ultimately been his decision to leave her, but there were so many aspects of his personality that if she'd not been so focused on keeping her family together may have given her reason to walk first.

Pulling herself to standing, Molly carefully kicked the half-empty box of patterns closer to the shelf and made her way upstairs. They could wait until morning. She just needed to put the TV on and block out her life for a while. There were reasons why people split up. There had been for her and Trevor, and there definitely was for Richie and Diane. Maybe she shouldn't have put things on the back burner with him. Maybe she should have trusted Richie's judgement.

Shaking her head, she flicked the kettle on. She'd done the right thing. Possibly. Anyway, at least this way she'd know for certain that she hadn't stood in the way of Marissa getting her family back together.

Turning her back on the kettle she pressed her index fingers against her temples. It didn't matter anyway. She'd done it now. She'd told him it was over.

24

Glancing down at her phone and back to the empty shop, Molly picked it up. 'Hi, Bea. Long time, no hear.'

'Hey, girl! I know, I know. I've been an absolutely rubbish friend.'

'Don't worry. How's everything with you?' Bea had always been the same, one minute calling and meeting regularly, the next disappearing completely. It used to annoy her, but now she figured it was just Bea being Bea.

'Crazy. Completely crazy. I got that promotion I told you about, remember?'

Promotion? How could she have forgotten? Perching on the stool behind the counter, Molly kept her eyes fixed on the door, ready to hang up if a customer walked in. Now it was her turn to feel like the rubbish friend. 'I'm so sorry, I meant to ring and ask you how the interview went.'

'No worries, you've had a lot going on too. What with opening the shop? How's that going? Are you turning over a profit yet?'

'It's going really well, actually. The village had a fete a couple of weeks ago and that's been bringing in new customers.'

'That's great!'

'Thanks.'

'You're welcome. I'm proud of you, Molly.'

Molly smiled. 'Have you been drinking?'

'Maybe a smidge. Sooo, tell me...'

'Tell you what?' She could clearly hear the clink of glass on glass as Bea refilled her drink. 'How come you're drinking so early? It's only three o'clock?'

'Ahh, but it's a Saturday.'

'It's still only three o'clock.'

'I know. I've just finished schmoozing a client for lunch and they barely touched the wine, I thought it'd be rude to leave it.'

'You're still at the restaurant? And you're working on a Saturday?' Molly shook her head. Their worlds were so far apart it was surreal.

'Anyway. Tell me.'

'Tell you what?'

'About our policeman friend. What was his name? Ralph?'

'Ralph? Richie. His name is Richie and there's nothing to tell.' Looking down at the counter, she picked up a pen and began doodling on the notepad.

'Now I know you're lying.'

Molly flared her nostrils and began drawing a flower, the stem first and two leaves.

'Tell me.'

'There really is nothing to tell.' One petal.

'Molly, if I hadn't been drinking I'd be jumping in the car. What's happened?'

Another petal. It was no good, Bea would just keep pushing until she told her. 'Okay. We were seeing each other for a bit, but only a bit. We got together at the dance after the Village Fete so it literally only lasted less than two weeks.'

'You've split up? Already? I thought he was a keeper.'

'He insulted us and complained about your car being parked an inch over his mother's driveway. Not to mention that he almost arrested me for speeding.'

'Umm, I guess he was a bit spikey but there was definitely electricity between you both. So, tell me more.'

'There's nothing to tell. His ex basically told me he was cheating on her with me.'

'Seriously? Wow, I hadn't seen that one coming and I'm usually such a good judge of character.'

Molly grimaced.

'I am. I told you Trevor was a prat from the moment you met him.'

'With your track record, I really don't think you can say you're a good judge of character.'

'Maybe not for me, although my darling hubby is lovely. But for you, I always get your men right, don't I? I really didn't see Richie as being a cheat though.'

'He's not. I spoke to him about it, and he told me she was lying. She then came to speak to me again and admitted she'd lied but she thinks she has a chance of getting back with him and doesn't want me swaying his decision.'

'So you've broken up with him? For her? Why? Why? Why?'

Molly shifted on the hard stool. It's not that simple. They have a daughter together and the break-up has really affected her, and Jessica upset Ellis and... you won't understand. You've not been part of a broken family.'

'Damn right I don't understand. You've met someone and by the sounds of your voice you really like him and he wants to be with you, but you broke it off?'

Pinching the top of her nose, Molly wished the headache creeping in would disappear. 'It's not that simple.'

'It sounds pretty simple to me. Look, I can't come tonight, but next Saturday me and you are going to go out. Properly out. Out for drinks and a dance.'

'No, I'm too old for that. Plus, I've got the kids next weekend.'

'You are not too old. And I'll sort the kids. My parents are having my two because Stuart is away with work so they can have yours too. And before you say anything, you know how much they love Lauren and Ellis.'

'I don't know.'

'Look, I've got to go now, the waiter is hovering with the bill but I'll text you the details during the week.'

'No, I...' Too late, she was gone. Great, so now Molly would have to come up with some excuse or other why she couldn't go drinking with Bea next weekend.

Placing her phone back on the counter, she checked the time. It was just gone three. If the last few weekends were anything to go by, then today was unusually quiet. Maybe it was the nice weather.

Of course, it was the river festival in the next village along. Everyone would be there. Looking across at the pile of orders she'd packaged up earlier, she grabbed a bag and bundled them in. She had planned to close up early and run to the post office, but she might as well do it now. Plus, she really needed to buy some painkillers if she had any hope of avoiding this headache turning into a migraine.

Picking the bag up, she smiled. It felt quite heavy and the bulging seams were proof that her idea of offering a range of stock online was working.

* * *

Tilting her head back, Molly placed the headache tablet on her tongue and took a sip of water before swallowing. Putting the bottle back into the cupholder by the gear stick, she pulled her seatbelt around her. The parcels would be safely on their way soon and so hopefully would her headache.

She looked across at the bag thrown on the passenger's seat. With a pizza and some ice cream, she had all she needed for an evening slumped in front of the TV. Just what she needed.

Hearing a noise from behind, she twisted her neck and looked behind her. Great, it looked as though a couple had decided it was the perfect spot for a row. Did she start the car which would hopefully shift them or sit and wait until they'd finished?

Placing her hands on the steering wheel, Molly looked ahead. A low fence ran around the perimeter of the car park, partitioning it from the high street ahead. Taking another sip of water, she rested the bottle against the steering wheel. The river festival must have taken the crowds from here too. Only a smattering of people weaved from shop to shop down the cobbled High Street, noticeably less than on a normal day.

Rubbing her eyes, she squinted ahead of her. A woman stepped down from a shop doorway and looked in her bags. Yes, it was her. It was Diane. She would recognise the high heels and sunglasses anywhere. Should she go and tell her she had walked away from Richie? She didn't particularly want to speak to her again, but now she'd seen her, she probably should go and mention it. Tell her she now had free rein to get Richie back.

Pulling the sun visor down, Molly glanced in the small mirror and tucked her hair behind her ears. She knew she shouldn't care what Diane thought of her, but with the large shadows under her eyes, she also didn't want it to be glaringly obvious how upset she was over breaking up with Richie.

Shaking her head, she shrugged. She'd have to go now, or else she'd lose her. Stepping out of the car, Molly put her hand up to wave and called across the road, 'Diane! Hold...'

Lowering her hand, she squinted against the sunlight. Diane wasn't on her own. A man, tall with a dark shock of hair, had followed her out of the shop. Molly watched as he walked in step with Diane before putting his arm around her shoulder. Maybe it was Diane's brother?

Shielding her eyes with her left hand, Molly frowned as Diane turned around and kissed him on the lips before slipping her hand in his as they made their way further up the High Street.

Opening the car door again, Molly slipped back behind the steering wheel, her hands gripping the black leather firmly. It didn't make any sense. Why would Diane want to get back with Richie if she was already seeing someone? Was she planning on cheating on him again?

Pulling her seatbelt on, Molly turned the key in the ignition. Whatever Diane was playing at, Molly had well and truly been taken for a fool. Why had she believed her? She'd known Diane was an accomplished liar. Richie was a policeman, and Diane had still managed to lie to him for years. Why had Molly thought she could tell truth from lie when he hadn't been able to?

Crunching the gear stick into reverse, Molly watched as the couple behind her looked across before rolling their eyes and moving out of the way. She couldn't wait for them any longer. She needed to get home.

* * *

Holding her now cold mug of coffee in her hands, Molly continued to stare out of the kitchen window. The red-bellied robin that had begun to visit the large oak tree in the garden behind continued his chirping whilst bouncing up and down on the window ledge oblivious to the whir of thoughts going through Molly's head.

How could she have been so naïve? She'd literally only been

trying to do the best thing for Marissa, and Richie. She'd thought she had been doing the right thing.

Taking a sip of the cold bitter liquid, Molly grimaced and swallowed.

She should go over and try to explain things to Richie, shouldn't she? He might see why she had reacted the way she had and forgive her. He should do, shouldn't he? He should understand why she had walked away from him.

Turning, she placed the mug down on the work surface with such force that the brown liquid ran down the sides of the ceramic. She should go and speak to him. She should explain how wrong she'd got it, that she should have realised that every couple split up for a reason and that was no different between her and Trevor as it was Richie and Diane. She should have realised that Diane couldn't be trusted.

She had no idea what game Diane was playing or attempting to play but she was sure that's what it was now, just a game, or maybe a way to try to stop Richie being happy with anyone else.

She shook her head. Picking up her mobile, she shoved it in the back pocket of her jeans and made her way downstairs. There was no time like the present.

* * *

Taking a deep breath, Molly tapped on the door again. Maybe Richie was out. Maybe she should just go back to Bramble Patch and carry on refilling the shelves.

Turning, she pulled her cardigan tighter around her against the evening's gentle breeze and walked back past his motorbike and car back onto the path.

'Hey, Molly.'

Twisting around, Molly looked behind her at Richie standing in his doorway, a towel wrapped around his middle.

'Sorry, I was in the shower.'

'That's okay. If you're busy, don't worry. I can come back another time.'

'No, it's fine. Here, come in. I'll just run and get some clothes on and then I'll be with you.'

Nodding, Molly made her way back down the drive and stepped into the hallway, closing the door behind her.

* * *

'Sorry about that. Everything okay? Can I get you a drink?' Coming back down the stairs, this time dressed in dark blue jeans and a grey T-shirt, Richie rubbed a towel over his hair before hanging it on the banister.

'No, I'm fine thanks. I just wanted a quick word, if you've got time.'

'Yes, of course. Come through to the kitchen. Marissa's upstairs as you can probably guess from the noise of her latest favourite band.'

Following him into the kitchen, Molly stood against the counter and watched him switch the kettle on.

'Are you sure you don't want a drink?'

'Honestly, I'm fine.' Waving his offer away, Molly fiddled with the hem of her cardigan and cleared her throat. 'I just wanted to apologise for the way I've been recently. I just thought I was doing the right thing.'

'I get it. I can't pretend that I'm not hurt, but I get why you did what you did.' Ignoring the kettle as it clicked off, Richie leant against the work surface and ran his fingers through his hair. 'I really get it and I respect you for your decision. It's not what I wanted. I really thought we had a real chance of making things work, but I get why you can't.'

Nodding slowly, Molly glanced down at her feet before looking back up at him. 'That's the thing, I saw her, Diane, again this afternoon.'

Shoving his hands in his pockets, Richie tilted his head. 'I'm sorry, Molly. I can't do this. Not again. I understand why you can't be in a relationship with me. I get that, and I respect you for making that decision, but I really don't want to hear what else she's been saying. I'm not with her for a reason and I don't need to still be dealing with her issues. I'm sorry. I'd like to still be friends though.'

Looking down, Molly hoped the fierce heat racing across the back of her neck wouldn't reach her face. She got it. She understood where he was coming from, but it didn't make it any easier for her. 'Okay, I understand. I had come over to apologise and to tell you I realised that I shouldn't have listened to her in the first place, but I get it. You just want to be friends.' Nodding, Molly bit down on her bottom lip and made her way back through the hallway to the front door.

'Molly, I... wait...'

'It's fine, Richie. I just need to get back now.' Slipping through the front door again, she closed it carefully but purposefully behind her. As she made her way back up the driveway and onto the street, she kept her eyes down, focusing on the path beneath her feet. She didn't blame him. She really didn't. She'd probably react the same way if he had believed Trevor over her. It was her own fault, she shouldn't have listened to Diane – she'd known what she was like from what Richie had said about her before.

Glancing around quickly, she checked that no one was about before pulling the sleeves of her cardigan over her fingers and wiping her eyes. She'd brought this on herself. She didn't deserve to find a partner, to find someone to be happy with. Richie had been the first person she'd felt remotely comfortable and happy with in years, and now she'd pressed the too familiar self-destruct button. She deserved to be alone.

* * *

Letting herself into Bramble Patch, she flung the keys down on a nearby shelf and headed up to the flat.

Sinking against the sofa cushions, Molly curled her legs up in front of her and wrapped her arms around her knees. She never learnt. She probably never would. Bea was always telling her to look out for herself more, to not be so trusting and to put herself first. Well, she hadn't followed her advice, again, and look where it had landed her. Alone, grieving for a relationship that hardly ever was with the first man she'd actually felt a connection with. It served her right. She'd just have to get used to the idea of being alone forever.

Wiping fresh tears away, Molly sank her head back against the cushions. She'd actually really liked him, more than that. She'd had proper feelings for him. Yes, their relationship hadn't really even took off before she'd ruined it, but the night of the Village Dance she'd actually thought she'd be with him forever.

25

Opening her eyes against the bright force of the sun, Molly reached out to the coffee table, knocked Lauren's pile of magazines to the floor and located her mobile. Hitting the off button, she silenced the alarm and pushed herself to sitting. Rolling her neck, she rubbed her shoulders in an attempt to ease the pain. She must have fallen asleep crunched up on the sofa. Momentarily closing her eyes, she forced herself to open them again. If it really was quarter past nine, she'd already slept through her eight o'clock alarm and numerous snooze intervals.

Standing up, she surveyed the living room, Ellis' school PE kit still laid sprawled across the armchair where she'd asked him to empty his bag, obviously failing to specify to empty it into the laundry basket rather than just where he had happened to dump his PE bag. Lauren's nail varnish bottles were still scattered across the coffee table, the accompanying nail varnish remover and stack of cotton pads encircling them, and a stack of clean washing teetered on the edge of the sofa. How she hadn't kicked it off in her sleep she'd never know, but for that, at least, she was grateful.

With Sunday being her only day off, she had to cram all the

housework into one day alongside doing a food shop and any other jobs such as sewing up the hole in the knee of Ellis' school trousers.

Slumping back down, she remembered she still hadn't finished restocking the shelves downstairs. There was too much to do and she really couldn't face doing any of it. Least of all going to the local supermarket. Sunday was usually one of Richie's days off too and she really couldn't face running into him in the fruit and veg aisle.

Rubbing her eyes with the heels of her hands, she set her jaw. There was only one thing for it, she'd have to go to the supermarket on the retail estate two towns down. It was a longer drive, but maybe she'd pop to the nature reserve which skirted the town. A brisk walk along the canal with a takeaway latte might be what she needed to blow the cobwebs of yesterday's encounter with Richie away. The housework would be here when she got back, and if she didn't have time to dust, she was quite certain that it would still be there mocking her the following weekend.

* * *

'Mum, Mum. Look what Jessica and Dad got me! Am I'm allowed to play it now?' Running towards her, Ellis brandished a computer game in her face before dropping his rucksack at her feet and running upstairs, the door to the flat swinging loudly shut behind him.

Molly rolled her eyes. That was how they'd made it up to Ellis then? Gifts.

'Hey, Mum. Can I pop over to Marissa's house? I've just arranged it and Dad's going to drop me off on his way back, aren't you, Dad?' Glancing quickly at Trevor, Lauren looked back at her mum. 'Can I, please? We've got this art homework that we both forgot to do and we thought if we did it together it would take less time.'

'Okay.' Molly nodded.

'Thanks. You're the best.' Dropping her rucksack next to Ellis', Lauren turned back to her dad. 'I'll wait in the car, Dad. Don't be long though please, I've told her I'll be there by now.'

Taking a deep breath, Molly looked at Trevor who shifted on his feet. Why didn't he just leave? 'Thanks for Ellis' game.'

Shrugging, he stared at her.

What was wrong with him? What did he want from her now? Pinching the bridge of her nose, she could feel the little piece of her heart that the walk in the fresh air along the canal had healed breaking again. She really didn't have the emotional capacity to deal with one of Trevor's tantrums. Not today. 'What's the matter?'

'Oh, nothing. I just thought you'd apologise now you've seen Ellis actually did have a good time at mine.' Crossing his arms, Trevor smiled smugly.

Seriously? And she was feeling sorry for herself that she was single? Walking past him towards the front door, she held it open. 'I apologise for worrying that our son was upset because your new wife had called him a bully and you had brought him home without dinner last time you had him. I'm sorry I was concerned because he understandably didn't want to go to yours in case you and Jessica treated him like that again. I am, however, pleased that you have all moved on from the, shall we say, incident, and that he obviously feels settled again at yours. I'm so sorry that I put the interests and well-being of our son ahead of my own. Is that what you want to hear?'

Huffing, Trevor walked out of Bramble Patch before turning back to her. 'Jessica warned me not to expect an apology from you.'

Shutting the door quietly but firmly behind him, Molly sank to the floor. She didn't need to apologise. If anyone should apologise it should be Jessica, to Ellis, and she apparently had. Plus, hadn't Molly already justified her actions? Was everyone against her at the moment? And to top it off, she'd have to go and collect Lauren up from Richie's house in a few hours and see him again.

* * *

Putting her mobile down on the kitchen table, Molly pushed her chair back and stood up. Great, Lauren had just called, now was the time she'd have to face Richie.

Shrugging her cardigan on, she pushed open Ellis' bedroom door. 'Ellis, sweetheart, we need to go and pick Lauren up now.'

'Can't she walk?' Pulling his headphones off his head, he quickly glanced at his mum before focusing on the screen in front of him again.

'No, it's dark. I don't want her walking home by herself.'

'How come? It's not far.'

'Ellis, no. I've said it's too dark. If we go now, we'll be back in ten minutes. It's only a five-minute walk.'

'Aw, but I need to finish this level.'

'I'm sorry, we won't be long. Besides it's getting late so you'll need to get off for bed soon anyway.'

'Can't we wait until I have to come off then? Or else I'm going to miss out on time.'

Tapping her foot against the floor, Molly leant her forehead against the doorframe. She couldn't very well tell him that she just wanted to get it over and done with because she didn't want to see Richie. 'I tell you what, as a special treat, if we pop out now and get Lauren without any fuss you can stay on your new game for half an hour past bedtime?'

'Really? Okay, cool. Thanks, Mum.' Putting his controller on the bed next to him, Ellis jumped up and turned the console off before Molly had time to change her mind.

* * *

'You didn't tell me we were walking.' Kicking a stone along the path, Ellis trudged behind.

'Yes, I did. Besides, it would have taken longer to get in the car, drive there and park up. Look, Marissa's house is the one on the end of this street so it's not far at all.' Glancing back at Ellis and then back towards Richie's cottage, Molly pressed her fingers tips against her temples. 'In fact, why don't you run ahead and get her? You'll be able to get back to your game even quicker that way.'

'Aw, no. Can't you go ahead and I'll wait here? My legs are hurting from going on a big walk with Dad.' Leaning down, Ellis rubbed his shin.

'Nice try. Come on.' Why did they always refuse to go on walks with her and yet they always seemed happy to go on long walks with Trevor? Molly shook her head. She should stop comparing. It didn't matter.

'Are we there yet?'

'Yep, it's this one here.' Taking a deep breath, Molly led the way down Richie's driveway and tapped on the door.

'Molly, hi. Hi, Ellis. How are you?' Opening the door, Richie grinned at them.

'Tired. Mum made me walk all the way from home.' Leaning against the wall next to the door, Ellis sighed.

'Wow, that must be miles, right?' Chuckling, Richie ruffled his hair.

'Yep. Is that Rocco?' Bending slightly, Ellis patted his hands on his knees. 'Come on, Rocco. Come say hello.'

As a black nose nuzzled its way past Richie, he stood aside letting Rocco out onto the driveway where he immediately made for Ellis, his tongue hanging out and his tail wagging in excitement.

'Did you want to go in the garden and throw some balls for him while Lauren and Marissa finish up?'

'Yes okay. Can I, Mum?'

Biting down on her bottom lip, Molly nodded.

Standing back, Richie waited until Ellis and Rocco had raced past before waving Molly inside. 'I just wanted to clear the air and see how you were?'

Molly nodded. 'I'm fine, thanks. You?'

Richie nodded. 'To be honest, I've not had much sleep. I wish things could be different between us...'

'Don't worry, I understand.' She'd messed up, and that was it.

'Mum, you're here.' Giggling, Lauren and Marissa walked down the stairs.

'I am. Are you ready? Did you manage to get the project finished?'

'We sure did. I'll show you when we get home.' Slipping her trainers on, she picked up a roll of paper.

'Great. Thanks for having her.' Nodding at Richie, Molly called down the hallway, 'Ellis! Time to go.'

26

'Here, try this one.' Holding up a bright red satin top, Bea slipped it off the hanger and threw it to Molly.

'Oh no, not that one, I've never liked it much.' Catching it, Molly added it to the pile of discarded tops on the bed next to her.

'Is there anything you own that you actually like?' Turning back, Bea continued to rifle through Molly's clothes.

'Not anything that I could wear out. I don't go out normally, remember.' And that was for good reason. The last thing she wanted to do after being on her feet all day was to spend her free time walking across sticky carpet in pubs and clubs and trying to have a conversation above the angry tunes of today. No, the sofa, a tub of chocolate ice cream and a TV series to binge-watch was just what she needed.

'Umm. I still can't believe you forgot. It's a good job I came early or we wouldn't be getting out until goodness knows when.'

Molly grimaced. Yes, she may have forgotten, but in her defence, she'd never actually agreed to go out with Bea. That had been all assumption on her part. 'I still feel bad you dropping the kids off with your parents. I wasn't even able to thank them.'

Bea waved her hand dismissively. 'Don't worry. Honestly, they've been looking forward to having them. Now, what about this little number? It's grey, so still one of your go-to colours, but it actually has a bit of colour on from the pinkie flowers?'

Holding out her hand, Molly accepted the top; she did actually like the style of this one and with its slightly gathered hem it distracted from her belly. She'd bought it at least a year ago to go on a date, but then the man had called off due to sickness or more than likely a change of heart, and it had sat forgotten in the back of her wardrobe since then. She didn't even remember unpacking it. 'Yep, that one will be fine.'

'Okay, great. I'll leave you to get changed and go and call a taxi then.' Closing the wardrobe door, Bea went towards the door, pausing before leaving the bedroom. 'Hurry up.'

'Will do.' Pulling her T-shirt off, Molly slipped the grey silky top on. It felt good next to her skin, cool. Standing up, she looked in the full-length mirror on the back of the door and sucked her stomach in, tightening her belt. Breathing out again, she turned to the side before loosening her belt again. She was what she was.

And anyway, she was only going out to have a catch-up with Bea. Men were definitely off the table. The way she'd ruined her relationship with Richie due to her own insecurities had told her that even after all of these years she wasn't ready for another relationship. She needed to get herself to a place where she felt worthy enough and confident in herself before even attempting to find a partner.

* * *

'So, what do you think of him then?' Holding her wine glass up, Bea pointed her finger towards a blonde guy near the bar.

'No comment. Anyway, I thought you promised talking about

men was off the table?' Sipping her orange juice, Molly laughed. Bea was relentless in her pursuit to pair her up.

'Fair enough. I did promise.' Bea stared ahead at the dance floor. 'Hey, I've got an idea for your shop!'

'What's that?'

'You could start doing art classes!'

Molly grimaced. 'Don't you remember what my drawing is like? The best I can do is a blob for an apple or a stick person. Why the sudden interest in art? I didn't think you had time for anything like that, what between Stuart and the kids and your new promotion?'

Leaning into her, Bea clinked glasses. 'Ah, I would make the time if it was a nude life drawing session.'

'Bea! I bet you would!' Rolling her eyes, Molly laughed. Bea's banter was one hundred percent worse when she drank, which was the main reason Molly hadn't – she didn't want to wake up in the morning to find out Bea had dragged her up on stage in some karaoke bar or something.

'You know me!' Standing up, Bea slammed her glass onto the table and held out her hand. 'Come on, let's go and dance.'

Looking at the dance floor, full of kids who could only have been barely eighteen if not younger, Molly shrugged. Why not? No one from the village would see her here, and she didn't have to come back.

* * *

'Ooh, don't look now but I think those two are having a bit of a disagreement.' Leaning in towards her, Bea whispered loudly in Molly's ear.

As they danced, Bea swung Molly around so she could see what she was talking about. It certainly did look as though they were in the middle of something. However, the word 'disagreement' seemed a little understated. Two men, or boys as they looked barely eighteen if they actually were, were sat opposite each other at a table at the edge of the dance floor. Their shouts, though muffled, could be heard over the incessant base of the music, which was saying something the volume it was turned up to.

Rolling her eyes at Bea, Molly moved closer to her, keeping her steps in time with the music, as best she could anyway. 'Let's hope they sort it out soon or they're going to end up getting chucked out.'

'Yep. Do you remember the time those two, what were their names? Wayne and Michael or Mickey or something, ended up having a boxing match in the club when we were younger?'

Laughing, Molly shook her head. How could she ever forget that? 'That had been your fault, you know that, don't you?'

'I can't help it if I was that irresistible that I had boys literally fighting over me.' Flicking her hair over her shoulders, Bea grinned.

'I don't think it helped much that you'd told them you were taking them both to the college dance the following week.'

'Oh yeah. I'd forgotten about that! What's happened to us? It barely feels like a few minutes ago that we were in a place like this dancing the night away without a care in the world.'

'Life. Life happened.'

'Umm.'

'Hey, don't get all down on me. It was you who had wanted to come out.' Reaching over, Molly held Bea's hand and twisted her around. 'Just because we're a bit older than almost everyone else in here, it doesn't mean we can't still enjoy ourselves!'

'You're right.' Steadying herself from the twist, Bea smiled again. 'Yes, you are right. We're not that old, we just have a little more experience.'

'Exactly. Oh, watch out. Come this way, Bea.' Molly pulled Bea towards her just as one of the boys arguing stood up and came round towards the side of the table closest to the dance floor, signalling to the other one to join him.

Sidling across to the far side of the dance floor they watched as the other boy pushed back from the table and came to stand opposite the other, their shoulders squared and their jaws set. People around them stopped to stare at the altercation unfolding and two more teenage boys raced across the sticky floor to join the stand-off. The two girls who had been at the table stood between the boys, shouting and waving their arms in an attempt to break up whatever was unfolding.

'Huh, the bouncers are slow in this place, aren't they? Not that they would have been any quicker in our clubbing days, the idiots would have just been be left to fight it out.' Rolling her eyes, Bea continued to sway to the music. Flicking her hair over her shoulders, she tried to get Molly to join in.

'In a minute.' She hated any sort of confrontation, she'd rather know what was happening before going back to their oblivious trip down memory lane. 'Maybe we should just go. It's late anyway.'

'What? No way, the night's still young.'

'Still young' was one o'clock in the morning. Bea might have been used to dancing the night away but Molly's idea of a late night was getting so engrossed in a new TV series that before she knew it she'd eaten a whole tub of ice cream and Ellis had padded through for his 2am toilet habit.

Shaking her arms, Molly smiled at Bea. Bea was right, she needed to loosen up. She needed to forget everything that had happened recently with Trevor and Richie. She needed to learn to enjoy herself again.

'Here we go.' Bea pointed to two bouncers ambling over to the ever-increasing crowd surrounding the ongoing argument.

Turning, Molly watched as the bouncers forced their way through the throng of people, re-emerging, each holding one of the boys by their elbows. Walking them across the dance floor one of them twisted and broke free from his captor. Running from the bouncer, he jumped in front of the boy he'd squared up to earlier who immediately wrestled free from the bouncer who had been holding him.

Molly wasn't sure who pulled the first punch, but in a matter of moments one boy had the other in a headlock whilst the two bouncers flexed their muscles before jumping into the middle, each grabbing one troublemaker and tearing them apart. Dancers who had given up to stare inched their way closer to Molly and Bea, pushing them against the railings surrounding the DJ booth in an attempt to get out of the way of the unfolding fight.

'Come here.' Pulling Molly out of the throng, Bea led the way around the other side of the dance floor into an empty booth by the door. 'That's better, I thought we were going to get crushed back there!'

Nodding, Molly gingerly placed her elbows on the wet sticky surface of the table. She would definitely need a shower as soon as she walked back into the flat. Her hair stunk of cigarettes after being caught in a cloud of smoke on the way in and her skin felt as though it was crawling with germs. Shaking her head, she grinned. It had turned into a good night though. She'd forgotten how fun Bea was and even without having a sip of alcohol, Bea's happy tipsiness was infectious.

As a sharp scream cut through the general excited hubbub, Molly jerked her head around, ducking too late as a piece of glass flew through the air striking her square on the side of her forehead. 'What on earth?'

'Molly! Are you okay?'

Blinking, Molly stared onto the dance floor as two people dropped to their knees, one grabbing their hand and the other gripping their thigh. Bringing her hand up to her forehead, she winced as a sharp pain seared through down her face. What had happened? She hadn't seen anything. She'd only glanced away from Bea, for a split second. What could have happened in that short space of time? 'What happened?'

'Molly, look at you. You're bleeding. Come here.' Leaning forward, Bea cupped Molly's chin, bringing her face closer to hers.

Looking down at her fingers, Molly rubbed them together, smearing the red blood between her thumb and forefinger. Bea was right, she was bleeding. As Molly stood up, Bea pulled her back down out of the way as the bouncers finally escorted the two boys out.

'Come on, let's get you outside.' Standing up, Bea held Molly's hand and followed the bouncers down the stairs and outside.

As she followed Bea through the doorway leading to the foyer, a group of lads ran past elbowing people out of the way. Stumbling as a girl was pushed into her, Molly steadied herself just as another boy ran past knocking her to the ground, the back of her head jarring on the doorframe as she fell.

'Molly?' Leaning down, Bea pulled her to standing. 'You okay? Was that thump your head?'

Standing up, Molly rubbed the back of her head and nodded before following Bea down the stairs and out onto the street.

Leaning against the wall of the club, Molly closed her eyes against the cold breeze, the pain increasing as she scrunched her eyes shut.

'You okay, miss?'

Opening her eyes, Molly blinked at the woman standing in front of her. She was wearing the same black shirt as the other bouncers. She must work there.

'Yes, I'm fine.'

'You can see she's clearly not okay. She got hit by a piece of the glass from the bottle and then some idiot pushed his way through the crowds and she hit her head on the doorframe.' Stepping towards the bouncer, Bea pointed back at Molly.

'I can see. If you hold on we have an ambulance on the way and the police will be here in a moment too.'

'No, it's okay. I just want to get home.' Pushing herself away from the wall, Molly swayed as the world spun around her.

'I'm afraid I'm going to have to insist you wait. You're a witness, and the police will want to speak to you. Plus, you really should get that gash seen by a paramedic.'

Nodding, Molly slumped back against the wall, closing her eyes on the bright blue lights as a siren jarred her bones.

'Hey, Molly, don't you go to sleep on me will you?'

Opening her eyes, Molly looked at Bea as she leant into her. 'I'm hardly going to fall asleep standing up, am I? It's only a scratch, don't worry.'

'Umm, I'll worry less when one of the paramedics have seen you.' Turning around, Bea watched as a police van pulled up and two police officers immediately jumped out and ran towards where the bouncers were still holding on to the boys who had started the fight.

The noise of the protests from the boys and their mates as they were handcuffed and bundled into the police van and the hubbub from the onlookers was too much. It only made her head feel worse. She needed to get away. She needed the pain to stop. Pushing away from the wall again, the coarse brickwork catching her nail, Molly began walking down the road.

'Where are you going? You heard the bouncer, you need to get seen to.' Chasing after her, Bea put her hand on Molly's shoulder.

'I'm fine. I just want to get home.' Shaking her head, Molly focused on the floor in front of her, focused on putting one foot in front of the other. There had to be a taxi rank around here some-where. They'd come in a taxi. It couldn't be far.

'Molly, no.'

'Excuse me, miss. Are you the lady who got caught in the middle?'

Pausing and turning around, Molly looked as a woman dressed in the dark green of a paramedic's uniform jogged after her.

'Why don't we get you to the ambulance and get you cleaned up?'

'She fell and whacked the back of her head against the door as well.' Bea interrupted.

Looking down, Molly could see the paramedic's hand on her arm as she was guided back towards the waiting ambulance.

'That's it. My name's Karen and I'm going to clean you up, okay?'

'I really don't need any help. I've said I'm fine. There were a couple of other people who got hurt though.'

'Yes, that's right, but they're getting looked after now. Look.' Karen pointed back towards the club.

Following Karen's finger, Molly could see another ambulance had pulled up, with their doors already open and the two other people who had been hurt sat on the trolleys being dealt with.

'That's it. Come on, it will only take a few minutes of your time.' Peering over Molly's head, Karen questioned Bea. 'Did she black out at all?'

'No, I didn't. It's only a cut. Just a little cut, that's all.'

'Okay, Molly. That's good then. We'll still get you checked out though.' Leading her towards one of the waiting ambulances, Karen stood at the bottom of the steps, indicating Molly to go inside.

'Honestly, I'd really rather not get in there. I really am fine and don't want to waste your time.'

'You're not wasting our time. We've been pretty quiet tonight, to be honest, and I'd feel a lot better if you let me check you over.'

Sighing, Molly sank to the step of the ambulance. 'Okay, but I *am* fine.'

Nodding, Karen indicated to another paramedic who passed her a green bag. 'That's good to hear.'

'Molly, let Karen do her job. It's for the best.' Leaning against the open door of the ambulance, Bea crossed her arms.

Nodding, Molly followed the small torch Karen shone in her eyes. She really did feel fine. I little light-headed, but that was hardly from a cut. It was more than likely because she was sat here with people's cigarette smoke wafting up her nostrils.

'That's it. Now just hold this and I'll be right back.'

Holding a pad of white gauze to her forehead, Molly leant against the side of the ambulance.

'Evening, can I just ask you a few questions, please?'

Opening her eyes, Molly saw a police officer standing in front of her, a notepad and pen in his hands. 'I really didn't see much. All I saw was the two boys, sorry, men squaring up to each other. The bouncers then got hold of them and pulled them apart. I guess they must have shaken them off and got into a fight.'

'I see. And did you see which of the suspects threw the bottle?'

Molly shook her head. 'No, sorry I didn't. I was talking to Bea, here. It all just happened so fast. Sorry.'

'I see.' The police officer glanced at Bea. 'I'll talk to your friend in a moment, I just have one more question if that's okay?'

'Molly! Molly! What's happened? Are you all right?'

Looking up, Molly blinked as she saw Richie weaving his way through the small crowd towards her. Typical. Of all the police officers there must have been around here, Richie was called. And why did they need any more? There were already a couple of police officers standing by the van with the boys in, plus the one speaking to her. It had only been a little argument. 'I'm fine. It's just a cut.'

'Let me see.' Coming in front of her, Richie gently pulled the gauze away before wincing and returning it, covering her hand with his as she held it on her forehead. 'It's okay, Adam, I'll take it from here.'

'All right, boss.' Grinning at Richie, Adam turned to Bea and indicated the path a metre or so away. 'Can I ask you a few questions?'

'You look very pale. Are you sure you're feeling okay? Are you feeling dizzy or light-headed or anything?' Richie took a step back as the paramedic returned carrying another bag in her hand. 'Is she okay?'

'She's sustained quite a deep gash to her forehead, we believe from a piece of glass from a broken bottle. Of more concern is the fact that she also sustained a substantial knock to the back of the head. She'll need to come with us to the hospital and have a couple of stitches and get checked out properly. Her vital signs are good, but she does appear a little confused.'

Molly shook her head. 'I'm not confused, and I really don't need to go to the hospital. I'm fine. I just want to get home.' Standing up, she held her hand out, gripping Richie's arm as the floor swayed beneath her. She really was fine. Just tired. She just needed to lay down for a few minutes. That was all.

'Molly, listen to Karen. She knows what she's talking about and you're clearly not fine.'

'I am. I really am. I just want to go home. There's people who need help and ambulances and hospitals much more than me.'

'That may be so, but I'd feel better if you got the stitches and got checked out properly.' Placing his hand over hers, Richie guided her back to the step of the ambulance. 'That's it. Sit down again.'

Taking the gauze off of her forehead, Molly leant her chin in her hands. She wasn't meaning to be difficult, she just didn't want to waste their time.

'I tell you what, I'll pop your stitches in and then we'll see how you feel. Just lift your head for me.'

Holding her head up, Molly held still as Karen cleaned and stitched up her wound.

'How are you feeling now?' Leaning back on her haunches, Karen stared at Molly.

'I'm fine. Honestly. I just want to get home to my own bed.'

'I can't make you do anything you don't want to do, but I can strongly advise that you come back to the hospital with us and get checked out.'

'Thank you, but really I want to get home. Thank you for everything, though.' Holding the side of the ambulance door, Molly stood up, allowing her eyes to focus on the dispersing crowd in front of her. Where was Bea?

'I tell you what. Why don't I take you up to the hospital? My shift is due to finish now, anyway.' Placing his hands in his pockets, Richie looked towards his patrol car.

Shaking her head, Molly rolled her eyes. He wasn't going to leave it, was he? Maybe if he gave her a lift back to hers he'd see she was fine and didn't need to go to the hospital. 'Okay.'

'Come on then. Thanks, Karen.' Holding his hand up in acknowledgement to the paramedic, he wrapped his arm around Molly's waist and led her towards his car.

'Hold on, what about Bea? Where's Bea?' Twisting around, she tried to locate Bea.

'Bea's here, I'll drop her off at her hotel on the way.' Holding open the passenger door, Richie waited until Molly had slipped inside before shutting it and getting in the driver's side.

* * *

'See I told you I was fine.' Leaning her head against the passenger window, Molly closed her eyes.

'Umm, the nurse didn't say you were fine. She said you were

mildly concussed and not to let you sleep.' Keeping his eyes on the road, Richie gently shook Molly's arm.

'Yep, she meant I was fine.'

'Molly, please don't close your eyes. Here, why don't you find something to listen to?' Deftly opening the glove box, Richie pointed to the CDs before pulling out of the hospital car park onto the main road. 'You can stay at mine tonight. I'd offer to go to yours, but I've got Rocco to think about. Marissa's at her mum's tonight, anyway.'

Nodding, Molly picked through the pile of CDs. 'You like The Levellers?'

'Doesn't everyone?' Glancing across at her, he grinned.

'Well, I do, but I wouldn't have put you down for a Levellers type of guy.'

'What kind of guy did you think I was then?'

Yawning, Molly closed her eyes and lowered the CDs to her lap.

'Hey, Molly. Almost home.'

'Yep...'

Richie tapped his fingers against the steering wheel. 'I'm sorry things didn't work out between us.'

'I'm sorry too.' Rubbing her eyes, she looked across at him. His chiselled jaw was sporting more than his usual couple of days' worth of stubble. 'Are you growing a beard?'

'What? Oh, yes. Well, I thought I'd give it a go, much to Marissa's disgust.' Richie ran his fingers across his chin. 'What do you think?'

'I think you look very handsome.'

'Umm, and now I know that you're concussed! Shall we watch a film when we get in? I could make us a chip butty too. I didn't have chance to catch a dinner break and you must be starving.'

Molly shrugged. 'Okay.'

27

Yawning and opening her eyes, it took Molly a few minutes to work out where she was and why she wasn't at home. Lifting her hand to her forehead, she winced at the sharp pain as her fingers touched the gauze. Blinking against the sun seeping through the curtains, Molly looked around the room. She must have fallen asleep on Richie's sofa. She vaguely remembered him putting a film on but she had no idea what film it was, she must have fallen asleep almost instantly.

Pulling the blanket covering her down, Molly sat up and twisted her legs around, letting her toes sink into the plush cream carpet. How he got away with keeping it looking so clean with a dog around, she had no idea.

Standing up, she paused. She couldn't hear anyone else. Maybe he was still asleep, or maybe he had gone to work. No, Rocco would be milling around if he'd gone to work. Looking around the room, she noticed a note protruding out from behind the clock on the mantelpiece. Picking it up, she checked it was for her. He'd taken Rocco out for his morning walk. He'd be back soon and get her some breakfast.

Placing the note back on the mantelpiece, she ran her fingers through her hair, wincing as the knots pulled her scalp. She must look awful. Even after a normal night out, she used to get a fright when looking in the mirror in the morning. And, even though she hadn't been drinking, her throat still felt tight and her head heavy from the late night.

No, she needed to get home. All she wanted now was a shower. Taking the note again, she located a pen and wrote a quick reply thanking him and telling him she was heading back.

* * *

Scrunching her hair dry with a towel, Molly took the stairs two at a time as the doorbell pierced through the silence again. She hadn't thought to check what time Lauren and Ellis needed picking up from Bea's parents' house.

Letting the door up to the flat swing shut, she strode through the empty shop floor of Bramble Patch before pulling the front door open.

'Richie?' Taking a step back, she felt the gush of red flush through her cheeks. She had planned to text him and thank him again later. Maybe she should have done before she'd jumped in the shower.

'Morning! I've brought you over some breakfast.' Holding out two takeaway boxes from the local café, he looked her up and down. 'I've got to say you look a lot brighter this morning.'

Lowering the towel from her hair, she straightened the collar of her top. 'Thanks and thank you for everything last night. I'm sorry if I was a pain.'

Ducking his head, Richie smiled. 'You were a bit, yes, but it's absolutely fine. I think I'd be a bit of a pain too if I'd whacked my head the way you did.'

'Sorry.'

'Honestly, you were fine. I was just worried about you, that's all. How are you feeling today?'

Molly shrugged. 'Okay.'

'Still painful?'

'A little.'

Lifting the takeaway boxes a little higher, Richie tilted his head. 'Can I come in?'

'Sorry, yes, of course. Come through.' Leading him into the back kitchen, Molly wrung the towel in her hands before hanging it over the back of a chair.

Placing the boxes on the table, Richie opened the lid. The warm sweet smell of Scotch pancakes and syrup filled the kitchen. 'I got us pancakes. I hope that's okay? Mrs Hopkins makes the best Scotch pancakes I've ever tasted.'

'Ooh, lovely. They smell amazing.' Holding her hair back, she leant over them, breathing in deeply.

'They really are. I would have made you something, but there's no way I can compete with Mrs Hopkins.'

'Thank you. You didn't have to though.' Smiling at him, she held his gaze.

'Do you feel better after your shower?' Richie indicated her top. The pale purple fabric deepened in colour as water dripped from her hair. Picking the towel up, he came to stand behind her. 'Here, let me.'

Closing her eyes as Richie gently dried her hair with the towel, Molly smiled. His warm, gentle fingers felt good against her head. Safe. Homely.

Tucking her hair gently behind her ears, Richie passed the towel back to her.

As she took the towel from him, their fingers brushed, and they stood for a minute facing each other.

Shaking his head, Richie stepped away and began plating up the pancakes before pausing and looking up. 'I can take mine back home if it's easier?'

Molly shook her head. 'No, it's fine. I'll pop the kettle on.'

'Thanks.'

With her back to him, Molly busied herself by spooning coffee into two mugs. Blinking in an attempt to contain the tears stinging the back of her eyes, she reminded herself it was her own decisions and actions that had led to them doing this ridiculous dance. It was her fault they were no longer in a relationship. 'One sugar, isn't it?'

* * *

'I can't believe you got in a fight! Wait until I tell my friends at school!' Leaning over his pasta, Ellis touched his mum's forehead.

'I did not! I told you what happened.' Laughing, Molly passed him the pesto. 'Do you want some?'

'Yuck, no way! Ah, but it'll sound a lot cooler if I tell them you got in a fight.' Shrugging, Ellis pushed a forkful of pasta and cheese in his mouth.

'Umm. Please don't.'

'Does it still hurt? I'll ring Marissa and get her to get her dad on the case. The police will find who did it.'

'No, it's fine. Just a little sore. Besides, he knows already, and it's all been sorted now.'

Lauren nodded. 'So can I have some money for these trainers I saw in town with Dad?'

Grateful for the sudden change in conversation, Molly smiled. 'We'll see. Let me see how much I've got at the end of the month, okay?'

'So that's a yes then?'

'It's a maybe.'

'Right, I'm done. Can I go on my game now?' Pushing back his chair, Ellis stood up, a single piece of pasta falling from his T-shirt to the table.

'Yes, okay. Not for long, though. It's school in the morning so you need to get a good night's sleep.' By the time she'd returned the pasta to the plate, he had already disappeared into his room.

'I'm done too. I'm going to ring Marissa about some homework that's due in tomorrow.'

'Okay.' Standing up, Molly yawned as a wave of tiredness hit her. Piling the plates up, she dropped them in the sink before slumping back at the table.

28

Rolling her shoulders back, Molly plastered a smile on her face before picking the tray up and kicking the kitchen door open. Weaving out from behind the counter, she was careful not to spill the coffees, teas and glasses of squash.

'Ooh lovely. Thank you, Molly.' Taking the mug from the tray, Gladys took a sip before placing it on the coffee table and turning back to her knitting.

'You're welcome.' Molly made her way around the circle of chairs, passing mugs and glasses out. The Knit and Natter group was busier today than it ever had been. Another two new members had turned up this morning and everyone else had made it too. 'How's your granddaughter's cardigan coming along, Pat?'

'Okay, I think.' Holding up a tiny pale pink cardigan, Pat tilted her head. 'I'm struggling with this part though.'

'Ah, the cuffs. I always find them the trickiest, but it looks like you've done a really good job.'

'She has, hasn't she? And to think a few weeks ago you'd never picked up a pair of knitting needles.' Gladys nodded over at Pat.

'Yes, you've done really well. Learnt much quicker than I did when I was taught. When is it your granddaughter's due again?'

'Two weeks Sunday.' Bill beamed.

'Wow, not much longer to wait then!'

Bill picked up his mug. 'We can't wait, can we love?'

'Not at all.'

Straightening her back, Molly looked up as the bell above the door tinkled. It was Richie. Making sure to keep her smile in place, she turned to him. 'Richie, how can I help you?'

'You've come to join our knitting group, haven't you, love?' Gladys grinned. 'I'll find you some knitting needles if you haven't brought your own.'

Placing his hands in the pockets of his jeans, Richie grinned across at the group. 'Not today, I'm afraid.'

'Oh, that's a shame. You could have knitted your sweet little dog a jumper.'

Looking down at his feet, Richie looked back at Molly. 'Do you mind if I have a quiet word, please?'

'Umm, yes, okay.' Hugging the tray to her chest, Molly led the way into the back kitchen. 'How can I help you?'

'I just thought I'd pop by to see how your head is.' Touching his fingers to his own forehead, he looked at her.

Molly shrugged. 'It's fine, thanks. Ellis thinks it's really cool.'

Richie chuckled. 'I bet he does.'

Placing the tray down, Molly straightened the tea caddie. Maybe what he had done for her on Saturday night should have made things easier between them, but if anything because it had stirred up so many feelings for Molly, it had made things more awkward. Turning to look at him, she tucked her hair behind her ears and made her way towards the door. 'Thanks for coming.'

Stepping forwards as Molly held the door open, Richie paused, looked down at his feet and back up again. 'Actually, there was something else.'

Oh great, she'd known there was something up when he hadn't got into a conversation with Gladys. He was normally so chatty with everyone, especially with the Knit and Natter group who appeared to think very highly of him. What had she done? Had she made a show of herself on Saturday and he had come to talk to her about it? Why hadn't he said before? She'd asked him, and he'd said she'd been fine. Letting the door swing shut, she placed her hand on the work surface. She'd have to listen. She didn't have a choice. After all, if she'd done something wrong on Saturday, it was her fault and she has to face the consequences. 'Okay.'

'Look, I wanted to speak to you about what happened.'

Molly nodded. She was right. 'I'm really sorry if I said or did something embarrassing on Saturday night. I wasn't really with it after banging my head...'

'Oh no, you didn't do or say anything wrong, or embarrassing. It's not about Saturday. Well, it is in a way but it's nothing you did.'

Biting her bottom lip, she nodded. 'Okay. Has something else happened?'

'No. Well, yes.' Running his fingers through his hair, Richie shuffled his feet. 'I just wanted to talk about everything that's happened between us.'

'Clear the air you mean?' Molly looked back at the shut door, she didn't need this. Not now, not with a shop full of people she was supposed to be entertaining. Plus, she'd hardly had any sleep for the last couple of nights. Richie helping her to the car, Richie looking after her, Richie drying her hair for her as he had – it was too much. Every time an image of him popped in her mind it was all she could do not to cry. She knew it was her fault things had ended between them before anything had actually really started and every time she thought of what could have been... she just wanted to crumble. No, she couldn't do that. Not now.

'Sort of. No, not at all.'

Well, which was it? Did he want to clear the air or just rub her nose in it for being so trusting of Diane? 'I'm sorry. I can't do this. Not now. I really should get back out there, we've got a couple of newbies and I need to make a good impression.' Molly indicated to the shop floor.

'Of course. Right, I understand.'

Molly nodded. 'Thanks.' Opening the door, she slipped through ahead of him. She didn't want to give him any chance of calling her back.

'Have you changed your mind, Richie?' Gladys grinned and held out a set of knitting needles.

Halfway to the door out of Bramble Patch, Richie paused, looked ahead, and then back at Gladys before turning around slowly. 'Yes, I have actually.'

'Aw, I told you he would.' Gladys poked Susan with her knitting needle and nodded.

'Not about the knitting, I'm afraid.' Richie glanced at Molly. 'I'm sorry, Molly. I do need to discuss this now. Or even just tell you what I need to say. You don't have to answer and you don't have to have any sort of discussion with me, but I need to get this off my chest.'

Picking up a ball of pale turquoise Merino wool, Molly tucked in the loose end before looking across at him. Was he really going to air their grievances here? In front of everyone?

'I'm sorry if this embarrasses you, Molly, but I need to apologise. I'm sorry for ever letting you go. I'm sorry I let Diane's fibs split us up. I should have tried harder, and I should have accepted your apology. I'm sorry I didn't. I'm sorry because ever since I met you, even though I gave you a speeding ticket, and I'm sorry for that too, but even the first time I met you, I felt a connection between us. And it scared me. I haven't felt this way about anyone since me and Diane split up and even though I loved her, it barely touches what I feel for you. Did you feel it too? Did you feel that connection?' Taking a deep breath in, Richie ran his fingers through his hair, his face flushed, his eyes wide.

Gripping the ball of wool in her hands, Molly could feel a fierce blush sweeping across her face. A connection? He'd felt a connection? Even back then? Why had he been so awful to her then?

'I know I didn't exactly welcome you into the community with open arms. Heck, I probably made your move more difficult for you. And I know it's no excuse, but it took me some time to realise what I was feeling, especially with you having moved in here.' Hardly pausing for a breath, Richie swept his hand around, taking in the shop. 'But, I love you.'

'What?' The question had slipped out before she even realised what she'd said.

'I love you. This feeling, it's love. A love that's more powerful than I've ever felt before. I love you, Molly Wilson.'

Opening her mouth and closing it again, Molly stood still. The shop floor had become eerily silent. Had he really just said that?

Richie stood still, watching her, before looking at the floor and back up again. 'I'm so sorry I've messed up.'

With the soft Merino wool still in her hands, Molly watched as he walked away, quietly shutting the door behind him.

'Wow, I wish my husband said things like that every once in a while.' Lucy whistled through her teeth.

Looking across at the Knit and Natter group, Molly could barely focus.

'Go on, girl. Go get him. We all know you feel the same, it's written all over your face every time he comes in.' Gladys called across the room.

'Yes, Molly, go after him.' Susan, normally the quietest member of the group, stood up, quickly walking towards the door and opened it, holding it open as she looked across at Molly.

'Right, yes. Yes, okay.' Looking across at the group, Molly grimaced before letting the Merino wool drop back into the basket and walking out of the door.

* * *

Outside, with the cool breeze whipping her hair, it suddenly hit her – Richie loved her. He had told her that. In front of everyone, he had told her how he felt. Pausing at the top of the parking bays, Molly shielded her eyes with her hand against the sun and looked left down to the junction towards his house. There was no sign of him.

Frowning, she looked right towards his mum's house and the edge of the village. There was a lone figure walking along the grass verge out of the village, a golden Labrador at his feet. It must be him, it must be Richie. He must have left Rocco outside whilst he had come into Bramble Patch.

Walking in his direction, she picked up her pace as he turned down the bridleway running through the fields. 'Richie, wait!'

He hadn't heard her. Running now, she came to the bridleway and followed him. She was getting closer. 'Richie!'

Pausing, he looked behind him. His face red with emotion until he saw her.

She watched as a slow grin spread across his face and he began walking towards her, quickening his pace with every step. Meeting in the middle, Molly sank into his open arms before looking up at him. 'I love you too.'

EPILOGUE

Taking Richie's hand, Molly laughed as he led her onto the dance floor. Just as they got there, the DJ switched the music to something with a slower tempo. Leaning her head against his shoulder, Molly grinned and nuzzled into his neck. 'Who'd have thought a year ago that we'd both be here again together?'

Richie looked across at the large banner engulfing the wall behind the stage. 'I did. There's no one I'd rather be dancing with, and here's to many more Spring Dances with you.' Leaning back on his heels, he held her at arm's length before pulling her close again.

As their lips touched and Molly mumbled that she felt the same way, the song spun onto a faster track. With Debs up on stage barking her orders, Molly twirled into the arms of another man.

Laughing as she was spun around, Molly looked across at Richie, their eyes meeting. He gave her the thumbs up as Debs instructed them to swap partners again. Automatically drifting back towards each other, Richie took Molly in his arms again.

Spinning back towards the edge of the dance floor, both Molly and Richie held their hands out. 'Come on you three, join in.'

As Marissa and Lauren both rolled their eyes and their faces flushed in embarrassment, Ellis giggled and jumped up, dragging his friend, Charlie, onto the dance floor with them.

'Do you think Marissa or Lauren will ever enjoy dancing?'

Molly looked back at them as they giggled and pointed at a group of boys over in the far corner. Molly was sure she recognised a few of them from their year group. 'Yes, and I don't think it will be long either.'

* * *

As Molly pushed open the front door, Rocco bounded up to them, encircling their legs in his excitement. 'Hello, boy! Have you been good? Shall we get you a treat?'

'And you wonder why he favours you over me?' As Lauren, Ellis and Marissa trudged through to the kitchen carrying the boxes of takeaway pizzas they'd grabbed on the way home, Richie put his arm around Molly's middle and led her back out of the front door.

'Where are we going?'

'Just to the garden.'

Sure enough, he turned and unbolted the side gate. 'Why didn't we just go through the kitchen?'

'You'll see. Come here.' Gently manoeuvring her in front of him, Richie covered her eyes with his hands. Pushing the gate open with his foot, he slowly walked them through.

'What is it?' Grinning, Molly stepped through, the familiar brush of wisteria against her shoulder. She still couldn't believe they'd managed to find this cottage, on the edge of the village so close to Richie's mum's and to Bramble Patch and yet big enough for the five of them. It was the wisteria that she'd first fallen in love with when they'd viewed it, she'd always dreamt of a home covered in the delicately scented purple petals of wisteria.

'That's it. Just come this way a little.'

She could feel the gravel pathway giving way to lawn underneath her feet. As Richie gently turned her, Molly worked out that she must be facing the back of the cottage. She could feel a different kind of warmth hit her. It wasn't the last of the spring evening's sunshine; it was warmer, as though the sliding glass doors from the kitchen/family room had suddenly been opened.

'Right, that's it. Keep them closed.'

Squinting her eyes shut, she fought the urge to open them as Richie's hands lifted. Tilting her head, she listened to his steps as he walked away and tried to listen to the whispering that ensued.

'Okay, one, two, three. You can open them now, Mum!' Ellis stifled an excited giggle.

Opening her eyes, it took her a second to focus and realise what was happening. The glass doors stood open, and Ellis, Marissa and Lauren all stood looking out. In front of them, the garden table had been set up with champagne flutes and a bottle of champagne sat chilling in an ice bucket.

As her eyes focused on Richie, tears welled up, and her heart skipped a beat. There he knelt in front of her, a small red box held in his hands.

'Molly Wilson, this past year has been an amazing whirlwind. You've made me believe in true love again and me and Marissa would love our families to join. Will you, Lauren and Ellis join us and will you marry me?'

A silence spread across the garden as Molly looked up from Richie to Ellis, Lauren and Marissa and back again. They'd known. They'd known what Richie had been planning. 'Yes! I, we, say yes!'

Slipping a platinum solitaire on Molly's ring finger, Richie picked her up and swung her around, laughing before setting her back down. Cupping her chin with his fingers, he gently tipped her head back, their lips meeting.

'Urgh, gross!'

'Ellis! You can't say that! They're engaged now.' Lauren's voice quietened Ellis' gagging noises.

'I suppose so.'

As they both pulled apart, Richie and Molly held their arms out just as Marissa, Lauren and Ellis ran towards them.

ACKNOWLEDGMENTS

Thank you, readers, for taking the time to read to read *Bramble Patch Craft Shop*. I hope you've enjoyed reading about Molly's escape to the beautiful Payton-on-the-Water and her journey to love with Richie as much as I enjoyed writing her story.

A huge thank you to my wonderful children, Ciara and Leon, who motivate me to keep writing and working towards 'changing our stars' each and every day. Also to my lovely family for always being there, through the good times and the trickier ones.

And a massive thank you to my amazing editor, Emily Yau, who reached out and believed in me – thank you.

Thank you also to Shirley for copy editing and proofreading *Bramble Patch Craft Shop*. And, of course, Clare Stacey for creating the beautiful cover. Thank you to all at Team Boldwood!

ABOUT THE AUTHOR

Sarah Hope is the author of many successful romance novels, including the bestselling Cornish Bakery series. She lives in Central England with her two children and an array of pets, and enjoys escaping to the seaside at any opportunity.

Sign up to Sarah Hope's mailing list for news, competitions and updates on future books.

Follow Sarah on social media here:

- facebook.com/HappinessHopeDreams
- twitter.com/sarahhope35
- instagram.com/sarah_hope_writes
- bookbub.com/authors/sarah-hope

ALSO BY SARAH HOPE

The Seaside Ice-Cream Parlour

The Little Beach Café

Christmas at Corner Cottage

The Bramble Patch Craft Shop

The Wagging Tails Dog's Home Series

The Wagging Tails Dog's Home

Boldwood

Boldwood Books is an award-winning fiction publishing company seeking out the best stories from around the world.

Find out more at www.boldwoodbooks.com

Join our reader community for brilliant books, competitions and offers!

Follow us
@BoldwoodBooks
@TheBoldBookClub

Sign up to our weekly
deals newsletter

https://bit.ly/BoldwoodBNewsletter